SHADOW
SWORN

COLLEEN VANDERLINDEN

Shadow Sworn
Colleen Vanderlinden

Published in the United States
by Building Block Studios LLC

ISBN 0692529756

ISBN-13 978-0692529751

http://www.colleenvanderlinden.com
http://www.buildingblockstudios.com

DEDICATION

In memory of my grandmother, Frances Kuczewski. The first stories I wrote were at your kitchen table, scribbled with green pen on the back of junk mail that you stockpiled so I'd always have enough paper. Thank you.

DEDICATION

In memory of my grandmother, Frances Kuczewski. The first stories I wrote were at your kitchen table, scribbled with green pen on the back of junk mail that you stockpiled so I'd always have enough paper. Thank you.

CONTENTS

Deep in their roots,
all flowers keep the light.

— Theodore Roethke

CHAPTER ONE

Sophie ran.

She ran, and no matter how fast she ran, it wasn't enough. There was no outrunning the ceaseless emptiness and maddening hunger, or the terrifying slow creep of insanity that had become her reality.

She forced her legs to pump harder nonetheless, propelling her body between the trees in the woods west of her house. Fallen leaves crunched and swished beneath her feet. Sweat trickled down between her shoulder blades, and her chest felt ready to explode from the pressure of her pounding heart.

Not enough.

Calder shadowed her steps, as he had every day since the morning he'd woken beside her to find that she'd taken his curse. His presence was steady, comforting, and distracting all at the same time. All she wanted was him. She craved him the way a starving person craves nourishment.

And she would know about that well. The curse ensured she was always hungry. Always thirsty. Always on edge and in need of *something*. Never satisfied.

She envisioned punching her ancestor, Migisi, right in her stupid regal face. This was her fault.

What kind of complete nutcase curses and entire line of people because she caught her lover with his pants down?

She let out an irritated shout, needing something, some way to release the frustration and anger inside her. It mingled with the Shadow, making her feel wrong and filthy and like a stranger in her own body.

A warm body hurled into hers, and she felt strong arms around her waist, pulling her down to the ground.

Calder was straddling her, glorious in his nakedness, having shifted back from his bear form. His blond hair was a halo, the sun high in the sky behind him as he looked down at her. Golden hair trailed over his broad chest, down...

"You know you can't dangle all of that in front of me like that, Calder," she groaned, out of breath. She was opening her thighs to him before she even realized what she was doing, and he shook his head.

"You wanted to learn control, right?" he asked, his ice-blue eyes meeting hers.

"Not now, though," she said. "That's just mean."

A small smile curved his lips, and he shook his head. "I can smell you. Settle down."

She growled at him, a sound that, just a few weeks ago, would not have been one she'd ever imagined herself making. She was finding, living with his curse, that words weren't enough. Screams, shouts, groans, grunts, growls.... none of it made her feel better, but they articulated, better than words, the frustration and anger she was feeling.

"Settle down," he repeated. "Come on, kitten."

She stopped thrashing, stopped trying to open her thighs to him. She went still.

"Breathe," he murmured. "Good girl."

"I'm not a pet," she said.

He smiled. "You like it when I call you that."

"Not unless you're rewarding me with something."

He laughed. "Nearly there. Your heart rate is slowing. A few more good, deep breaths." He watched as she took several breaths of cool autumn air, filling her lungs and then releasing each breath slowly. "You're getting so much better at this," he said softly.

"I hate it."

"I know," he said. "Should I say it, or…?"

"Shut up, Calder."

"What was I going to say?" he teased.

"You were going to remind me that I shouldn't have taken your curse," she said. "Which is crap, because it would have meant losing you. I'd rather have the curse."

His gaze softened, and he lowered his forehead to hers, and they stayed like that for several long moments. "I love you," he murmured.

"I love you too," she said. She tilted her head so she could kiss him, and when their lips met, just like every time they kissed, it was like a cool drink of water on a hot day; like warm buttered bread to someone who was starving. "Love you," she repeated between kisses.

He slowly pulled away after feathering a few more soft kisses over her lips, her jawline. "Come on," he said. "Race you back." She watched as he ran, muscular human body shifting, changing before her eyes into a huge, shaggy black bear. Sophie shook her head and followed, her feet pounding the ground again. She slowed only when she reached the fenced-in area where her vegetable garden had once been. She'd since cleared all of the dead vegetable plants out, and it sat empty. It was a lost cause unless she figured out a way to work her way back to the Light.

She'd given up everything she believed in, turned her back on her faith, turned to the Shadow to save Calder. Because she'd seen what he would become, and she couldn't let him go on the way he had, especially when her ancestor was to blame for the curse that had doomed him and so many males in his family before him.

3

She'd watched him kill his own father, who had long since lost his own humanity in the grips of the curse. He still dealt with the grief, the nightmares of what he'd been forced to do. It had made her decision all too easy, to take the burden on herself rather than let him fall to the same fate.

The advice Migisi had left for her in one of the journals, to destroy Calder and end the curse, wasn't even worth thinking about. Ending anyone's life, let alone someone she'd loved since she was eleven years old, was something she'd never do. It went against everything she was, even now.

Especially now, maybe.

He stood on the back porch, buttoning the flannel shirt he'd been wearing before they left for their run, and she was sorry to see him all covered up again.

"So mean," she repeated as she walked toward him, and he smiled.

"You wouldn't learn any control at all if I gave you what you wanted all the time. You decided you wanted it this way," he reminded her.

She didn't answer, grabbing a large bottle of water off of the railing instead and chugging over half of it before forcing herself to calm down. He wasn't lying. He'd been prepared, more than willing, once he realized what she'd done, to do everything in his power to keep her satisfied. He'd fed her, endlessly. Ensured there was always something to drink, that she was well-loved as often as she'd wanted it, which was often.

After a week, she'd realized how tiring it was for him. He'd never said a word, had kept to his promise to care for her, but she hated it. So she'd decided to learn control instead, so she could at least act, for the most part, as if everything was fine.

And every time she lost control and started acting like a mindless animal, she remembered how well he'd hidden the ravages of the curse from her. She would do the same for him, and, at the same time, retain some of her pride.

They'd made it through the solstice, which would have been a nightmare for him, as a shifter, but was just one more intolerable day for her, no better or worse than the day before.

"Don't you think we should try going into town for a while?" he asked.

"Nope."

"Sophie."

"Not a chance in hell." She watched him. "You can go, though. I know you need to pick up those parts that came in."

"Your leave from work ends in three days," he reminded her.

"Then I'll deal with it in three days," she said.

He crossed his arms, watching her. He blew out an irritated breath. "Okay. I'll go then. I'll stop at the grocery store, too. Do you need anything in particular?"

"You," she said, and he shook his head.

"You're not playing fair," he said, stepping toward her and pulling her into his arms. "Control, remember?"

"You already said no once. That counts, right?" She leaned forward, stood on tiptoe, and pressed a row of open-mouthed kisses to his throat. A low growl vibrated deep in his chest.

"Good point," he said, picking her up and taking her into the house, barely remembering to close the door behind them before he started pulling her clothing off.

A while later, she watched as he pulled his truck out of the driveway, waving to her before he backed out onto the road. She watched until she couldn't see the truck anymore.

God, was this what his beast had gone through every time she'd walked away from him? It took everything in her not to chase him down and drag him back. Sophie took several deep breaths. She focused: breathe in, breathe out, over and over again until she felt less insane. There was panic there, that he wouldn't come back. She wasn't sure if that was her own fear, or something caused by the curse. Either way, she hated it.

She turned toward the living room, went to work cleaning. She washed windows, swept and mopped the floors, polished the wood furniture with beeswax until it gleamed. Her house had never looked so good; it got this treatment on an almost daily basis now. As with many things regarding the curse, Calder had been right about this as well. The need to keep her hands busy, to stay active, was almost overwhelming. Sitting and just reading, which she'd always loved, drove her mad. She couldn't stay still long enough and, even when she and tried to read, she couldn't focus. That, almost as much as anything else, was what she mourned. Reading, gardening, taking care of her animals, soap making… all of it was lost to her, at least for the time being, either corrupted by the Shadow or impossible to do because of the curse Migisi set on Calder's family.

So she ran, and she ate, and she drank, and she let Calder ravish her as often as he wanted. When she wasn't doing those things, she cleaned.

She guessed she'd be really, really good at her job when she went back to work, she thought as she scrubbed the kitchen sink. Her boss at the Falls Resort had been very understanding when she'd asked for a month's leave due to "health issues." It was time to go back soon despite the fact that leaving her land terrified her. Interacting with people other than Calder and her best friends, Layla and Cara, had her on the verge of panic.

She was Shadow now. She was a Shadow lord's plaything, destined to do his bidding. The fact that Marshall hadn't made a single appearance since the day she'd let him turn her to the Shadow only made her more stressed out. When he finally did demand something of her, she knew it would be something she would hate.

This was the price. This was the cost of keeping Calder sane and alive. This was the cost of trying to keep control of the darkness that was beginning to consume her. And she promised herself every single day that she was still a daughter of the Light, that she would find a way to work her way back to Its grace.

That was another reason why getting some semblance of control over her curse was so important. It was distracting, and when all she could think about was when she could eat next, or how best to get Calder naked, it was nearly impossible to focus on learning about the Shadow magic she now wielded. In those rare moments when she felt like she had some form of clarity, she could almost see the structure of the magic, just barely, and then it was gone.

Control first.

Sophie looked around. There was nothing left to clean. She'd sorted through the rest of the attic, even cleaned out the barn and two small garden sheds her aunt Evie had filled with stuff during her years on the property.

Cooking. That was something she could still do well enough. Sort of.

She looked through the pantry and realized she had ingredients for brownies. She assembled her ingredients: flour, cocoa powder, semisweet chocolate, eggs, salt, butter. She forced herself to focus on the task at hand: measuring, mixing. She chopped walnuts and more dark chocolate, added it to the batter. Every time her mind wandered, she tried to bring herself back to the moment, to the rich scent of the chocolate, the feel of the well-worn handle of the wooden spoon in her hand, the sight of the light filtering through the butter-yellow curtains over the kitchen sink. It was another trick Calder had taught her, and for a moment, she was lost in the memory of his lesson.

"Focus on the moment. This moment. Nothing else."

"You say that like it's easy," she complained. *She was in bed beside him, at the end of a particularly frustrating day.*

COLLEEN VANDERLINDEN

"I didn't say it was easy, kitten. But it's worth a try."

"I don't even know what you mean."

He pulled her into his arms and rolled both of them over until she was trapped beneath him. "My worst moments, before you took the curse, I held myself together with you. I'd look at your eyes, the way your lashes contrast with your gorgeous skin." He gently kissed each of her eyes. "The scent of your skin. You're like vanilla and lavender, maybe a touch of something smoky. Delicious," he murmured, kissing his way down her jawline. "The way your skin feels against mine." He ran his palms down to her hips. "I think I need a reminder of how you taste, though. You know, so I can describe it better…"

She shook her head, aware that she was smiling like a fool, blushing at a memory. He tended to have that effect on her.

She finished making the batter, but despite how hard she tried to focus on concrete things, her hunger came roaring to the forefront. Her stomach was growling. She was truly in pain, her stomach cramping from the emptiness, and she bit back a whimper as she placed the pan of brownie batter into the oven and set the timer.

"Control," she whispered to herself.

She put the flour back in the pantry, placed the eggs and butter back in the refrigerator. She was wrapping up the baking chocolate when, before she could even stop herself, she began shoving it into her mouth.

It was bitter. Dry. It tasted chalky and foul, and she couldn't stop eating it. She inhaled what was left of the bar and she needed more. Before she could think, she grabbed the canister of cocoa powder off of the counter, started spooning it into her mouth in huge heaping tablespoons, gagging on it even as she shoveled more in.

The entire canister was gone before she realized what was happening, and she pulled the refrigerator door open, grabbed the last gallon of milk and started chugging it, just trying to fill herself, trying to satisfy the emptiness inside.

8

Even after it was empty, she wasn't full. She was still ravenous, and now the smell of the brownies baking suffused the air in her house.

She was barely even aware of where she was anymore, as if she was floating, somewhere between dreaming and reality. She wrenched open the oven, pulled the pan from the oven.

Her fingers were burning, and she didn't even care.

She dropped the hot pan on the floor and got ready to start pulling the searing-hot, mostly raw brownies right from the pan.

"Stop!" Calder shouted from the living room. He'd just walked in, and he dropped the bags of groceries he was carrying as she snarled at him and turned back to the pan. She'd nearly gotten her fingers into the molten hot batter when he grabbed her, pulling her back from the pan and its contents, and all she wanted to do was scratch his eyes out for getting between her and satisfaction.

"Stop," he repeated as he held her close to him, her back to his chest, his arms like iron around her, holding her arms to her sides as she struggled with him. "Sophie, stop," he said in her ear, and she tried to head butt him. He dodged it and only growled when she brought her heel down hard on his toes.

"Shh," he soothed, still holding her as she struggled. "Shh, kitten. Come on, Sophie," he said, his voice even and calm, and she felt the fight go out of her. She slumped, and she released an ashamed, frustrated wail, her sobs wracking her body. Calder turned her gently, folded her into his arms. "It's okay," he murmured against her hair, and she shook her head.

"I'm sorry," she said between sobs.

"You don't have anything to be sorry for," he said, still holding her. He backed up a little, took her wrists gently in his hands and turned her hands, palm up, so he could look at them. "You blistered yourself up pretty good," he said, and she could see that muscle jumping in his jaw. Stressed out, angry.

"I couldn't stop," she whispered. "I knew what was happening, and I couldn't stop."

He pulled her close to him again. "I know, honey," he said. "It's getting worse."

"I'm fine."

She heard him take a deep breath. "Clearly," he said. Then he shook his head. "Let's get these taken care of."

Calder led her into the small bathroom, lifted her so she was sitting on the counter. He dug the small first aid kit out from under the sink.

"Back in the day, I could have healed this," she said shakily, at a loss for anything else, looking at her red, blistered hands. They hurt so much she was nauseous with it, and she gritted her teeth.

Calder didn't answer. He gently swabbed her hand with warm water on a soft cloth, and she hissed in pain, tried to pull her hands back. He held her wrist until she stopped moving, went back to work on that hand, then cleaned the other one. He applied ointment, and, though he tried to be gentle, the feel of his fingers on her blisters hurt so much tears soon ran down her face.

"Burns are the worst," he said quietly, focusing on her hands. "One of the rough things we went through with my dad was the time he decided that picking up the iron stove in his pen and bashing the gates with it was a good way to get himself free." She'd seen where Calder's father had lived after he'd lost control of himself; a tiny cabin enclosed by a tall, reinforced fence. "There was a fire in it at the time. He was a mess for months after."

She wanted to soothe him. Memories of his father haunted him. All she could do was lean forward and press a kiss to his temple as he wrapped her right hand in gauze.

"And I'm making you live through it again," she said softly.

"You're not making me do anything. I'm here because I want to be. I love you. This will never, ever be okay with me," he finished, meeting her eyes. She knew what the "this" was. Her, taking his curse. Her, suffering in his place.

"Well, watching you lose your mind was not okay with me. We're both irrational about one another that way," she said softly. "I love you. I'd do it again in a second. But I'm so—"

"Do not apologize to me, Sophie. Not ever," he said, the tenderness in his voice underlaid with anger. Not at her, she knew. He wrapped up her other hand, and she watched his face, watched him working through his emotions as he dealt with the task at hand. Taking care of her, which, she worried, he'd grow to resent.

She bit her lip. "Promise me something," she said.

He looked up at her. "What?"

"If this ever starts getting to be too much, if it ever gets to the point where you resent what our life is—"

He stood up and walked out. "Fuck that," he said.

She looked down at her hands, which he'd just finished wrapping. "I just don't want you to stay because you think you owe me something. I'm a big girl and I made a choice. That's all."

He came back, stood in the bathroom doorway. He crossed his arms over his chest and watched her as she hopped off of the counter.

"And I'm a big boy and I made a choice, too. I love you and you're mine and the day I resent you or our life together will never, ever come. Jesus, Sophie," he said, shaking his head. "What part of 'I love you' do you not understand?" She didn't answer, and he kept watching her. "This is something you actually worry about?" he asked quietly, and she nodded, looked away from him.

"Would you have resented me, if our situation was reversed?"

"No," she said, meeting his eyes. "Never."

"I believe you. Now do me a favor and have the same faith in me."

"I do…"

"Then stop, Sophie. Just stop."

She didn't answer, and they stood there for a few moments. She didn't know what to say or do. He took two steps into the bathroom, ending up standing directly in front of her. He tilted her face up toward his, gently, with his fingers, and she met his eyes. "There is nothing I wouldn't do for you. I'd do anything, happily, for you. Okay?" he said softly, and she nodded. He leaned down and kissed her, once, gently. When he drew back, there was a small smile on his lips. "If you'd have waited like five minutes, I brought brownies home with me," he said, and she laughed weakly and leaned against him.

"Must learn control," she said against his chest, and he held her tighter. "I ate cocoa powder."

"That's nothing compared to some of the weird shit I've eaten," he said, and then he pulled her out into the living room and fed her and held her, and she felt almost sane again.

After spending most of the weekend either running, cleaning, or trying to work up the courage to go into town like a normal person, Sophie was less ready than ever to go to work.

With people.

Where she would have to pretend she wasn't starving and thirsty and on the edge of losing her mind.

"I should quit," she said for about the twentieth time as she pulled her white work shirt on. Calder was sitting on the daybed watching her lazily, a tiny half smile on his lips. "Stop staring," she said.

"You should see yourself. Goddamn, sweetheart."

"Are you trying to make me late for work?" she asked. "I should quit," she said again.

"And do what? Hide here?"

"You don't have an actual job you go to anymore either," she pointed out irritably.

"Nope. I work for myself. And this isn't about me. This is about you. We'll get your magic back the way it's supposed to be, and you'll be able to start your soap business back up."

"By then I won't need to be able to stay home," she grumbled.

"What? Do you want me to tell you I'll support you if you quit? I will. I would in a heartbeat. Do you want me to do that?"

"No."

"No," he repeated. "You've been doing for yourself your whole life and it would drive you nuts if I even tried to take care of you that way."

"Don't be smug," she said, struggling with the top buttons on her top. Her hands were better than they had been after the brownie incident, but a few blisters still remained, making it tricky to do certain things.

Calder stood up, pushed her fumbling hands away, and started buttoning her top. "This is the opposite of what I usually do to your clothing," he murmured.

"Feels wrong, doesn't it?" she asked, squeezing her thighs together, trying not to whine with need for him. The smell of him, the warmth of his body, the slight brushes of his knuckles against her body as he buttoned her up.

He let his hands linger at the top-most button, where she knew he could feel her pulse jumping at her throat. Her breathing felt shallow, ragged. She was looking up at him, and a look crossed his face. He turned away.

"What?" she asked quietly.

"Nothing. I was just thinking how much I'm used to us being together all day. And I'm worried about you and I know it's going to be hell." He paused. "But you don't want me to rescue you."

She shook her head. "Just be here when I get home," she said with a small smile, even as her body went insane, as she hungered for anything and everything, but especially him.

He grinned. "You know I will be." He came back to her, gave her a soft, quick kiss, and walked her out the door and to her car. "Have a good day. Remember: control. If you need me, call me. Right?"

She nodded, kissed him again, and got into the car. Calder shut the door behind her and watched as she pulled out of the driveway and onto the highway.

"Okay. I can do this," she whispered to herself as she drove toward town.

CHAPTER TWO

"I can't do this!" Sophie hissed into her phone as she crouched in the cleaning supply closet on the second floor of the resort.

"Yes, you can," Layla's voice said in her ear. "You're a badass. You can handle a day at work, Soph."

"I can smell the food from the dining room. And every time I pass a vending machine I want to break it and take everything. And there are *men* here."

"Yes. It's a resort in an area where fishing and hunting are things people do. I am sure there are men." Layla's tone was firm, and bordering on bored. She'd expected her best friend to be a little more comforting.

"I swear if one of them even looked at me I'd jump him and I don't even want them but," she broke off with a growl.

"Then control yourself," Layla said, saying each word more firmly than the last. "This is exactly why we were trying to get you into town at least sometimes. Calder said—"

"I know what Calder said. I've heard it about ninety million times," Sophie said, rolling her eyes.

"Well since he's the expert in the curse department, maybe you should have listened."

"You know you're supposed to be commiserating with me, right?"

"Nope. You're a big girl. Get your ass back to work. Love you." And with that, the line went dead.

"She hung up on me," Sophie said in disbelief, staring at her phone. After a few more seconds of trying to force some sense of calm, she stood up, got out of the supply closet, and started pushing her cart down the hallway. She knocked at the first room, and found it empty. After chugging two bottles of water, she got to work scrubbing, vacuuming, making beds, dusting, and polishing.

"Better," she murmured to herself. She locked up and headed down the hallway, handling the next two rooms in the same way. When she knocked on the door to the third room, she was irritated that someone was inside. A tall, dark-haired man answered.

"I can come back later," she said, already starting to walk away.

"No, not at all. I was just packing up. Come on in."

"Really, it's okay," Sophie said. "I have another floor to do, I can come back and do this later."

"Why make another trip?" He gave her a disarming smile, and she nodded, followed him into the room. She kicked the doorstop to keep the door open. This wasn't uncommon — many of the resorts guests were repeat visitors and knew most of the full-time staff by name. She recognized this guest. He was into fishing, from what she remembered. A lawyer or something.

"I'll start on the bathroom then so I'm not in your way," she said, and he nodded.

Sophie grabbed her cleaning supplies and gritted her teeth. She wasn't remotely attracted to him. At all. Her mind, her heart, belonged to Calder. But her body had other ideas and she was ashamed to find herself reacting to this strange man almost as strongly as she reacted to Calder. It was wrong.

She scrubbed the sink and countertop, probably with more force than she needed to. She could hear him moving around out in the main part of the room, opening and closing drawers.

"Excuse me," he said, reaching around to the back of the bathroom door, where a tie was hanging. She nodded. He stopped, glanced at her. "Are you all right? You look a little flushed."

"I'm fine," she said. She looked away from him, grabbed the spray to wash the mirror, and stated wiping it down.

"Do you need a break?" he asked, seeming genuinely concerned.

She shook her head.

"Hey," he said, reaching out as if he was about to touch her.

She closed her eyes and hated every single thing she was physically feeling.

"I'm fine. I think I'm going to come back later though, okay?"

He nodded, looking confused, and she left as quickly as she could, wheeling her cart to the service elevator and taking it to the next floor up.

By the time her shift was over, Sophie had a sore jaw from keeping it clenched against the craziness running through her. She'd run out of change after making way too many trips to the vending machine, and walking past the kitchen had nearly been a disaster. She quickly bid her co-workers goodbye and sped toward home.

She drove down the highway, the windows down, the radio off, the cool wind blowing through her hair. The sky was darkening, the sun low on the horizon. The trees had long lost their leaves, and it was as if the Earth was breathing its last breath before winter buried everything.

17

They had already had their first snowfall; such a thing wasn't uncommon where they were, at the very top of Michigan's upper peninsula. Soon, the whole world would be under a blanket of snow.

The highway was empty, and before Sophie knew what she was doing, she pulled her car over the the shoulder, got out, and headed through the scrubby trees at the side of the road, emerging on the edge of the river. If she followed it, she would soon be on her own property.

And as much as she needed to see Calder, it wasn't what she wanted. Not then. Suddenly, she wanted the silence she could only find in the woods and near the water. Stopping hadn't made sense to her when she'd first done it, but all of a sudden, it seemed like a fabulous idea.

She stuffed her hands in the pockets of the wool sweater she'd tossed on, and strolled along the edge of the river. She let herself be soothed by the sound of the water rushing over rocks, babbling its way toward the falls. Her legs carried her along the shore, almost of their own volition. There was no thought behind it, just the sensation of movement.

Sophie kept walking, and stopped, freezing when she came upon a doe drinking at the edge of the river. She remembered the last time she'd used her healing powers. She'd healed a doe. Not this doe, of course, but seeing her made Sophie remember it just the same. The doe raised her head and watched Sophie, her large, long-lashed eyes reflecting Sophie in the dimming light. She raised her snout, and sniffed at the air.

And then she bounded away, spooked.

Sophie closed her eyes and took a deep breath. For just a moment there, she'd dared to hope that not everything was as changed as she'd believed. Of course the animals could smell it on her. The stench of Shadow. Marshall's dark power flowing through her where once there was only Light. She knew Calder smelled it. Sometimes, she could as well, a smoky, intense scent that clung to her like a veil and never seemed to fall away.

She stood there for several moments, and then she felt another presence nearby. A presence that she was tied to. A presence that owned her, no matter how much she hated it. Him.

"Finally. It is impossible to get you alone. Does loverboy ever take a break?" Marshall asked, his smooth voice cutting the sunset quiet like a blade. "Of course, not that you would be avoiding me now, would you?"

Sophie didn't answer, merely turned and looked behind her. The man, warlock, who had haunted her steps, who had ensured she was alone, who had terrified her, tarnished her every moment, whether she was asleep or awake, stood there. His nearly-black eyes seemed to take in every detail, and even that, even a look from this particular man, felt like an assault. She felt bile rise in her throat as her stomach twisted. Not so much in fear, the way it used to. In pure, hot hatred.

That was Shadow. That was what it did. At least, that was what she tried to tell herself. She had been convinced she was pure, that she was Light, and the hatred that lived in her for Marshall could never have been her own. She wondered, the longer she lived with Shadow coursing through her veins, how much of that was true.

"You're still obsessing over that Light bullshit?" Marshall asked irritably. She was linked to him now, in every way. Her power linked to his, her emotions, his to know and play with as he desired. So far, he had kept his distance.

"Why are you here?" Sophie asked, crossing her arms over her chest.

He didn't answer. Instead, he just stood there watching her, and she hated it. She despised the hungry look in his eyes, the possession there.

"You look just like her, you know that?" he finally asked.

Sophie took a few steps away. Somewhere, in the back of her mind, she was relieved that she didn't have any kind of reaction to Marshall. At least there was that. At least she didn't have to feel her body responding to his presence the way it had earlier, to the men she passed at work. "Like who? Migisi?" she asked.

He shook his head, still watching her. "No. Before her."

"What? Her mom? How long have you been stalking my family, you creep?"

He smirked. "I told you. Hundreds of years, 'kitten.' I can't believe you let him call you that."

"That is none of your business."

He shrugged. "Not Migisi's mother. Before her. Long before. Some of Migisi's ancestors came over from Spain, settled in the Americas back when the Conquistadors sailed here. I met her before that, though." He shoved his hands in his pockets, still watching her. "You were never meant to be Light, kitty cat. She was pure Shadow, and she was perfect."

A chill went up Sophie's spine. "I swear, lying is as easy as breathing to you, isn't it?"

Marshall let out a cold laugh. "What reason would I have to lie?" He stepped closer to her, and she did her best to avoid flinching back. She refused to allow him any more satisfaction in seeing her afraid of him. "Your hair, your eyes, even the shape of your lips, Sophie. Of course, she was a lot thinner. I think you'd probably look better in a corset though. More to push up," he said, holding his hands cupped in front of himself, at chest level. Sophie felt her lip rise in a snarl, and he laughed. "She was gorgeous."

"So, what? Is this one of those stories where the girl you wanted never gave you a second look, so you became a stalker freak in response?" Sophie asked.

He stepped toward her, towering over her, and she refused to step back.

"You've grown a backbone. I like it. This is what Shadow does. And for the record, she was mine for most of her life, and she loved every minute of it."

"Oh. Right. So are we supposed to be having our Darth Vader moment now?" She cocked her head, looked up at him. "Is that what this is?"

"What in the hell are you talking about?"

"Is this the part where you tell me you're my great great grandfather or something? And then I'm supposed to scream my denial and swear I'll never be like you?"

He sneered. "You are ridiculous. I said she was mine. I never said she gave me children. She was married to some other fool." And then he gave her that cold smile again, the one that had chilled her since the first time she'd seen it. "No, no grandfatherly feelings here for you."

Sophie didn't answer.

"Migisi was pretty. She was strong as hell. And when I finally pushed her over the edge, the chaos she caused was beautiful. But she always lacked something. You, though... you're the first that reminds me of her." He raised his hand and traced a fingertip down her jawline.

Sophie swallowed, tried to keep her breathing calm, steady. She flinched back. Him touching her was about as pleasurable as being swarmed by maggots. She wished she'd never stopped the car, wished she was home with Calder.

Marshall dropped his hand back to his side and laughed. "You don't get it yet. You stopped here because I wanted you to. Part of you knows that. My power over you is a glorious thing. I could have you bent over and begging me with nothing more than a thought."

Sophie wanted to argue, but she wasn't feeling brave enough to test him on that. Part of her feared he was right.

"Smart girl," he muttered. "Though I would have enjoyed proving myself."

"So, what? You want a replacement for her? Is that why you've been... the way you've been?" she asked, looking down.

"If you ever wanted to warm my bed, I'd take you in a second, and I'd make it worth your while. That's not why I started hanging around though. That part came later," he added, looking her up and down. "I made her a promise, that her descendants wouldn't suffer as she did, unable to unleash their power, suffocating under it. She came to love her power in the time we were together. And I made her a promise, that I would keep her line pure. Shadow. And at some point, one of you dumb bitches went and fucked a powerful Light warlock and had kids. And then another did the same thing. And that screwed everything up. I don't have their influence out of your bloodline, especially the second one, but I'm working on it. I'm so close now. You were a surprise," he said.

"I am Light," she said, raising her chin.

He laughed. "Keep deluding yourself. About this and about a million other things."

"I'm not the delusional one here," she said.

He smirked again. "You're the one who believes that bear you're fucking will be there through all the shit you're going to put him through. You really think he won't get sick of you? That he won't get tired of holding your hand all the time, of trying to keep you satisfied? You really think he means it when he promises you forever? He will resent you and everything you are." His voice was a low hiss, the words he said so perfectly echoing her own fears that she could do nothing to dispute them.

Sophie clamped her mouth shut.

"You know he will. And when he's gone, when he decides he's had enough, I'll be here. And you'll know where you belong."

"You are insane. Even if I believe what you're saying, even if she... what was her name?"

"Micaela," he answered, and the longing in those four syllables twisted something inside Sophie.

"I'm not her," she said.

Marshall closed his eyes, took a deep breath, and opened them again. "I know you're not. You could never hope to be. But you're as close as I'm going to get, and I'm getting really fucking good at pretending."

She turned toward the road, started stalking back to her car.

"Run. Just know that the second I want you back at my side, you'll be there, whether you want to be or not." She'd already reached her car, but his words followed her, sliding over and around her in a way that made her feel filthy just for having heard them, for allowing herself to be in his presence.

She started her engine and hit the gas, wanting nothing more than her house and her land, even if it no longer protected her the way it once had. Calder.

"Must learn control," she muttered to herself. She could not allow herself to become Marshall's puppet, Marshall's plaything. Not a chance in hell.

She would start by not letting Calder see how freaked out she was. That only made him worry, made him want to take care of her. She didn't want that, no matter how much she'd come to depend on it, no matter how easily she'd let him start doing it. She'd always stood on her own two feet, and she was going to keep on doing it. In the few miles until she got home, she forced herself to breathe normally, to numb out the fear, the anger, the unease she felt at Marshall's appearance.

She pulled into her driveway, glanced across the road. The lights in Calder's big white farmhouse were on, the living room and kitchen windows glowing warmly. Bryce's ugly blue car still sat in the driveway, though it was looking much less ugly than it had. She knew Calder planned to repaint the vintage monster soon, and she had no doubt it would look a lot better.

She ducked into her house, jumped into the shower, then slipped into clean clothes. The simple act of coming home from work and changing centered her. It was so normal. She'd started to forget what normal feel like.

Once she'd changed into some yoga pants and a top, she pulled her hair up and headed over to Calder's.

Her stomach growled, and her thirst was overwhelming.

Sophie closed her eyes and took a deep breath. "Control," she whispered to herself. She could be starving. She could be out of her mind with all of the things she needed. But she couldn't let herself be controlled by it. She had to at least try, or she would end up Marshall's toy, or worse.

CHAPTER THREE

As soon as her left foot hit the bottom step of Calder's front porch, the front door opened, and there he was, backlit, the warm light from the living room bathing his flannel-clad shoulders, picking up the golden ends of his hair, the ones that curled up under the bottom of his baseball hat when he worked. For just a moment, all Sophie could do was stare at him

Calder smiled. "What?" he asked with a laugh.

She smiled and shook her head. "I love you. Do you have any idea how much?"

His gaze softened, warmed even more. "Back atcha, Sophie."

She climbed the last few steps, reached him, and put her arms around his waist. She rested her face against his chest, breathing him in, letting the scent, the feel of him bring her back from the slimy sensations Marshall raised in her.

"How was it?" he asked softly, resting his chin on the top of her head.

"It was okay. I nearly bashed in the front of the vending machine a few times, but I held it together."

Calder let out a short laugh. "Yeah?"

"Yeah. They had Cool Ranch Doritos in there. It was almost too much to take," she said, and he laughed again. They stood there for a few minutes, and she felt the tension and fear flow from her.

"What do you want first? Me or dinner?" Calder finally asked.

"Is there any doubt which one I'd want more?" Sophie asked, grinning up at him.

"I made cheese lasagna," he told her.

"We can have it in a bit," she said, taking his hand and leading him into the house.

Later, she lay in Calder's arms, sweaty, exhausted, her body sore in the best way.

"You're going to get tired of this eventually," she said, hating that she remembered Marshall's words at a time like this.

Calder moved his hand from her hip to her chest, gently squeezing a breast, and she gasped. "Clearly you have no idea how the male mind works. Or at least how this male's mind works," he amended. "I don't think that's something you need to worry about."

"What about the rest of it?"

He sighed, rubbed his thumb across her nipple lazily, stirring her body anew. "You've got to stop this, Sophie. If I get sick of any part of us, I'll let you know and we'll work it out. I don't see that happening, though, and I don't even think about it unless you bring it up."

They lay in silence, Sophie cocooned, curled next to Calder's big body, his fingers lazily rubbing, tweaking, pinching her aching breasts.

"That warlock freak was around you today, wasn't he?" he finally asked. "I can smell him on you."

She nodded.

"What did he want?"

"To make a point," she said. He tweaked her nipple, and she let out a loud gasp.

"Which was?" he growled.

"That I'll come when he summons me, whether I want to or not," she said.

"Did he touch you?" Calder asked, and she shook her head.

"No. He didn't. And I would have fought him off if he tried."

"He forced you out to meet him," Calder said, and after a moment, she nodded. "He could force more."

"I won't let him," she said.

"I think I should talk to him," Calder said again, the growl in his voice both terrifying and alluring. She knew this part. He was possessive, and the control Marshall had over her, which he hadn't bothered to prove until that day, made Calder want blood. It made him want to protect her, keep her, make it clear who she belonged to.

He gave her breast one more firm squeeze, then stood up. She turned and watched him as he pulled on his jeans and a t-shirt.

"You know you can't. He would kill you without a thought, Calder," Sophie said.

"You really think that little of me? That I can't defend myself against a warlock?" he asked her. She stood up and pulled on one of his t-shirts.

"It's not that and you know it. I know you're strong. I know you can fight. I don't doubt you. But he would play dirty. He's the kind to hit from behind, except it's magic, not fists. You can't really fight someone who has no intention of fighting," she finished irritably. "And do you know what I really don't need right now? For you to go off on some stupid macho... *thing* because you feel like you have something to prove."

He crossed his arms, gaze boring into hers from across the room. She kept her gaze on his, knowing he was still in that half-animal mode, the one she was beginning to recognize as all shifter. Looking down or away, which was what she was most comfortable doing during a confrontation, would not do when he was like this. So she kept her eyes on his, and finally he took a breath and shook his head.

"You're right," he finally said.

"I know," she said, and he laughed.

"I still would love to kick his ass, though."

"I know. And I know that, if you took his stupid magic out of the equation, if you made it impossible for him to play dirty, you would wipe the floor with him. You probably would anyway. But I don't want to find out," she said.

He nodded. "I know. I'm sorry for being an asshole."

"A stupid macho asshole," she corrected, and he laughed again. "And wasn't there something about lasagna earlier?"

He shook his head and held out his hand, and they walked downstairs to the kitchen together. He reheated the lasagna, and they sat at the round table in his kitchen.

The urge to shovel the warm, cheesy bit of heaven into her mouth as quickly as she could was almost impossible to ignore. But she forced herself, thinking "control" over and over again, making sure she put her fork down between bites. It was like all of those stupid little tips she'd ever read for how to eat less when you are on a diet, except that everything felt about a million times harder.

"Bryce and I cut down those dead pines behind your house today," Calder said. "You'll have a good amount of firewood."

Sophie nodded. "Thanks." She couldn't say more. The trees were another sign of the blight the Shadow was causing. Everything around her either died or weakened. She wondered why, thankfully, that hadn't been true of Calder. She kept an eye on him, watching, waiting for signs of sickness or anything else wrong. What she would do if she saw them, she had no idea. But she watched and waited, just as she watched and waited for signs he was becoming fed up. So far, there had been neither.

Then again, it had only been a little over a month.

"You'll have plenty of wood to split," Calder said, and she nodded, remembering him splitting wood like a madman in an effort to keep the madness at bay. "But if that doesn't do it for you, I'll do it. I still find it kind of relaxing." He took another bite of lasagna, and she watched him as he ate.

God, he was gorgeous, she thought to herself. That wavy blond hair, those icy blue eyes. Broad shoulders and muscles for days, and the way his mouth quirked up at the corner, just a little, when he was amused. The smell of him…she gave her head a tiny shake, and took another bite of her dinner. Control.

"Bryce is gonna pop the question," Calder said, putting his fork down, his plate clear.

Sophie's mouth dropped open in shock. "He is?" Bryce and her best friend, Layla, had been nuts about one another for most of their lives, but had only recently made it to the point of admitting to one another what everyone else already knew.

Calder grinned. "You can't say anything, though. He's still kinda freaked out by it all."

Sophie laughed. "Well, the boy moves fast, I'll give him that."

"If you consider twenty-plus years fast, then sure," Calder said with a laugh.

Sophie pushed her plate away and rested her elbows on the table, her chin in her hands. "I'm so happy for them. Layla's in heaven."

"So's Bryce," Calder said. "You know what, though?"

"What?"

"As happy as I am for them, I've even happier for us." His face was serious, his eyes on hers. "This was a long time coming, and it's better than I ever could have imagined. And I could imagine a hell of a lot."

29

She reached across the table and took his hand in hers. "Same here. I can't believe we're finally here together."

"All we need is you and me, Sophie," Calder said, gently stroking her wrist with his thumb. "We have those two things, and we have everything."

She smiled, and squeezed his hand, and felt Shadow rise up inside her, as if reminding her that it was there.

As if she could ever forget it.

After they did the dinner dishes together, they'd made their way up to Calder's bedroom, and he'd loved her in the way only he could, tirelessly, thoroughly, bringing her to the edge of sanity over and over again until she was limp and exhausted in his arms. She was lying beside him, his body wrapped around hers, his hands each cupping a breast as he quietly snored behind her. The only other sounds were the occasional "hoot" of an owl in the woods nearby and the ticking of the old grandfather clock in the hallway. She lay there, and lazily replayed their lovemaking in her mind. He was never rough with her, though he'd finally, after bringing her to the edge with his mouth and fingers so many times she'd lost count, taken her hard and fast, knowing it was what she needed. The memory of it, of the look in his eyes as he'd thrusted into her, along with the glorious ache between her thighs, the feel of his warm, strong hands on her breasts had her shivering in a combination of need and pleasure.

She had to stop thinking about it, or she would be out of her mind with need for him again.

She slowly, gently extricated her body from his embrace, then looked down at him and watched him sleep for a few moments. The fact that he hadn't woken made her grin. To say that Calder was a deep sleeper was an understatement. Working, running as his bear, doing all of the miscellaneous things he did around both of their houses while she was busy with work and other things, and then loving her as enthusiastically as he always did all made for a sound night's sleep. Still, she sometimes woke in the night to find him awake, and when she asked him what he was doing up, he usually told her he was double-checking the locks or making sure they'd blown the candles out. She guessed that was anxiety, that desire, maybe, to control the small things because the big things seemed too insane.

She slipped into his t-shirt, then quietly headed down the stairs to the living room. She clicked on the lamp next to the ugly brown recliner he liked to kick back in when he was watching baseball, and she grabbed the canvas backpack she'd been lugging around with her, the one carrying Migisi's journals as well as the file folders of copies her friend Thea had made for her from her archives as they'd tried to trace Migisi and Luc's story.

She'd been through all of it, of course. She always let her eyes skim over Migisi's instructions for how to truly break the curse, by destroying the one she loved.

Migisi was nuts. What the hell did she know, anyway, Sophie thought to herself.

It wasn't the words that drew Sophie's attention anymore. Those, she had memorized. It was Migisi's artwork, the sketches and watercolors scattered throughout two of the journals that held her interest. Of course, there were those early ones, the ones Migisi had done of the falls and of Luc in his bear form, the dead woods and moonlight. In the past month, Sophie had made her way through the rest of the thick journal. While most of the writing had been messy, sometimes indecipherable, it mostly focused on Migisi learning about using her Shadow powers.

Sophie's stomach turned as she read through some of it again. Migisi had embraced the Shadow fully, once she'd finally succumbed to the curse Marshall had cleverly hidden in Luc, making it so that the more time Migisi spent with her beloved, the deeper she was pulled into Shadow. In the journals, she'd called it a "fear curse," and berated herself for not seeing it for what it was early on. "Any fool with an ounce of magic should have seen what was happening. And I was so focused on Luc that I never even saw it until after it was too late," she'd written.

Luc, Calder's ancestor. And Calder had carried that curse with him, as well, so that the longer Sophie had spent with him, the more she felt Shadow pulling at her. Her magic had gone haywire, and then finally fizzled to nothing. Not that she'd had much to begin with, she thought sardonically. She'd been a weakling, as far as witches were concerned.

The words faded away as Sophie became lost in thought. She'd started losing her Light magic, because of the curse on Calder's line, and whatever it did, however it worked, that made Shadow rise within her line. And to break the other curse, the one that Migisi had put on Calder's line, she'd embraced Shadow so that she would be strong enough to take his curse. She still was not a strong witch. Her Shadow magic was not any stronger than her Light magic had been, which was a relief.

But when the Shadow flowing through her was combined with the madness of Calder's curse, it was a combination that terrified her. She could see, easily, how she could come to be a force for destruction. It would be all too easy. With no effort at all, plants died around her, and healthy animals became unable to produce milk or eggs, unable to reproduce.

It would be all too easy to bring that Shadowy magic to the people of Copper Falls, to watch the town slowly but surely die around her. Would it all extend to people? Would children fail in the womb? Would they become sick if she was around them too much?

All of the questions weighed on her, and so she turned, ironically, to Migisi's journals. Not the words, but the drawings and paintings. Her artwork had changed with the Shadow as well, Sophie thought, turning her attention back to the journal on her lap. For a while, it had had an angry, uncontrolled feel to it. Black, bleak, and tired, were the feelings she got from it all. But, over time, it began to change again. It regained its control, the refined feel of Migisi's earlier work. But it was different, too. Deeper, perhaps, though she wished she could find a better word for it. The drawings of the landscape around Copper Falls held a sense of yearning, of deep love that Sophie could easily relate to. It was in the careful lines, the intricate detail. Migisi had returned to the falls over and over again, and in at least a few of the drawings, the very boulder that Sophie and Calder had first kissed on could be seen.

Sophie wrinkled her brow. There were two enormous oaks, one at either side of the boulder. They had shaded Sophie when she'd sat there on hot summer days. She'd figured they were quite old, but they were not in any of the drawings Migisi had done of the falls. "Weird," she murmured. Maybe Migisi had left them out to show the falls better.

What really made Sophie wonder, though, were the later watercolors. The watercolors of an enormous, shaggy black bear, sometimes with his head lifted majestically, sometimes looking mad, feral.

Luc.

She'd known, from what she'd learned from Thea, from that visit to the Copper Falls cemetery, that they'd found their way back to one another somehow. They'd been buried side-by-side, had died on the same day. She hadn't quite believed it at the time, but here was the proof. And she was sure, for some reason, that these were not merely things Migisi had remembered and then painted. She recognized that feral look to Luc, because she'd seen it so often in Calder when he'd been burdened with the curse.

No, these had come later. After the curse, after whatever had happened between them. She wondered if they'd managed to love one another again somehow, even through it all.

She wondered if they'd somehow managed to be happy, in the end.

With a sigh, she closed the journal and placed it back in the bag, then clicked off the lamp and went back to Calder's room, pulling the shirt from her body before she crawled back into bed beside him. As she watched Calder sleep, she hoped.

She hoped Migisi and Luc had found a way to make it all work.

CHAPTER FOUR

July 12, 1870

Migisi stood on the dirt road looking toward the neat clapboard house. It was long past sunset, and the windows were lit from within, the dim light that comes from candles and firelight. She had watched the house all that day, unseen but clearly sensed, the wrongness that surrounded her making the inhabitants tense and jumpy as they had gone about their business.

The forest, normally so full of the sounds of wildlife, was silent around her.

She could hear a baby crying, and her gaze hardened.

Luc's child. The child he'd gotten on his new bride.

A child he had managed to make with another, when the ones he and Migisi had tried to make together had each faded away, her womb unable to support the life they'd so wanted to create.

She rested her hand on her own swollen belly. She was in her final month of pregnancy, and the baby kicked, strong and energetic, in her womb. A daughter, she knew.

She would have a daughter. A daughter likely born to Shadow, when Migisi herself had had the glory of having been born to Light.

She watched, and she listened, and soon the baby's cries quieted. The door of the cabin opened, and Migisi's breath caught.

Him.

Light, his body was the same as always. Strong, broad. Her fingers ached to run themselves through his beard, and her body yearned for his touch.

After all this time. After nearly ten years of living in the Shadow, after cursing him and his entire line in a moment of loss and rage… After all this time, she still wanted him.

He stopped still, and his gaze swung in her direction. She made no effort to hide herself.

He closed the door behind him, then stalked to where she was, stopping when he was a few feet away from her, where the narrow road cut through the endless wildflowers.

They stood, and she regarded him in silence, as he did the same to her.

"What did you do to me, Migisi?" he asked, his deep voice low in the dark, the familiar French words soothing despite the anguish in which they'd been uttered.

"We both know what I did," she answered quietly in his native tongue, the language one she hadn't spoken since the day she'd turned her back on him.

"I still don't understand what happened," he said, watching her closely. "I did not know that woman. I do not remember meeting her, or touching her, or anything else. All I remember is sitting with my business partners, and then there I was, touching a woman I did not know, and you standing there with that stricken look on your face."

Migisi swallowed, trying to control the emotions running through her. She could not speak.

"And you cursed me," he said, as if he still could not believe it. "You made me this mad… thing. You did that to me, Migisi."

She nodded, unable to look at him with it stated so clearly between them. And it hurt her more, somehow, that instead of anger in his voice, she heard disappointment. Sadness. Anger, she could have handled.

"I don't know what you're doing here, Migisi, but it's time for you to leave. If I see you near my family again, I'll destroy you. I don't care about the bastard you carry."

"Bastard?" she asked, raising an eyebrow.

He came to her, took her chin roughly in his hand. "It's not mine, which makes it a bastard."

"You seem to have moved on, my love."

He let loose a rough laugh. "That shows how little you know me," he said. He released her and stepped back, running his hands through his hair in that way he always did when he was agitated. "It changes nothing. If you come near my family again, I will kill you. Keep your vile magic away from us."

"Once upon a time, you found my magic beautiful."

"Once upon a time, it was," he answered simply, and it felt as if he had punched her. "We both know that you are no longer what you once were. Stay away from me, Migisi. Go back to whoever got that child on you and live happily ever after. Or don't. I don't care either way."

And with that, he turned away, heading back to the cabin and the new family he had created without her.

CHAPTER FIVE

After two more days of struggling through work, a day off felt like reaching an oasis in a vast desert. She was grateful for the first time since she began working at the resort for the reduced hours that came with the end of the tourist season. Always, before, she'd had her aunt's debts and the possibility of losing her land hanging over her head. Autumn had always brought the scurry for part time jobs to fill in the missing income.

This year, her meager salary would be enough to cover her living expenses, now that the debt had been paid. Sophie stood in her kitchen and smiled a little to herself. Though, at the time, when Calder had bought her house out from under her at auction, she hadn't found the situation nearly as comforting.

She leaned against the butcher block counter in her warm kitchen, sipping a soothing herbal tea blend from her favorite antique tea cup. She forced herself to stay, to be calm, to focus on the moment. She forced herself to see the way the late afternoon sun gleamed across the newly-waxed wood floor, the way the light picked up the subtle floral pattern on the area rug in the living room. She held onto Calder's advice, and hoped that if she could do this one thing, if she could slow down, and focus, and truly exist in the moment... if she could do that, then she could stay mostly sane.

So she stood, the herbal scent of her tea wafting toward her, sun shining in the windows.

And she needed it. She'd spent the entire day with Calder, but he had left a while ago to see Bryce about his ugly car and the hunt the two of them were planning. They did a long hunt every fall — Calder, Bryce, and Calder's brother, Jon. Calder had initially called it off for that year, and, at Sophie's insistence, he'd agreed to reschedule with his friend and his brother. She didn't want his entire life changing, and she didn't want him to feel like he was singularly devoted to babysitting her.

Though how she would manage for a week, when she was nearly out of her mind having him away from her for even an hour, made her break out in a cold sweat. Stupid, insane curse. This possessiveness was part of it, and she'd only gotten more possessive the longer she lived with the curse. Every time he walked away from her, even if it was simply to leave the house to grab the mail or feed Merlin, it made her edgy, as if she wanted to drag him back and keep him. She'd wondered, at first, how much of that was just her. After a lifetime spent wanting him, she had Calder. She had the one man she'd ever truly wanted, and she knew the rest of their lives wouldn't be enough.

She smiled, remembering that conversation. How pleased Calder had looked to hear her say those words, the way his face had softened, the warmth in his gaze. The way he'd slowly run his hands down her sides, over her hips, and pulled her toward him. How he'd told her that the insane possessive thing was all the curse, but that she should remember that idea about forever not being long enough for those times when he would undoubtedly manage to piss her off.

She shook her head with a smile and gulped down the last of her tea. She had a quiet house, and time to focus, and she had other things to do besides stand there mooning over Calder. She glanced at the potted plant she'd picked up the day before, sitting on the windowsill near the table where she and Calder ate their meals. She'd bought it on clearance from the local nursery because it was wilted and potbound. That was reassuring, in its way. If she killed it as she seemed to kill so many other plants of late, at least she would have the comfort of knowing it was likely on its way out, anyway.

It had wilted a bit more in her presence, and she supposed it could have been from her Shadow magic. But it could not, as well.

She walked over to the windowsill and picked up the plant, its terra cotta pot cool in her hands. She carried it back to the kitchen and set it on the counter.

And she focused.

She called to mind the magic she'd worked so often, that healing, life-giving magic that had once come to her. It had never roared through her, and it had never come easily. Always, working her magic had been like coaxing a shy animal out of hiding. It had been delicate, painstaking work.

She looked at the plant, and focused first on her gratitude for the Light, for its beauty and richness, for its life-affirming energy.

The fact that she could not longer feel it was something she forced herself not to think about.

She spent a moment sending her apologies to the Light for what she had allowed herself to become. For allowing the Light within her to be profaned, to the point that she'd lost it completely.

She sent a prayer that she would once again be worthy, that the fact that her intentions had been those of a Lightwitch would be enough.

Those things done, she turned her attention once again to the plant. It was an English ivy, and its leaves wilted horribly. Some were brown, some a sickly yellow.

She focused, and recalled the spell she'd used so often.

She could see it. She could see the way the spell was supposed to work, just as she always had. She could see the way she was supposed to cast the spell, the way the magic was supposed to work, the way her power was supposed to wrap itself around the plant, the Light's power combining with the inherent life force within the plant.

She could see it, and yet she could not call forth even a spark of the Light magic she'd once had.

She focused harder, no longer coaxing. Calling. Commanding.

Begging.

To her utter dismay, instead of Light answering her call, she felt Shadow rise within her. She tried to stop focusing, tried to let the spell drop. She could still envision the way her spell was supposed to work, and as she stood there, she could see Shadow twisting, working its way into the spell she'd been trying to perform.

Sophie gave a strangled cry and closed her eyes, shook her head to break her focus. She felt the spell fall apart, this time with some relief.

The plant looked no worse for wear, she noticed as she looked it over. It didn't look any better, either, but at least it wasn't worse.

"One more time," she murmured to herself. She knew she was reaching the end of her ability to focus at all, as she stood there with her stomach growling in insane hunger, her throat dry with thirst, her body yearning for release. She forced herself to focus. She would have to learn to ignore the hunger. Master it, somehow.

She rebuilt the spell until she was able to see it. This part, she could do. It felt familiar to when she was learning to use her magic, when she was in her teens and early twenties. At first, all she'd been able to do was see the spells

41

she read about online. See the mechanics of them, how they went together. Eventually, she'd learned to fill them with her Light magic, and had been delighted to see plants grow healthier, animals heal, and humans find themselves feeling heartier. She'd worked the magic over and over again, putting a bit of that healing power into the soaps and lotions she'd once made.

She focused then, holding the spell in her mind, her eyes closed, her hands in front of her, fingers moving every once in a while as she imitated the gestures she'd so often made when casting.

She coaxed. Pleaded. And once again, she was rewarded only with Shadow slithering its way through what she'd made. She groaned in frustration, and the spell shattered.

She plopped down onto one of the dining room chairs and looked at the plant in frustration. She held some hope. At least she could still see the way her magic was supposed to work. As she sat, she looked at the plant without really seeing it, her mind racing as her body nearly screamed with her endless hunger. She could see the way Light magic worked. Did Shadow work the same way? Would she be able to build the spells the way she did with Light?

She shook her head, pushing the thought away. She had no desire to learn how to work Shadow magic. She didn't want it, and she certainly didn't want to learn about how to use it.

That crazy, restless energy she'd inherited with Calder's curse had her gritting her teeth, and she finally gave up. She stood and stepped into her sneakers. She let herself out the back door of her cottage, and headed for the woods, stopping to scratch Merlin's ears on the way. He gave her a cranky bleat in return, and she shook her head, then took off toward the woods.

She would run off this energy. And then she would come home and try to cook. She hadn't had the greatest luck in the kitchen since the brownie incident. The two times she'd tried, she'd burned everything, distracted by Calder's curse.

But today, she'd surprise Calder with dinner, and she'd try to pretend that everything was just fine.

Calder pulled into his driveway and climbed out of his truck. He pulled the box he'd picked up at the post office out of the back. The taillights he'd been waiting for to complete Bryce's slightly-less-ugly car had finally come in, which was a good sign because the details like this were signs that he was getting close to the end of the restoration. He opened the garage and looked the vintage Dodge over. It was coming along. It ran now, and he'd completed the body work, getting rid of the dings and rust that had accumulated over the years. Of course, there was still the interior to deal with, but he was happy with his progress so far.

He had two more restorations lined up after he finished Bryce's, and one he was working on while he waited for parts to come in. He glanced at the other car he was working on, a 1970 Barracuda. He'd had more requests for Barracudas in the past few months, and he wondered at the sudden popularity again. There were cycles to all things, and which old cars were trendy was apparently one of them.

Calder stowed the box on one of the crowded workbenches, then pulled the garage door shut and looked toward Sophie's house. Maybe they'd go out to dinner that night, he thought to himself. He didn't feel like cooking, and she seemed less freaked out by the idea of going out where other people were. He felt his guilt crash over him, the way it did every time he thought of the woman he loved bearing his curse. And while he understood her reasoning, while he understood that she was stronger and better able to handle it than he was, he still couldn't deny that he was angry with her for taking it. Her reasoning had been based on love and logic, but all he could see when he saw that insanity in her eyes, the insanity that had been so familiar to him, was the fact that the woman he loved was hurting because of him.

And he'd had no say in the matter.

He loved her, more than he'd ever loved anyone. He would do anything for her. And she'd told him time and time again that she couldn't stand by and watch him fall into insanity, the way his father and every first-born male in his family before him had. She couldn't do it, because she loved him.

Yet he was supposed to be okay with watching her fall apart. The love of his life, who'd lived through hell already and now had a whole new kind of hell to deal with. He was supposed to be fine with watching her suffer under a curse that was his to bear.

He closed his eyes and took a deep breath. They'd been over and over it. They'd both said everything they could on the matter, more times than he could count. And it always came down to the fact that what was done couldn't be undone, and that she was stronger and better able to deal with his curse. His bear didn't work well with the insanity the curse brought. It was a deadly combination that would have resulted, eventually, in Calder having to be kept imprisoned the way his father had.

I can't do that to you, Calder. I couldn't lock you up, and you'd end up killing me or someone else. Is that what you want?

Words thrown at him when she'd reached the breaking point. Words he hadn't been able to refute, no matter how much he'd wanted to.

Calder swallowed his anger and guilt and crossed the road to her house. As he walked up the gravel driveway, he could hear music coming from the house. The Supremes, he realized. And, the closer he got to the house, he realized he could hear Sophie singing along.

He raised his nose into the air, scenting it. Venison. She was cooking.

And it didn't even smell burned, he realized with a smile.

He stepped up onto the small porch at the front of the cottage and walked in, the scent of venison and herbs surrounding him, overlaid with her scent, that clean, wild scent that was his woman. Her back was to him as she stirred something on the stove, and she sang, and he watched as her hips moved side to side with the music. Her long, thick curls cascaded down her back, nearly reaching her luscious ass. He practically salivated at the sight.

And this was why, no matter how pissed he was that she'd taken his curse without asking, it was all too easy for him to forget to be irritated with her. One look, and he was a goner.

She turned then and saw him, and she smiled, her dark eyes sparkling.

"Hey, sexy," she said, coming over to him and wrapping her arms around his waist.

"I don't think I'm the sexy one here," he murmured as he lowered his lips to hers.

"Mm. You have no idea," she whispered against his lips. Then she smiled up at him. "I didn't burn anything," she said, and he laughed.

"It smells fantastic," he said. Together, they set the table, and she plated up a fragrant stew of venison, potatoes, carrots, parsnips, and a rich sauce for him. For herself, a baked potato and a side of roasted carrots. They sat and Calder lifted his fork to his mouth. The rich, meaty flavor of the stew only made him feel hungrier, and he dug in, finishing off one plate and getting up to grab a second helping before he even realized it. Sophie laughed a little, and he threw her a grin.

He polished off his second plate, and contemplated a third. There was enough left in the pot for one more helping, he thought.

He looked across the table at Sophie, mesmerized by the sight of her lips around the tines of her fork. The stew was promptly forgotten, just as quickly as his thought of a third helping had come on. He watched as she took another bite, her lush lips closing over her fork, then sliding down the tines as she pulled the fork back out.

"What?" she asked with a bit of a laugh.

Busted.

"You have the most gorgeous mouth," he said, aware of the low growl in his voice. She stilled at his tone, and he could smell another scent now, even stronger than the stew, than her wild scent.

The intoxicating scent of her desire.

"Calder," she began softly. He watched her, the way her ample breasts heaved with her shallow breaths, the way her skin flushed a rosy pink under his gaze. He stood up, and without another word, he picked her up and carried her over to the daybed in the living room, dinner completely forgotten in the maddening haze of his need for her.

Hours later, once they'd exhausted one another, he lay in bed beside her and watched her sleep. Her hair was an unruly mass of curls, tumbling around her, slightly obscuring her face as she lay curled beside him. Her lips were swollen from his kisses, and he could see the red bite mark he'd left on her neck.

He flexed a bit, feeling the long scratches she'd left down his back. She'd been wild, needy, single-minded in her need for relief.

And he had been just as insane with it. It had taken him no effort this time to keep up with her, to give her everything she needed. In fact, for once, he'd outlasted her, to the point where she'd finally moaned that she couldn't take anymore after coming down from her final orgasm.

He would have been swelling in male pride if he hadn't had that moment, that insane, stupid moment after she'd said the words, in which he wanted to ignore them and keep going. It was only an instant, and not even enough of one that Sophie noticed. She had no idea that for just a moment, he'd been back where he was before she took his curse away from him. For an instant, he was drowning in his need and lust.

And that instant was enough to scare the hell out of him.

He'd stopped, of course, and she'd kissed him and fallen asleep beside him. And as he lay there watching her sleep, he knew he'd have to watch himself with her. Maybe he'd attributed too much of his maddening lust for her to his beast, to the curse, when it had just been him all along.

She trusted him, and she loved him. And he swore he'd never give her a reason to stop doing either of those things. He watched, wondering if she'd sleep through the night. He closed his eyes, and eventually drifted off to sleep.

He woke a while later to find her side of the bed empty, and he swore at himself. A glance toward the bathroom told him she hadn't merely gotten up to relieve herself.

He cursed himself again as he pulled his jeans on. Every night, he told himself he'd somehow manage to keep tabs on her, and every night, he ended up sleeping the sleep of the dead, and she'd drift away.

He opened the back door and ran toward the woods. He knew, by now, that he'd find her in the same place. For the last two weeks or so, more often that not, he'd woken to find her missing. The first few times, he'd panicked, and run as his bear, picturing the worst — usually involving the warlock. So far nothing terrible had happened, but the fact that she was having these episodes where she wandered and had no idea she was doing it... the fact that she was having them at all was not a good sign. The fact that she couldn't remember them afterward, the fact that she didn't recognize him when she was in one of them was something he tried not to think about.

He came to the edge of the woods, just before the clearing along the edge of the river. She stood there, naked as she'd been when they'd fallen asleep. She was like a marble statue in the dark woods, still as stone. A shiver went up his spine at the blank, unfocused look in her eyes.

47

It was the same every time. She stood there with that emptiness in her eyes.

"Sophie," he said quietly, calmly.

She didn't respond. It was as if he wasn't even there, and he tried to ignore the sick feeling that rose within him, the reality that he knew this look from his father. He'd likely worn the same look himself a few times.

He stifled a growl of rage over the curse, over the fact that she was suffering from it. Instead, he took a deep breath and walked up to her. He wondered if at some point, she'd lash out either physically or with her magic, but so far, she hadn't done that when he'd found her.

"Come on, kitten," he said softly, hoping without hope for a flicker of recognition in her eyes.

Nothing.

He took a breath and picked her up, carrying her in his arms back toward the house. She rested there, staring at nothing with those dark, empty eyes, and he could barely breathe around his fear.

She'd wake in the morning, and not remember a thing. And he didn't want to burden her any more than she already was. If she knew, she'd be completely freaked out.

He just had to get better at making sure she didn't slip out of bed in the first place.

Everything would be fine.

CHAPTER SIX

The post-tourist season meant work was generally quiet for Sophie, which made it both better and worse in terms of dealing with the curse. Better, because there were less people around to see her when she had one of her panic attacks or became overwhelmed. Fewer men around as well, which was always a good thing. Worse, because there was just less to do. During the tourist season, they'd often have no vacancies, every room full, every room needing to be cleaned on a daily basis. There would be mountains of linens to help fold, or customers to assist. Once tourist season was over, the resort was quiet as a tomb, at least until skiing season started.

Sophie only had a handful of rooms on her three floors to clean, though she did open and refresh the others as well. As she did, her mind wandered, either to the night before, and the way Calder had been with her, or, less happily, to that morning, to the strange distance in his eyes as he'd pulled away from her, preventing her from touching him, from loving him, before their day began. He'd tried to joke about how he was still tired from the night before, but she knew him. That look in his eyes was not one he usually had with her.

She pushed the thought away again. She couldn't think about it now, and she couldn't do anything about it now, anyway. Maybe he'd been telling the truth.

She was demanding too much of him, she thought as she walked through the lobby to check on the brochure display to see if anything needed to be replenished. She demanded too much time, too much energy, just as she feared she would, and it would eventually drive him away. And as she thought it, she felt a spark of irritation. As if he had anything to complain about, considering that he was no longer under the threat of losing his mind now that she lived with his curse.

She shook her head a little as she surveyed the brochure rack, pushing the thoughts aside again. They were running low on brochures about the lighthouse, she noted. She smiled briefly at Janice, the woman who had manned the check-in desk since Sophie had started. Just as she did every day, Janice wore her resort uniform under a gaudy orange sweater that she'd filled with all manner of novelty buttons. "I'm with stupid." "Kiss me, I'm Irish." "WTF?" Anyone else couldn't have gotten away with that particular breach of protocol, but apparently it paid to be related to the owner of the resort.

"How are things, Janice?" Sophie asked politely, knowing what was coming.

"Ah, I can't complain. My hip hurts like the dickens, and that ingrown toenail of mine is paining me something awful. It's hell getting old, girl."

Sophie nodded in commiseration, then turned and headed toward the supply room for the brochures. She busied herself with straightening the rack, then offered to water the plants for Janice, who accepted gratefully. The large front windows of the lobby overflowed with ferns, ivy, and pothos. Sophie tried not to spend too much time nearby as she watered them. The last thing she needed was to kill Janice's prized gargantuan houseplants with Shadow magic.

There was only one other person in the lobby, a guest sitting in one of the chairs studying a guidebook. A cup of coffee sat on the table beside her, and Sophie wondered if she was meeting someone there. As she carried the watering can back through the lobby, the woman caught her eye.

"Excuse me — do you work here?" she asked. Sophie nodded. She looked young, maybe in her early twenties, and she had the look of someone who enjoyed the outdoors, tan, trim, and strong. She was dressed as if she was about to go on a hike or something, right down to the well-worn hiking boots.

"I do. Can I help you?"

"Yes, please! I'm looking through this," she tilted the book she'd been reading so Sophie could see the cover. *Paranormal Copper Falls*, Sophie read, suppressing a smirk. Oh, it was more supernatural than that book could ever hope, she thought to herself. "And it's talking about this 'witch in the woods.' Do you know anything about that?"

Sophie scrunched up her face. "That's a child's story, kind of a play off of Hansel and Gretel with a local twist. A witch who lives alone deep in the forest and those who go to see her never return," Sophie said, widening her eyes for dramatic effect. She'd forgotten all about the story, though it had come up nearly every Halloween when she was in elementary school.

The woman laughed. "So you're telling me not to get my hopes up," she said.

Sophie grinned. "That's what I'm saying."

"Do you think there's anything to any of this?" she asked, nodding toward the book in her hand. "I mean, like this witch. It says she lives deep in the forest, alone, and that those who go to her don't return. It says that for acres around her home, the forest has died and even animals fear to tread. That can't be real, right?"

Sophie stared at the woman as a chill went down her spine. She clamped her mouth shut for a moment, then remembered herself.

"No. That can't be real," she finally managed. "Though I would check out the Marsdale. I keep hearing they get reports about a ghost in their bar all the time."

The woman's face lit up. "Thank you! I'll definitely check it out." Sophie plastered on a smile and gave her a nod, and then headed back to the storage closet with her watering can.

A woman, a witch, who lived in the woods, yet the woods had failed around the place she called home. Sophie went over and over it, and then pulled out her phone and Googled. She knew the general area where the house was supposed to be. There weren't many roads leading into that part of the forest.

She only hesitated for a moment, glancing at the clock and realizing her shift was over in less than twenty minutes. She hit Calder's number on her phone.

"Hey, kitten," his deep voice said, and she smiled at the sound of it.

"Hey, you sexy thing. I just wanted to call to tell you I'm going to be home a little later tonight. I want to meet with Thea for a bit and see if she's found anything else."

"Oh, okay," he said, and she wondered if that was relief in his voice. "Come over when you get back, okay?"

"I will. I love you."

"Love you more," he said, and she smiled.

He hung up, and she realized that for the first time, she didn't entirely believe him when he said the words.

Sophie left work a while later, tossing her bag onto the passenger seat of her car as she climbed in. She started her car, which ran better than it ever had, thanks to Calder, and turned toward the highway that wound its way through the forest. Happily, that meant taking Rockway, which was one of the most scenic driving routes in the entire state.

Rockway Mountain looked over the city of Copper Falls, out to Lake Superior. The combination of forest, lake, and lighthouses made for an absolutely beautiful view. The sky was deep blue overhead, and autumn's last leaves clung to the trees. For the most part, branches were bare, and the world was caught in that breath of waiting, that phase between the pleasantly cool days of autumn and the brutal freeze that came with winter. It was as if everything, including those last remaining leaves, wanted to cling to the comfort of autumn for as long as possible.

Sophie could relate.

As she drove, she listened to the soothing piano sonatas she'd put on her mp3 player. She'd been trying all manner of things to try to deal with the curse, knowing, even before that morning, that she could not rely on Calder to help her with everything. First of all, because she'd always done for herself and wasn't about to change that now, and secondly, and perhaps most importantly, because they both deserved so much better. She would rely on herself, and keep herself together. Meditation, yoga, soothing music... she was using all of them with varying degrees of success to keep the insanity at bay, to keep the fear of what she now was from completely overwhelming her.

Shadow. She was Shadow. She was death, and blight, and violence. She was everything she'd never hoped to be. The Light, her beloved Light, was about life and love and honor. And she had lost it, and Marshall waited in the wings, biding his time until he decided to truly use her in a way she knew she would hate herself for. His kind were strengthened not only by how many Shadow witches they controlled, but also by how much violence and chaos happened around them.

His presence alone caused a bit of that. She'd noted through the grapevine that in the past few weeks, which lined up with Marshall's arrival in Copper Falls, arrests had quadrupled. Theft, vandalism, and violent crimes were all on the rise, which was shocking to the tightly-knit year-round community of Copper Falls. It was because of Marshall and his influence, and she knew he planned to use her to somehow add to his power even more.

Which was why she was driving through the national forest chasing a child's story.

The marks of a Shadow witch were all there in the story the woman had mentioned. And if there was another Shadow witch around, one who was perhaps not under Marshall's control, maybe she could learn from her. She had these powers, and she hated them. They felt filthy and oily and wrong. But she had them, and she knew that if she didn't learn about them, if she didn't figure out how to do things with them, she would truly be at Marshall's mercy. He wouldn't teach her anything other than the bare minimum he would need to to reach his goals and demonstrate his control over her. She had a feeling, as with so many other things in her life so far, that staying a step ahead of Marshall would mean taking control of her magic, learning what she could do with the meager amount she possessed.

Maybe this Shadow witch, if she even truly existed, could help her. At this point, Sophie was more than happy to place her hopes in fairy tales. It wasn't like she had much else at the moment.

The two-lane highway snaked its way through the national forest, towering white pines and oaks flanking the road, branches stretching overhead making it feel like driving through a tunnel of trees. Through spring and fall, it was a shady, soothing drive, surrounded by shades of green. Now, with most of the leaves gone, it was much brighter than usual, and she could see the sky peeking through the latticework of branches over the road. As she drove, she looked for street signs. If the guidebook was right, this witch could be found just off of South Mine. Sophie still couldn't quite believe she was even bothering with this.

After another few minutes, she spied the black and white street sign that said *S. Mine*. She turned onto it, trading asphalt for rutted dirt road. The trees were even thicker once she turned off, and she watched a deer bound across the road a few yards ahead of her, then disappear into the forest again.

As she drove, she began to notice the forest becoming less robust. At first, the forest just seemed less dense. Then the trees began to seem shorter, stunted. Some looked deformed, as if they'd grown despite whatever it was that wanted them not to. Another mile or so, and the trees had thinned to just a scattered few, twisted and stunted, almost painful looking. The land between them was gray; not even the hearty wild plants that thrived in the northern Michigan sand were able to withstand whatever was affecting the earth there.

This was what would happen to her land, given enough time. Her beautiful, lush, life-giving acreage would become just like this unless she did something. Unless she found her way back to the Light.

She shook her head. She'd never let it happen. She would rather leave the land she loved than see it turned into this wasteland.

She kept driving, nothing but gray soil and the occasional spindly, dead tree on either side of the road. There were no more deer bounding past, and, though her window was down, she couldn't decipher a single bird call. Nothing but dead silence surrounded her, the sound of her engine cutting through it.

The sense of wrongness there was overwhelming, and Sophie's Shadow magic responded to it. She felt calmer than she had in a while. Of course she did. Shadow loved destruction, she realized. Her magic would have hated every moment spent on her land, with life all around, with Calder there, loving her through even her most desperate, insane moments. But here, in this desolate, sick place, the Shadow magic within her hummed.

She navigated one more bend in the dirt road, and a house came into view. It was not the type of house Sophie expected to find there, deep in the forest. This was the domain of log cabins and little stone houses, the occasional clapboarded Cape Cod or manufactured home. What rose before her was nothing short of something out of a fairy tale. It was a tall Victorian, complete with rounded turrets, fish scale siding, and a porch that wrapped around from the front of the house to both sides. It was painted a stone gray color, with dark red trim.

It looked wrong. Sophie was used to seeing Victorians with lush plantings in front of them, bushy ferns hanging from the porches. She wondered at the appearance of this huge house here, so out of place with everything else, so prominent against the desolation. This house had not been mentioned in the guidebook or any of the stories she'd heard.

The realization crept in that the stories claimed that those who actually ventured far enough to see the house never returned.

She pulled the car to a stop. She was still quite a way away from the house. She could just turn around and go home.

And do what? she asked herself. Sit and wait helplessly for the moment when she either loses her mind or Marshall makes her do something she'll hate herself for? Wait for Calder to decide he's had enough, or for her life to slowly but surely become as desolate as the land around the Victorian in front of her?

She took a deep breath and put the car in "drive" again. She pulled into the driveway, aware that the only thing keeping her hands from shaking uncontrollably was her grip on the steering wheel. She felt cold, and her stomach flip-flopped with nerves.

She pulled to a stop in the long, winding gravel driveway. She could see that it lead behind the house, probably to a barn or garage, she figured. She took one final deep breath and pushed her car door open.

Her footsteps sounded too loud to her ears, the only sounds in this emptiness. First the crunch of gravel, then the crinkly sound of dead grass beneath her sneakers. She took hold of the railing and was raising her foot to the bottom step when the front door opened, and Sophie froze.

A woman stepped out onto the porch. A woman who had powers, magic that Sophie's Shadow magic recognized and welcomed. She had a cold, hard look about her that had Sophie thinking again that this had been a phenomenally stupid idea. Her long red hair fell in a silky curtain to her waist, and greenish-gray eyes stared at her from the woman's expressionless, porcelain face. She wore jeans and a long black sweater that fluttered around her as the wind picked up.

She and Sophie stood studying one another for a moment.

"I could kill you with nothing more than a thought," the woman said, and her voice was deep and rich, with an underlying seductiveness to it that, despite her words, made Sophie feel flushed, confused.

"Probably," Sophie admitted, trying to pull herself together. "I'm Sophie."

"I really don't care. I am giving you to the count of ten to get back in your car and drive away. And that is only because I am feeling generous today."

"I was hoping you could teach me," Sophie said quickly.

The mask of indifference slipped, and for just an instant Sophie saw disbelief. And then it was gone so quickly Sophie wondered if she had imagined it. "You wasted your ten seconds," the witch said. With a flick of her fingers, Sophie felt herself lifted from the ground, tossed through the air like a rag doll. She landed, hard, on the driveway behind her car, the sharp gravel cutting into her palms as she tried to stand.

"Are you one of Marshall's?" Sophie asked, realizing that if the witch was going to kill her anyway, she could at least get an answer or two before she died.

"I am nobody's," the witch said.

Sophie stared at her. "Are you one of them, then? One of those who turns witches and grows fat from their power?"

The woman sneered. "I have no need of anyone else. And while I'm not sure if you're brave or stupid, I really..."

"I need to learn how to control myself. I don't want him to control me," Sophie said quickly, begging. "I don't know who else to turn to. I followed a ghost story to you, because I have no idea what else to do. I was Light, and the Light abandoned me, and then I was Shadow. And I don't know how to make it work."

The woman stood there watching her, her hair blowing behind her, sweater fluttering around her legs. "Then you will die," she said with a shrug. "I have no interest in killing weaklings, but I can't speak for the others out there. Put your affairs in order. Walk away now, before I change my mind."

Sophie watched as the woman crossed her arms over her chest, waiting impatiently for Sophie to get into her car.

"I have nothing to lose," Sophie said quietly.

"Don't you? You have the aura of a woman in love, though the love is wreathed in darkness. You have the aura of foolish hope. And so much fear, so much that it chokes everything else out."

Sophie swallowed, her throat dry at the woman's words. "Yes. I have all of that."

The witch shook her head. "I have no interest in teaching you. You are like a little lost puppy. Go home to your man, and live fully in what little time you likely have left. If I see you here again, it will be the end of you." With that, she turned and went back into the house, leaving Sophie standing on the driveway, the day growing darker as it got closer to sunset. Her hands were still shaking, though now it was a mix of fear and anger coursing through her. Frustration. She knew she was grasping at straws. She knew it, and yet she'd been stupid enough to hope.

She shook her head and climbed back into her car, slowly pulling out of the driveway and making her way back down the dirt road toward the highway. She knew she should be grateful to be getting away with her life. She could feel the witch, could feel how the other woman's power dwarfed her own — not that that was overly difficult to do, she reminded herself. That instant when she'd sent Sophie flying through the air had taken no effort at all.

Yes. She should be grateful to still be alive, to be able to drive down the tree-lined highway and back home to Calder. She knew it, and yet she chafed against the idea that she was helpless, that she was basically just supposed to wait until Marshall showed up and used her, or until something went wrong and she pushed Calder away. As she drove, she thought. Migisi had had this same Shadow magic flowing trough her, a Lightwitch who had turned Shadow thanks to Marshall's influence. Marshall, who had been on his own little crusade to steal the Light from her family in a deranged personal quest to keep a promise to a long lost love.

How she hated that ancestor. Even more than she hated Migisi, and that was quite a lot. How could anyone ever love Marshall? And how could anyone try to control their descendants, even from their grave? How egomaniacal could you get?

Migisi, at least, she could somewhat understand now that she was living through the same thing. Turned to the Shadow thanks to a curse planted on the one she loved. She was still living that nightmare. And that could not be blamed on Migisi. That was all Marshall, using Luc in his desperation to turn Migisi from the Light.

If only Migisi hadn't totally lost her ever-loving mind and cursed Luc with the endless hunger that drove him and his descendants insane. If only she'd held it together enough to keep the evil to herself.

Sophie leaned her elbow on her car door, breathing a sigh of relief as she left the gray soil and twisted trees of the

Shadow witch's domain behind. She turned onto the highway, toward home.

If only's didn't actually get her anywhere, she thought. She was sure Migisi had had a few "if only" moments of her own, especially since she and Luc had likely become close again later in life. It perhaps hadn't been the smartest idea, going to see the Shadow witch. She knew of Sophie now, and if she decided at some point that she was not happy with Sophie knowing where her home is, or what she looks like, or whatever, that could be a problem. She shook her head a little. It couldn't be changed now. And the other witch had made it clear that she didn't see Sophie as any kind of an actual threat.

Sophie let the cool air revive her and calm her as she drove toward home. She let herself be soothed by the smell of the forest around her, the sight of the sun setting over the horizon. This land, her blood. They were one and the same and she would find a way out of the Shadow before she ever let the land become what she had seen around the Shadow witch's home.

She promised this to herself, among so many other things, and silently hoped that she'd have enough time and sanity to manage it all.

CHAPTER SEVEN

Calder was greeted with several shouted greetings as he walked through the front door of Jack's. He waved and smiled, traded good-natured insults with some of the shifters he'd known his entire life. For most of his adult years, this had been as natural as breathing, a weekly tradition. A way to blow off steam and relax for a few hours from the tension involved in watching his father and trying to find a way to ward off his own impending insanity. Him, Bryce, Jon, beer, and a dark bar. It had been so easy.

Until Sophie.

He spotted Bryce and Jon at one end of the bar, nodded at a lynx shifter he knew, clapped another wolf shifter on the shoulder as he walked past.

He should have stayed home. What if she had a rough night? What if she tried to cook again and didn't manage to hold it together the way she had the other night? What if the fucking warlock showed up?

What if some guy showed up, and Sophie couldn't control her needs?

As soon as he had the thought, he hated himself. Was he really that shallow, that she had sacrificed pretty much everything for him and he was focusing on the fact that some other asshole could find his way into her bed?

As he sat down on the stool between where Bryce and Jon were sitting, he tried to keep an impassive expression on his face. They'd finally managed to convince him to come out with them, and Sophie had practically pushed him out the door, telling him that he deserved a break from babysitting duty and that she was perfectly able of managing for a few hours without him.

And, damn it, he knew she was. He knew it, and he still felt like he should run back to her little cottage as quickly as he could.

Part of it was that edge of madness he saw in her eyes.

Part of it was the fear that, yeah, some other guy would take advantage of the situation.

And part of it was the fact that he knew she'd lied to him. She'd told him a couple of nights back that she was stopping to see her friend Thea at the reservation, yet when she'd gotten home, her car was dusty as if she'd been driving dirt roads, and she seemed on edge. Tense.

There were no dirt roads on the reservation. At least, not the part Thea and Sophie usually spent time in.

It wasn't that he didn't trust Sophie. He trusted her. What he didn't trust was the fucking curse he'd lived with for so long, or the Shadow warlock who'd made it clear that he could force her to his will whenever he decided he wanted to.

He didn't even realize he was starting to stand up again until Bryce and Jon each put a hand on his shoulders and pushed him back down onto his bar stool.

"You can't watch her every second," Bryce said in a low voice. "And you need a break, man."

"And she doesn't *want* you to watch her every second," Jon continued from his other side. Calder glanced over, briefly meeting his brother's serious gaze. "You remember how it is. I know you do. I know how it was with dad. She's ashamed enough of how she's feeling, how crazy she feels. You watching her every second, waiting for her to lose it, doesn't help."

"And if she loses it and I'm not there?" Calder shot back.

"Then you pick up the pieces after, and you're there for her when she needs you."

"This is so much worse than when it was your dad," Bryce muttered. "This is your woman. You can't babysit the woman you're supposed to see as your equal."

"I do see her as my equal. More than my equal," Calder corrected himself.

"Then start freaking listening when she gently tries to tell you to back off," Bryce told him, taking a swig of his beer.

Calder stared at him, dumbfounded. "She never told me to back off. Where is this shit coming from?"

Bryce furrowed his brow. "Layla said Sophie was upset the other day. And if Sophie's upset, then I know enough to know that you're not much better."

"She could have told me," Calder said, irritated. He wasn't sure who he was more irritated with: himself, or with Sophie.

"She tried to. Layla said Sophie told her she kept hinting that you should get back to work on my car, which, by the way, man, I totally agree with," he added, and Calder shook his head. "And she said you just kept sitting there, watching her until it felt like you were this close to putting her in a playpen or something."

"Oh, bullshit," Calder answered, stinging from Bryce's words.

"I don't think so," Jon piped up. "With as much trouble as it was to get you to come out tonight, I'm surprised you're not following her to work and watching her."

Calder felt a blush heat his face. He'd been tempted. He had. He heaved a deep sigh. "Fine, you dickheads. Point taken. Can we stop talking about it now?" Bryce and Jon nodded, and they all sat for a few minutes, attention directed toward the large TV behind the bar. The Tigers were in the playoffs, and the bar was more full that night than usual as the local shifters took in the game. Of course, there were non-shifters there, too, but for the most part Jack's served a very specific clientele. Shifters weren't all that common, for the most part living in wild, wooded areas like that around Copper Falls. There were maybe five thousand of them in the entire country, from what they were able to gather about their notoriously reclusive brethren. Maybe around ten times that across the world. Part of the reason there were so few of them was that they didn't breed easily. Most shifters were only children; he and Jon, and Sophie's friends, Layla and Cara, were the only siblings Calder knew of. It was likely another reason shifter communities were so close-knit; lacking brothers and sisters, shifters usually sought out other shifters to befriend. And, unless two shifters bred together, their offspring would be normal humans. It took both a female shifter and a male shifter to create a shifter child.

His children with Sophie, should they have them, wouldn't be shifters. Really, one would have thought that his ancestors would have stopped breeding with other shifters to keep the curse a little more manageable. And some did. But even if you weren't a shifter, the genetic code for shapeshifting might still be there, sometimes buried back several generations, so two people who seemed totally human could find themselves with a shifter child if they'd both had shifters somewhere in their ancestry.

He hadn't considered that before, that if he and Sophie had kids, they would just be normal. Or maybe they'd be Shadow witches, he thought with a grimace.

"Stop thinking about her for like five seconds," Jon muttered, and Calder raised his middle finger in response. "It's like you're thirteen all over again."

"Except worse," Bryce said with a smirk. "Thirteen year old Calder only had her kisses to obsess over."

Calder looked at the television again. The truth was, he'd felt more isolated than ever since the night Sophie had taken his curse. Yeah, he was sane now, and he had the love of his life... if he said it was everything he'd ever dreamed it would be, he'd be lying. He never fantasized about having to pull an insane Sophie away from a pan of raw brownies, or having to wonder if she would jump some random guy just because she happened to be in the right mood. The sex was everything and more he'd ever dreamed of, and in her sane moments, Sophie was a dream.

"I've never been so pissed at anyone in my life," Calder said quietly. He didn't normally do this confiding bullshit. He glanced at Bryce. "And this doesn't leave the three of us. Keep your mouth shut to Layla."

Bryce nodded.

"She had no goddamn business taking the curse. I hate seeing her like this, and there's not a goddamn thing I can do about it. She never asked me. I never, ever would have let her take it," he said. He rubbed his hand over his face. "Part of me hates her for it," he finished quietly. "And I feel like an asshole for saying that."

"Because you are an asshole for saying that," Jon said, and Calder was surprised by the vehemence in his voice. "Fuck you, Calder."

Calder stared at his brother.

Jon went on. "She took the curse because we all knew, the second dad was gone, that the curse would hit you fully. She took the curse because no matter what else you think Sophie is, she's strong as hell. Not magic-wise or physically or any of that shit," Jon said, waving off whatever Calder had been about to say. "Emotionally. Dude, did you not hear even a tiny bit of what you told me about what she went through after they moved away from here? Did you not tell me she lived through not just leaving her home, but then losing everyone who ever mattered to her, having that freak-ass warlock stalking her, and coming out of it sane and strong and determined to take her life back? Do you remember any of that, or is your mind totally gone under your pathetic 'poor Calder' bullshit?"

Calder stared, dumbfounded, at his brother. "You don't even like Sophie," he said, incapable of putting together anything else in the face of his brother's impassioned speech.

"I like Sophie just fine. I didn't like her when it looked like she couldn't break the curse. I didn't trust her line. Didn't trust her. But she showed more strength in the moment she decided to take your curse than I've ever seen, and from what you told me about what she went through before she got back here, I think she deserves some kind of damned medal for sheer strength of will. So get the hell over it and appreciate what you've got. Asshole," Jon added.

Calder turned to Bryce in disbelief.

"What he said," Bryce said with a grin. "Stop being an asshole. Give her a little credit, man."

"I do! I am! You haven't seen her when she's losing it—"

"Did you ever once think of dad as being weak or helpless when the curse was on him?" Jon interrupted.

"No," Calder said without a thought.

"Then stop thinking of Sophie as those things," Bryce said, and Jon nodded.

He was about to argue. He was about to tell them that he never thought those things about Sophie. But the fact was that he had, more than once, thought her helpless, too weak to face the burden he'd lived with for so long. And that was a big part of his anger with her: that she'd taken his curse and wasn't strong enough to manage it.

"So she loses it every once in a while. The woman is going to work every day and managing not to turn your dumb ass into a toad or something. She's already handling it better than dad ever did," Jon said quietly. "Dad hated it when he could tell we felt sorry for him. Remember that?"

Calder nodded.

"Sophie's likely not any different."

"Just a hell of a lot sexier," a deep voice said to Calder's right. He looked up to see Jack, the area alpha and owner of the bar standing there grinning at him. Jack was a big man, roughly the same height as Calder, but with a bulkier frame. He shifted into a wolf, but in his human form he looked more bear-like. He was about fifteen years older than the three of them, but shifters tended to age well. Calder knew the man's reputation among both the shifter and human communities and the idea of him even thinking about Sophie made Calder want to slug him. "What the hell are you doing here when you have a sweet little thing like Sophie Turner waiting at home for you?"

Calder gritted his teeth, suppressing the urge to jump over the bar and slug Jack for talking about Sophie.

"We barely got him pried away as it is," Bryce said to his alpha. Bryce was in Jack's pack, as a wolf himself, as were Layla and Cara. Being bears, Jon and Calder belonged to no pack. And Calder was grateful for it.

"I bet," Jack said. "The things I could do with a woman like that. Damn. That ass—"

Calder saw red, and before he even realized what he was doing, he was lunging over the bar. He got one hit in on Jack's mouth before the alpha recovered enough to fight back.

After that, it was all punching and snarling. Jack tossed Calder over the bar, and Calder crashed into one of the small tables, which cleared out just in time, patrons scattering to get out of the two shifters' ways. Jack jumped over the bar, and Calder was ready for him.

"Come on, teddy bear," Jack taunted, and Calder launched himself at the larger man, hitting him hard once, twice, in the ribs before taking a quick jab to the stomach that had him gasping for air. He recovered in time to dodge another swing, then landed a solid hit to Jack's kidney.

"You're lucky I have customers in here tonight," Jack growled at Calder as they scuffled, then swung out and Calder didn't duck in time to avoid the solid hit to his right eye.

He barely felt it.

All he could feel was the need to rip Jack apart, to see him beaten and bloody for even looking at what was Calder's. For having thoughts about Calder's woman that he had no right thinking.

Calder was on him, punching, hard, and when Jack fell to the floor under the onslaught, Calder was on him, punching him repeatedly. He was vaguely aware of Jon and Bryce pulling him off of Jack, and turning his rage against the two of them.

Even Jack seemed to have seen something that had him trying to calm Calder down. "All right, man. Okay. I'm sorry," he said, holding his hands out in a gesture of peace. "You feel better now, though, right?" he asked with a grin.

Calder watched him as he tried to get his breathing under control. Blood was dripping from Jack's nose, and his eyes were blackening. The alpha laughed.

"It's okay, man. That was a stupid thing for me to say."

"I've seen you looking at her," Calder snarled.

Jack smiled in a disarming way. "There's not a straight man in the vicinity who wouldn't look at her. Come on. Calm it down there, son."

Calder shook his head, and as his sanity returned, he realized what he'd done: he'd attacked the alpha of the Copper Falls pack in his domain.

Jack laughed as he watched Calder work it out. "It's okay. I could see you had a bug up your ass when you walked in here. Sometimes all you can do is fight that shit out," the older man said, still grinning.

"So you did that on purpose?" Calder asked.

"I didn't really think you'd hit me. But I'm glad you did. It's been a while since I've had to kick anyone's ass."

"Pretty sure I kicked your ass, old man," Calder said, and Jack laughed again, stuck his hand out. Calder took it, and they shook.

"You're not of my pack, but I like you, kid. I liked your father. Damn shame, what happened to him," Jack said, too much knowledge on his face. "And an even bigger shame that his sons have to live with the memory of what their old man became. You ever need anything, come to me. Yeah?"

Calder nodded, and Jack gave his hand another firm shake, then turned back to the rest of the bar. "Right. Show's over. Round on me to make up for the interruption," he said, and the patrons cheered, started righting chairs and tables. One of the bartenders grabbed a broom and dustpan to clean up the broken glass, and within moments, life was back to normal.

Calder sat on his stool and gratefully accepted the beer Jack handed him.

He stared at the television without seeing it. It had been weeks since he'd felt that pissed, that insane with rage. Not since he'd been freed from his curse.

Jon and Bryce talked about the Tigers, and about Bryce's ugly car, and Calder answered noncommittally when they asked him how it was going with the cars he was restoring. His mind was a million miles away, something just out of reach bothering him.

He shoved another palmful of peanuts in his mouth, and the barmaid replaced the empty bowl with a full one.

"You really like those, huh?" she asked with a smile.

"Huh?"

"That was your fourth bowl," she said with a laugh.

Calder shook his head. "Oh. Well, they ate some, too," he said, glancing at the bowl.

"Uh-huh. Sure they did," she said with a wink. He watched her walk away, then tore his eyes away and looked back at the television screen.

"I should get home to Sophie," he said. This time, Jon and Bryce didn't bother arguing with him, and he left, clapping each of them on the shoulder. When he opened the door and stepped out into the cold night air, he finally felt like he could breathe again.

It was late. Sophie was likely in bed already, he realized. And the though of Sophie lying in bed in that sexy sleep bra and panties she showed him had him hard as a rock in an instant, his erection almost painful in its intensity.

Yeah. Definitely time to go home, he thought. He climbed on his bike, started it, and roared down the highway toward home.

When he pulled up to Sophie's house, he could see that there was still a light on inside. She probably fell asleep looking through those journals of Migisi's again, he thought to himself as he unlocked the front door with the key she'd given him. When he entered the living room, he stopped, frozen, struck by how gorgeous she was. She was asleep on the daybed in the little nook off of the living room, the wall sconce over the bed casting her in a warm glow. Her riot of dark curls cascaded over the pillow, and her full, gorgeous breasts rose and fell with every breath. She was wearing the sleep bra and pajama pants she'd showed him, the same ones that had him running hot on his way home, and now his desire returned tenfold. The white blanket on the bed was tangled around her legs as if she'd been tossing and turning.

Regaining his senses, he slowly walked toward the bed, still staring at her. Her eyes fluttered open, and at first she smiled. Then her expression turned to one of alarm.

"Calder! What happened to you?" she asked, sitting up.

"Later," he said, gently pushing her back down. He untangled the blanket from her legs and tossed it aside.

"Your eye—" she protested.

"Later," he repeated, settling himself between her thighs, the painful erection he'd been sporting the entire way home cradled between her thighs, and she gasped.

Damn, he loved that sound. She tried to say something about his bruises again, and he lowered his mouth to hers, kissing her with all of the hunger he was feeling, all his need, all his love… everything. He was rewarded with a moan, and it kicked his need into overdrive. He pulled her bra down, watching as her gorgeous breasts popped free, and then he was licking, sucking, biting her sweet flesh as she writhed beneath him, moaning his name, urging him on.

He didn't need any encouragement. He reached between them and pulled her pants down, and she helped by kicking them off.

He was too impatient to even bother with his clothes. He unzipped his fly, and the second he was free, he plunged it inside Sophie in one hard thrust that had her crying out, her fingernails digging into his shoulders.

He took her in a frenzy of need and lust, as if he couldn't get deep enough inside her, and nearly lost his mind when she clenched around him as she fell apart.

"Oh, don't stop, Calder," she moaned as she came down.

He couldn't stop if he wanted to. If nothing else, he was stirred into an even higher frenzy. He took her faster, harder, out of his mind with need for her. The scent of her arousal only drove him crazier, her moans and cries, the way she clawed at his back and repeated his name like some kind of prayer as he took her.

He finished, thrusting into her, hard, holding her hips down and plunging into her with a series of hard, fast movements that had her screaming with another orgasm.

He collapsed on top of her, and within moments, he was asleep, still buried deep inside her, the haze of lust and anger finally abating, at least for a little while.

CHAPTER EIGHT

Sophie lay under Calder for a long time, trying to catch her breath. His snores started even as her heart pounded from what they'd just done together.

He was so heavy on top of her. So solid. She closed her eyes. His face was pressed against the side of her neck, where he'd bitten her as he loved her. His hands were wrapped around her wrists, her arms stretched over her head.

Even in his sleep, he occasionally moved his hips, still connected to her, and she trembled in need and exhaustion.

He hadn't taken her like before. It was exactly what she'd wanted, during the worst of the need she felt for him due to the curse. Clearly, being away from her made for an enthusiastic homecoming, she thought wryly as she tried to shift a little beneath him. His hands tightened on her wrists, and she stilled.

"Mine," he murmured in his sleep, voice muffled against her neck.

"I'm yours," she whispered. "Always."

"Lied to me," he murmured, and she wasn't sure if he was asleep or not. She didn't answer. "Car was dusty."

She closed her eyes. Of course he'd notice something like that. He hadn't asked her about it. Of course he'd noticed and knew she'd lied. And she felt even guiltier for lying to him.

"I'm sorry," she said quietly.

"Where'd you go?" he asked, and now she knew he was awake. He rolled off of her, then gathered her into his arms. She wrapped her arms around his waist and kissed his chest, the light hairs there gently tickling her face as she did. He raised his hand to her hair and gently tugged it, forcing her to look at his face.

She did, and was met with the sight of that black eye. "You need ice," she said, pulling herself out of his arms. He sat up in bed with a sigh, and she was well aware of his eyes on her as she crossed the cabin. She'd long passed being self-conscious around Calder. Truly, he made her feel like the most gorgeous, most desired woman on Earth, and she was almost embarrassed by how much that pleased her, how much his approval meant to her.

She opened the freezer, then popped several ice cubes into a bag of ice, then put the bag onto a dishtowel that she'd lightly dampened at the sink. She twisted the dishtowel around the bag of ice, then carried it back to the bed, blushing a bit under Calder's unabashed appraisal. He'd removed his pants, and sat in bed naked. She climbed onto his lap, straddling his thighs, and gently pressed the ice pack to his eye. He rested his hands on her hips, and when she tore her eyes away from the icepack and focused on his face, he was looking at her, intensity, love, seriousness in his gaze.

"You do that like a pro," he said quietly.

"The ice pack?"

"Yeah."

Sophie shook her head a little. "After my mom died, my dad worked nonstop. When he wasn't working, he didn't know what to do with himself, so he drank. And when he'd drink, he'd fall. A lot," she added. "I can do stitches too, by the way. But don't make me have to give you any."

"Okay," he said quietly. They sat in silence for a few moments.

"So are you going to tell me how you got this? Who slugged you?" she asked, continuing to hold the pack to his eye. His hand rubbed over the curves of her hips, his fingertips gently tracing up the curve of her waist, then back down, over and over again. She glanced down at his hand, noting the red, scraped knuckles. "And who did you hit?"

"Are you going to tell me where you went?" he asked.

She nodded. "You first, though."

"I got in a fight with Jack," he said, and she looked at him in surprise.

"Why?"

He didn't answer, and she ran the fingers of her free hand through the stubble on his chin. "Why, Calder?" she repeated.

"He was a little too complimentary toward you," he growled, and, after a moment of surprised shock, she found herself laughing, just a little. "It's not funny," he said.

"No, it's not," she said, sobering. "You seriously got into a fight over something like that? Do you know how stupid that sounds?"

"I know. It was stupid. He said it, and kept going, and I was leaping at him before I even realized what I was doing. All I wanted to do was punish him for even thinking about you," he finished quietly. "I haven't been that pissed in a long time."

"Well. Maybe it was a case of the straw that broke the camel's back. We've both been tense, and I know you've been worried about me." She paused, shifted the ice pack a little. "I know you're angry with me."

"Sophie—"

"You are. And I can even say that I understand it. I would be angry if the situation was reversed," she said. He

74

put his hand over hers, and lowered the ice pack from his face so he could look at her.

"I have no right to be mad. You did what you thought was right. It's who you are. You're a Lightwitch. Expecting you to let me continue on that way would have been impossible. I get that. I love that about you, that you care so much. I'm pissed because I hate seeing you suffer. I'm pissed because I hate that I wasn't strong enough to hold it together better—"

"You held it together better than I ever imagined!" she exclaimed, interrupting him. "Now that I have it, I can't believe how together you were all that time."

He rested his forehead against hers, then took the ice pack out of her hand and set it on the small table next to the bed.

"Your eye," she began to argue, and he stopped it with a kiss. Sophie let herself melt into him, let herself focus on everything she knew he was trying to tell her with his kiss, with lips and tongue, with the gentle nip of his teeth on her lower lip. When he finally pulled away, he stayed close, his lips a hair's breadth away from hers, his gaze intense as he looked into her eyes.

"You are the strong one, Sophie. You always have been. And I am the world's luckiest bastard, because you managed to make your way back here, and out of all of the men you could have chosen, you chose my undeserving ass. I love you."

The words hit her, the sincerity of his tone nearly undoing her. She felt tears spring to her eyes. "It's always been you, Calder. It always will be," she said.

"And it's always been you for me," he murmured, running his fingertips up her sides again. "Now tell me where you went, kitten."

So she did. She told him about the woman in the lobby of the hotel with her guidebook, and her ride to follow a ghost story. She told him about the dead and barren land, the huge Victorian house, the cold woman and the way

75

she'd tossed Sophie around like a rag doll. Her refusal to help Sophie figure out her powers. She left out the part about the Shadow witch's advice to put her affairs in order. She had no intention of giving up that easily. When she finished, Calder's hands were tightly gripping her hips, his hold on her firming more as the story had gone on. They sat in silence for a few moments.

"So she knows about you now," he finally said.

"And she knows I'm not any kind of a threat to her," Sophie said. "I had to see, Calder. I can't just sit here and wait for him to decide to use me, to depend on him to teach me, because we both know he'll only teach me those things he wants me to learn. Nothing more." She paused. "And I keep trying things. I feel like I'm on the verge of breaking through, on the verge of making it work, but I'm not quite there yet. Part of it is, I can't see the way the magic works, not the way I could see the way Light magic worked."

"That makes sense, I think. You're of the Light, so it would maybe reveal itself to you that way."

She nodded. "That's what I think, too." They had talked often, laying together at night, about magic and how she'd learned to wield what little power she'd had, about how she could see the mechanics of a spell, even though she'd never heard another Lightwitch describe it that way.

"I still see the Light spells," she said quietly. Calder ran his fingertips up and down her spine, gently, soothingly. "I see them, and they're just out of reach, like an oasis in the desert. It looks so close, so real, and every step, thousands of steps, miles even... nothing brings it any closer."

She paused, and they sat in silence. "I would feel better, maybe, if I could at least see the Shadow spells. If I can do that, I could probably make them work eventually. That was what happened with the Light. All I can do is feel the Shadow inside me, but I can't actually do anything with it. I hope that eventually, I'll see Shadow so I can figure out how it works." She closed her eyes. She had neglected telling Calder, ever, what it felt like to have the Shadow power inside her. It felt like she was never clean. It felt like there were millions of foul, many-legged insects writhing, crawling just beneath her skin. It made her nauseous and uncomfortable, and she'd found herself, more and more often, contemplating the fact that death would be a welcome respite from it. As soon as the thought came, she pushed it away angrily.

She could never tell him that. She could barely admit it to herself. She had been though this before, had been through a time when death seemed like the only way out, and she still had the scars on her wrists to prove it. She'd failed that day, the Light keeping her alive, even as it fled her for the way she'd lost faith, for the way she'd tried to turn her back on Its life and power. She could see herself there again, all too easily, trying to drift away in a hot bath, or by leaping from one of the cliffs near Rockway. A long, slow descent into nothingness.

"Sophie," Calder said in a low voice, bringing her attention back to him.

"It'll work out. I'll keep working at it."

He lay down, and she snuggled into him, relishing the strength of his embrace, the safety she felt there. She knew it was only the illusion of safety.

There would be no true safety unless she figured out how to make the Shadow magic work for her.

And as long as she did it before the curse she'd taken from Calder wore away at the remains of her sanity.

Sophie had the next day off of work, and she woke the way she always wanted to, to Calder's kisses, the excruciatingly perfect way his hands teased her. After her Calder time and a shower, she stepped out of the steamy bathroom to the scent of pancakes. Calder stood over the stove, dressed in a blue flannel shirt and the stained jeans he wore when he worked.

"You are perfect," she told him, planting a kiss on his bicep before stepping past him to pour a cup of tea. He'd already boiled the water, as he so often did for her.

"Not even close. But you are," he said, setting her plate in front of her and capturing her lips for just an instant before going back to the stove for his own plate. They sat at her little kitchen table, the local classic rock station playing on the kitchen radio. That was a Calder thing. He always had the radio on. She usually preferred the silence in her house, the sound of the birds out her windows. They dug into the pancakes, and she let out a little hum of appreciation at the first bite.

"You are so much better at making these than I am," she said, taking another bite as her hunger became almost overpowering. She shoveled more into her mouth, then reminded herself to settle down. She forced herself to set down her fork and take a sip of tea. *I will be sane, I will be sane, I will be sane,* she repeated in her mind.

"Me and Jon practically lived on these when we were teenagers," Calder said. "Dad was already losing it, and it was the one thing I knew how to cook at the time."

Sophie smiled a little, though her heart ached at the thought of what Jon and Calder had gone through.

"Jon still asks for these when he comes over sometimes," he added, and she laughed a little.

"Are you working on Bryce's car today?" she asked, nodding toward his work clothes.

He nodded. "He's been real patient, but he deserves to have this done. And I have other jobs lined up that I want to get to. That Barracuda is going to be a big job, but I can't wait to get started. It'll be fun to bring that bad boy back to its former glory."

She smiled, loving the boyish expression, the enthusiasm in his voice when he talked about his work. She knew it was the same way she'd sounded when anyone had asked her about her soap making, her lotions, her perfumes. She missed it.

"I know it'll be gorgeous when you're done with it. But I don't quite believe that Bryce's big blue monster will ever be pretty."

"Oh, ye of little faith," he said with a grin. "Just wait."

She watched with amusement as he dug into his third plate of pancakes. She would be right there with him if she let herself go, but she was holding as tightly to self-control as she could. Her stomach ached from hunger, from the need to gorge herself on the stacks of pancakes she knew were in the oven.

Control. Control.

Another mantra she used. At first, she had tried to keep control for Calder's benefit, so he would not have to see the chaos his curse wrought in her. But, as the past few weeks had gone by, she'd begun doing it more for herself. She hated herself when she lost control. She hated the sense of helplessness she felt. She had vowed, upon returning to Copper Falls, never to feel helpless again. And she hadn't. Even when aunt Evie's debts had come in, even when she'd been in danger of losing the house, she'd kept hold of herself, she'd worked harder, she'd insisted on doing everything she could to save it. In the end, that had meant doing what Calder asked her to do, and working to find an end to his curse.

She hadn't expected to fall in love with him again. Not then, not when he was holding her house over her and acting like he didn't remember her. But she'd fallen anyway, and he with her. And she hadn't broken his curse, but stealing it had been a compromise she was happy to deal with.

It gave her a hell of a lot more practice in control.

"What are you doing today?" he asked her as he finally pushed his empty plate away from him.

"Layla and Cara keep bugging me about going to yoga. I'm going today, mostly to get them to stop, but also because I feel a little calmer after," she said, looking at the pools of syrup on his plate, imagining smearing it all over

Calder and then licking it off. She shook her head a little, trying to rein it in.

He gave a low growl, and she met his eyes. The way he was looking at her, as if he wanted to devour her, had her heart racing, her need increasing.

"You are driving me insane," he said in a low voice. "Do you have any idea what it does to me, when I can smell you like that?"

She didn't answer, though her face flooded with heat at the tone of his voice. "We both have things to do today," she reminded him quietly.

"All I really want to do is keep you here and make you scream my name."

She swallowed and squeezed her legs together. Control. This was just another time she needed to force herself to have some. "You can make me scream later," she said, meeting his eyes. "I'm already looking forward to it."

He captured her lips with his, and she grabbed his shirt, holding the fabric tightly in her fists. She kissed him back with equal fervor, her entire existence seeming to depend on the feel of his lips on hers, on the feel of his heart pounding against her body, the sound of his low growl as she gently bit his lip. She started to pull away, and he held her tighter, kissed her harder, hungrier, and she gave a helpless whimper against his lips as she let herself drown in him.

Finally, when she was nearly out of her mind with lust, she forced herself to push him away, and he let her, though she could tell he didn't want to. He had that intense, hungry look in his eyes that never failed to make her ache for him. "Later," she promised him.

"Later," he agreed, his voice rough, his hands still tightly holding her hips. "The things I want to do to you, kitten…" he said in that low, rough voice, and she could barely breathe.

"I want them all," she said, promising him. She knew, when he was like this, that she needed to soothe him, reassure him. His bear was so close, in those moments, that he was more animal than anything else. Instinct and power and possessiveness. She hadn't been sure whether that was all the curse or not. The curse made it worse, twisted it, but that animalistic need was all shifter. She'd seen the same thing in Bryce when he was watching Layla, and in Layla when she was watching Bryce. It was one of the many shifter things that she hadn't understood, that Layla had had to explain to her.

He seemed to calm down a bit, soothed by her words. "Glad to hear it," he said, clearing his throat a little. "You should go though, before I take you out into the woods and do a few of them."

Her face warmed, and hot need curled deep inside her, but she nodded, then kissed him quickly before grabbing her yoga mat and bounding out the door.

Once she was outside, she breathed in the cool air as if she couldn't get enough of it. The intensity between her and Calder was almost too much to handle at times, and that had been just one more example of it. She unlocked her car, and breathed, and tried to get her traitorous body under control. It was perfectly happy with the idea of Calder taking her out into the woods and having his way with her.

Control, she chided herself again. She started the car and pulled out of the driveway, heading toward town. She managed, even as the curse had her nearly insane with her need to go back to her cabin, to stuff herself with pancakes and milk and let Calder have his way with her as often as he could manage…

No. She rolled the window down, and drove, and breathed.

She would not let this curse control her, just as she sure as hell had no intention of letting Shadow destroy her.

CHAPTER NINE

Main street in Copper Falls was pretty much what you could expect of any northern Michigan small town. Low brick buildings flanked the street, a mix of shops, bars, and restaurants. The library and post office were at one end, and the town's only church, St. John's Catholic, rose in the distance at the other end. During tourist season, it was nearly impossible to even find a place to park, but now that summer had ended, it was much quieter. There was always an upsurge during the peak of fall color, but even that had passed and now the town was pretty much down to its year-round residents.

Which mostly meant shifters and witches. This was the time of year Sophie loved most in Copper Falls, when she was surrounded by familiar faces, by the faces of people she'd known as a little girl, by the faces of people who understood, at least partially, what she was. There were humans, too, but those that lived in the town year-round were either related to shifters and witches or married to them, and could be relied on to keep their secrets. That had been the bad thing about the school she and the other kids from Copper Falls had had to attend as kids; it was a combined district with three other nearby small towns, none of which had their particular type of residents. They had had to hide what they were, and, for Sophie, it was even harder because she'd been one of the very few non-white kids in the district. She remembered, smiling, how she'd begged her mother to go to the school on the reservation because she was part Ojibwe so why couldn't' she? Her mother had calmly explained to her that she'd always be "other" so she may as well get used to it.

At the time, Sophie had hated her mother for that. As she'd gotten older, she'd come to appreciate the lesson her mother had been trying to teach her.

She shook the memory of her mother, as well as the ache she felt every time she remembered her, away as she got out of her car and walked down the block. She was meeting the twins at their family's diner before heading over to yoga. Her thoughts drifted back to her mother as she walked. Her mother, who Marshall had very likely murdered in his sick, twisted plot to get to Sophie. Yet another reason she needed to hold it together. He would be forced to pay for what he'd done to her mother. Her father. Her first, young husband who'd never seen it coming, who had no idea what he was getting mixed up in when he'd fallen in love with her.

She pushed the thoughts away again and opened the front door of the homey little diner that Layla and Cara's family owned. Their aunt called a hello from the kitchen, and Sophie waved and smiled back. She sat in one of the booths near the front window, and within moments, the twins' grandmother, Faye, bustled over to her.

"You owe me a hug, girl," she said in a voice roughened by a lifelong love of singing and Virginia Slims. Sophie grinned and stood up again, and Faye pulled her into a strong hug. She stood a few inches taller than the older woman, who was wearing one of her seemingly endless supply of gaudy Western-style shirts, this one complete with rhinestones and fringe.

"How are you, Faye?" Sophie asked as they drew apart.

"Just fine, just fine. You meeting my granddaughters here?"

Sophie nodded.

"Pie?"

Sophie nodded again, this time with another smile. Faye bustled away, patting her shoulder as she did, and Sophie smiled after her. Like the rest of the twins' family, Faye had seemed to adopt Sophie as one of her own. She'd made sure Sophie was fed and warned some of the rougher men in the diner away from Sophie as if she was one of her own precious granddaughters.

She also wielded a mean flyswatter, which Sophie knew all too well from her childhood growing up with Layla and Cara. Sophie smiled at the memory, then glanced up as the bell on the front door rang. Layla and Cara came through, looking as gorgeous and fit as always. Amazons, she thought, every single time she saw them. And they had the temperaments to go with it. They sat down, each hugging Sophie quickly, and their grandma came to the table with three plates of pumpkin pie and three steaming mugs of coffee.

"Thanks, gramma," Cara said, and Faye blew her a kiss. She was about to bustle off when Layla took her hand.

"Stay here a second, gram," Layla said, eyes sparkling.

"What's going on?"

Layla was smiling, eyes shining, practically bouncing up and down in her seat, and Sophie had a notion of what had her friend looking that way.

"I'm getting married!" Layla screeched, and Sophie, Cara, and Faye all squealed in delight along with Layla. "He asked me before he left for work this morning!"

"Hold on. I'm going on break," Faye called to the other waitress. People were shouting congratulations to Layla, and Faye shuffled back to the table with a slice of pie and a cup of coffee for herself. She sat beside Sophie. Faye and Layla exchanged a long look, grinning at one another, and Sophie couldn't help but smile at the obvious adoration they had for one another.

"It is about damn time," Faye finally said, and Layla laughed, nodding.

"Amen," Sophie and Cara said, meeting one another's eyes.

"We haven't been dating that long," Layla said, rolling her eyes.

"Maybe not, but only because you're both blind. You and that MacEntire boy have been dancing around one another since you were kids. The only ones more obvious were this one and the Turcotte boy," she said, nodding toward Sophie.

Sophie blushed, and Faye patted her hand.

"Speaking of which, we need to get that boy moving. I'm not getting any younger," Faye added, and the three younger women laughed.

"I remember Bryce trying not to look like he was staring at Lay all the way through school," Cara said with a smile. "Remember how we used to tease her, Sophie?"

Sophie nodded. "I can only imagine that it got more obvious as you all got older," she said with a laugh, and Layla hid her face in her hands. Cara nodded.

"As if you can talk," Faye said. "I clearly remember, that summer before you all moved out of here, looking out that front window, and there's you and Turcotte. Kissing," she added for emphasis. "Which I wasn't happy with because you were both too young to be kissin' that way. But I'm not your momma." She paused. "So I'm keeping my eye on you, and I see his hands start moving." She pantomimed two hands reaching around and cupping a backside, and Sophie laughed.

"God, I'd forgotten that," she said.

"You remember what happened next, then?" Faye said with a wink.

"I don't know this one," Layla said. Cara nodded.

"Oh, I remember," Sophie said.

"What happened?" Layla asked.

"His hands were making their way to her backside, and I had decided he wasn't getting frisky on my watch. So I grabbed one of the big wooden dough spoons from the back, and I went out that door, and I gave his knuckles a good smack. Boy jumped about a foot in the air and howled like the devil."

Everyone at the table burst out in laughter, and Sophie wiped her eyes.

"Oh, that's perfect," Layla said, still chuckling. "See? At least you never had to smack Bryce with a spoon, gram," she added.

"No. But I was about to give him a good thwack if he didn't come to his senses about how perfect you are," she said, and Layla took her wrinkled hand. "I'm happy for you, sweetheart."

"I'm happy, too." Then Layla looked at Sophie. "She's right, though. Calder needs to pop the question now."

Sophie shook her head. "Not right now, maybe," she said, meeting Layla's eyes.

"Soon, though. Waiting is stupid," Layla said. "There's never going to be a perfect time. The perfect time is now, because it's all we have. We wait, and it can all be gone, like that," she said, snapping her fingers. "Which you well know," she added. She and Layla had talked, endlessly, about the curse and what it meant for her and Calder. Only Layla knew how many times Sophie had considered setting Calder free, just so he could hopefully have a normal life someday. And only Layla knew how even the thought of it tore Sophie apart. She exchanged a long look with her best friend, and Layla gave a small nod.

"He'll ask in his own sweet time, I guess," Layla said aloud, and Sophie nodded. An awkward silence rested over them, and Faye shook her head.

"His daddy was a good boy. Quiet," Faye said, remembering, and also breaking the silence. "He was friends with my boy. They were real close until junior high, and then Turcotte turned hermit. Never did come around much after that."

Sophie didn't say anything, and Faye watched her for a few moments, then gave a small nod.

"Well. Every family has their secrets, I guess. And a good woman will protect hers to the end." She patted Sophie's hand, then got back up and started taking care of the few customers in the diner.

Layla was still smiling. "Well," she said, "who's ready for yoga?"

They walked down the block to Bryce's studio, and when they entered the narrow brick building, Bryce and a few other women from town were already there. Sophie waved at the others, then she, Layla, and Cara strolled over to Bryce.

"Morning," she said in greeting. "Congratulations!" Bryce grinned and hugged first Sophie, then Cara.

"How's Calder this morning?" Bryce asked.

"I can't believe he got into a fight last night. How could you let him do that?" she asked with a laugh.

Bryce grinned. "Have you ever seen Calder when he gets pissed? It would have taken ten of us to stop him from jumping at Jack, and even that might have failed. That bastard is strong," he said, shaking his head. "I think Jack was afraid for a minute," he confided, and Sophie laughed, feeling a strange rush of pride at the strength of the man she loved. "He all right?"

"He has a black eye, but other than that he's fine," she said, and Bryce nodded. "Thank you for convincing him to go out. He needed that. He's been too cooped up with me."

"Seriously, I don't hear him complaining. If Calder had his way, he'd find a deep dark cave and keep you there forever and be perfectly happy with it," Bryce said with a laugh, and Sophie shook her head.

"Let's get started," Bryce called, and Sophie, Layla, and Cara unrolled their mats toward the back of the room.

Bryce's studio was a place of absolute serenity. Soft, ethereal music played over the sound system, and bright autumn morning sunlight cascaded through the front windows, gleaming across the dark wood floors. The scent of lavender incense filled the air, and, through it all, Bryce's voice was its own melody. Sophie tried to let herself be soothed by it. She pushed thoughts of Light and Shadow, Calder, obsession, curses, and everything else, out of her mind and focused on her breath: slow breath in, slow breath out. When thoughts of all of the crap going on in her life tried to flow in, she pushed them away. She focused on the way her muscles warmed as she used them, as she stretched, as she held each pose. Her body warmed, and she felt herself becoming more fluid, more relaxed, with each asana, and she was grateful for it. But it was a lot of effort to get there.

Everything was going well until she was in a downward dog, and Bryce came up behind her, gently using his hands to pull back on her hips, to deepen her stretch and fix her alignment. It was something he'd done several times before.

Before she'd had Calder's stupid curse.

A streak of hot need shot through her at the feel of his hands on her, the way he was positioned behind her. Calder had enjoyed the same position more than a few times, and it made her think of him.

She blushed furiously as Bryce quickly removed his hands.

"Hey," Layla whispered from her left. Sophie looked over at her, and her friend looked absolutely furious. "Don't fucking do that."

"What?"

"He can smell you. I can freaking smell you. Calm down."

"I'm not doing it on purpose," Sophie whispered, irritated with both Layla and herself. Layla just rolled her eyes and started ignoring her. Sophie shook her head in irritated disbelief. As if Layla didn't know exactly what Sophie was going through. As if she hadn't sat and listened to more than a handful of panicked phone calls from Sophie about the way the curse was messing with her.

"Screw this," Sophie muttered. She stood up and started rolling up her mat.

Bryce came over to her, and leaned toward her. "Hey. It's okay. Don't go."

Sophie shook her head again and stormed out of the studio. She tossed the mat into her car, then got in and roared down the road.

Not toward home. Toward the forest. Away from everyone. She could feel Shadow surging within her again, and Layla's attitude wasn't helping.

She drove to the entrance of one of the state parks, pulled into a parking lot, and started walking along one of the many trails through the forest. She had done this often, when she'd first moved back, when she'd felt as if moving was the only thing keeping the terror that Marshall would find her again at bay. The trails had become a second home, a place she out-walked her demons.

Now, she ran. She was glad she'd worn sneakers. She ran, and barely noticed the way the tree trunks alls seemed to blur into one, the way her feet pounded the mulched trail, the way the cool air made her face sting, just a little, as she ran. Hunger, rage, anger… all of it boiled within her, just below the surface, threatening to push her over the edge. She ran.

Starving. Empty. Nothing but a void, and she knew nothing would ever fill it. Not food, not drink, not Calder, not anything anyone could give her.

She ran, and her feet hit the ground harder, faster.

Her teeth clenched, her lips pulled back in a feral grimace.

Her heart was pounding, her stomach twisting with the emptiness that never seemed to leave her. Her flesh crawled with the sensation of Shadow within her, a filth she couldn't escape.

She stopped and raised her face to the gray sky overhead, and she loosed a shriek that sounded barely human to her ears. Her throat burned with it, her chest ached, and still, she screamed into the emptiness. She knew no one would hear it. Not this far into the forest, not during the off-season when few were around. She let it out: the fear, the anger, the lust, the hunger, the knowledge that she wasn't what she should be. She screamed it into the frigid air, her fists clenched at her sides.

When she stopped, she fell to the ground, exhausted, emotionally spent, terrified and sick at the way she was behaving. But she knew that, for a moment, at least, she'd felt better. How often in her life had she kept her anger inside, hidden every part of herself she'd thought she should be ashamed of? She'd hidden her magic at first, from her family. And when they'd discovered it, they'd proved her right, by freaking out and moving her away from Copper Falls. She'd spent most of her life hiding in general from Marshall.

She was so sick of hiding. So sick of wishing things were different. So sick of coming up short, over and over and over again.

She glanced around, and her gaze landed on a dead tree nearby, its trunk split, the top half of the tree having fallen and crashed into trees nearby.

She remembered the way she'd thrown Marshall across her living room and through her window. It was the one and only time she'd used her Shadow power, and she'd done it without thinking. She'd feared it, hated it, felt sick and filthy with it.

But it was what she had. And she was beginning to recognize that, for a witch, whether she was Light or Shadow, the fact that she had been trying so hard *not* to use her magic was having a bad effect on her as well. She'd been through that before, too. It never ended up well.

She focused on the tree, on the way the fallen top of the tree was crushing the smaller trees around it.

She felt Shadow rise within her, its destructive nature at the ready, an almost eager feeling to it.

She raised her hands, and felt Shadow surge within her, fed by her anger and hunger, and the top of the tree exploded, slivers of dead wood flying everywhere around her, bent trees springing straight after being freed from the weight of the dead tree. She looked at her hands numbly.

"Okay," she murmured, taking a deep breath. "Okay."

That time, she'd called it, and it had come. It had done what she'd wanted it to. She hadn't had to build a spell, not the way she did with Light magic. She just had to focus, and push her power forward. Was that all Shadow was?

No. There was more to it than that, she knew. Marshall's ability to manipulate people, to make them do bad things… that was part of Shadow as well. That was something she didn't want to mess with. But this part of Shadow… this could protect her from Marshall. Maybe. If she caught him by surprise. And it would likely only work once, if that, because she'd already done it to him once already.

But not quite this. Her mind wandered, briefly to what would happen if she wanted to make Marshall explode the way the tree had. She pushed it away.

Still. It was handy to have some kind of control. Even a little bit. Even if she had no clue what she was doing or what she was actually capable of. Sophie glanced around and spotted another fallen tree trunk, this one leaning heavily on a nearby sugar maple.

She focused on the tree trunk. Something less messy, maybe, she thought to herself. Could she turn it to sawdust instead of making shards of wood fly everywhere?

She stared at the tree. Felt Shadow rise within her again the longer she focused. Instead of envisioning a spell, building it the way she always had, she envisioned what she wanted to happen. Tree to sawdust. She focused, hard, raised her hands, and made that same instinctive pushing motion. A loud "crack" filled the air around her, so loud her eardrums hurt. Instead of falling to sawdust, the trunk of the tree split down the middle, each half falling in a separate direction, then falling loudly to the forest floor.

Once the echoes of the tree's fall ended, Sophie walked over to one of the halves. It was a clean split, as if a hot knife had sliced through a tree made of butter. Perfectly straight, no tears, no shredded bark. But it wasn't what she'd wanted.

"How the hell did that happen?" Sophie muttered. She chewed her lower lip as she paced back and forth along the length of the tree trunk half nearest to her. She crouched and ran her hand along the trunk. She felt Shadow rise in her again, and she went with it. A flick of her wrist, and the half of the tree trunk nearest to her fell away to nothing but cinnamon-colored sawdust, the clean, antiseptic smell of pine rising into the air as the tree fell apart.

She glanced at the other half. Okay. So Shadow was really, really good at destruction. Really good. That didn't help her in getting back to the Light, but it did help if it came down to having to protect herself or Calder. Then she grimaced. Something nagged at her. She looked at a healthy, living tree and tried to do it.

Nothing.

Interesting. She looked back at the two dead trees, and what remained of them, and then at the trees nearby. Those trees were now healthier, not being crushed by the bigger dead trees.

So it hadn't all been destruction. She'd saved the small trees being crushed by the first tree she'd exploded. Her gaze went to the remains half of the second tree. Destruction...

She smiled to herself. Destruction didn't have to be an immediate thing. She wondered.

She spied some bright green moss on the bark of the tree half. Slow destruction. Over time, the moss would help the tree decompose, and, soon, the tree would be nothing but rich humus, feeding the rest of the forest.

She pictured one of the Light spells she knew, one that had helped plants grow. Part of being of the Light had been knowing that life around her flourished, just because she was nearby. She'd lost that part of it, for sure. But she wondered if she could force Shadow to her will, considering that the ultimate, eventual goal of the moss was destruction of the tree trunk.

She held the structure of the Light spell in her mind, and focused on it, and the moss on the tree trunk, the tree trunk itself, and she felt Shadow winding its way around, through, between all of it, hesitant, but seeming to understand that destruction would be the outcome.

She held it all, her breathing growing shallow, a sheen of perspiration appearing on her forehead as she held the spell, as she tried to force Shadow into what she wanted it to be.

An eternity later, she began to see soft, velvety emerald moss spreading along the tree trunk, through the rough bark, up the thick branches. She wanted to cry. She wanted to shout in glee. She held it together, and watched the moss spread, until the tree was covered in green there on the forest floor. The moss would die with winter, of course, but come spring, the spores would still be there, and they would grow again, cover the tree, and begin the tree's long journey into decay.

She pulled her power back, drawing the spell to a close. Shadow seemed subdued within her, and she felt better than she had in a long time. She'd made something grow. She'd done the kind of work a Lightwitch would, even with Shadow flowing strongly within her. She'd hoped for maybe a spark, a whisper of Light magic, the sense that it hadn't completely abandoned her, but that hadn't happened. She tried not to focus on her disappointment over it. She'd managed much more than she thought she would.

She gave the moss-covered tree one last glance, then turned and started walking slowly back down the trail. She had no idea how long she'd been gone. The sky was very overcast. It was likely past noon, she guessed. Calder would have expected her back before now.

But he'd understand. He'd be happy to hear about the way she'd made Shadow work with her natural affinity, rather than against it. She knew it wouldn't mean a damn if she actually had to face off against Marshall, because that would require actually wanting destruction, and her magic just wouldn't seem to work that way.

She thought of Layla, of Bryce, and her face flushed. She'd have to deal with that eventually. While Sophie was irritated that Layla hadn't been more understanding, she could see it from her point of view, too. How happy would she be to see someone very clearly turned on by Calder? Wouldn't she want to scratch the person's eyes out, no matter who they were or why they felt that way?

I'll call her later, Sophie told herself. Bryce at least had seemed understanding, but that didn't surprise her, really. Bryce was one of the most laid-back people she'd ever met. He was good for Calder, she thought to herself, remembering Calder's black eye, those bruised, scraped knuckles. The two best friends had always been opposites, she thought to herself. Even as kids, Calder was the one always getting into trouble, getting into fights, and Bryce was usually the one pulling him off of whoever he was beating up.

She made her way, finally, back to her car, kind of surprised by how far she'd run. She got in and headed back down the highway toward her house. When she pulled into her driveway, she saw Calder across the road, in his driveway, crouched next to the passenger side door of Bryce's ugly car. He was rubbing something along the door, maybe sanding the old paint or something, she thought. The way his posture looked, she could tell he was tense, on edge. A glance at her dashboard showed her that it was well past three o'clock; she'd been gone for hours and hadn't even realized it. He'd probably been worried, she realized guiltily.

She walked across the road, and he didn't look up as she got closer, even though she knew he knew she was there. He'd told her that he could smell her anytime she was near, that her scent drew him in a way nothing else did.

She pushed down her annoyance. If he was pissed at her for being late, she really wasn't in the mood to deal with it. Her good mood over Layla's upcoming wedding and making her Shadow magic work was dampened. Again.

She approached, and leaned against the side of the car, looking down at Calder.

"Careful. You'll get blue dust all over your clothes," he said.

"These are old anyway," she said, looking down at him, at his dark blonde hair, his strong shoulders. "Sorry I'm so late. I lost track of time."

He just nodded.

"Aren't you going to ask me where I was?" she asked quietly.

"I think maybe I don't want to know," he said, getting up and stalking to the other side of the car. "But I can guess who you were with."

She stared at him.

"So what did he make you do this time?"

"Who?"

Calder rolled his eyes. "Please don't tell me you're trying to protect him now. I can smell him all over you."

"You think I was with Marshall?" she asked, dumbfounded. She felt Shadow responding to her anger, rising along with her temper, and she pushed it down.

He didn't answer, just ran a cloth along the opposite side of the car, though his jaw was clenched, his shoulders rigid.

"You think I'd lie to you about being with Marshall? I've told you every single goddamn time he's approached me,

Calder. And it's not him you're smelling. It's me, and if you actually gave two shits about me, you'd ask me how my day was instead of immediately jumping to the conclusion that I'm hiding something from you."

"You want to tell me what happened with Bryce?"

"You know what happened with Bryce. You had the curse. Or did you already forget the way it scrambles your brain? If they hadn't been goddamn shifters, they wouldn't have known a thing. It's not like—" she stopped. "You know what? Stay on your side of the road tonight. I don't need this crap right now." She turned on her heel and stalked across the road and up her driveway. She let herself in and slammed the front door soundly behind her, locking it. She headed into the kitchen, her stomach twisting painfully. She'd managed to forget her hunger, that endless emptiness, while she'd been working with her Shadow magic — something to keep in mind, maybe. But now that she was home, she felt bone-tired from using the magic, from trying to force it to her will. From dealing with Calder and his stupid jealous bullshit. She opened the fridge, grabbed a container of yogurt and dug into it, barely in control. She finished it, tossed it aside, and pulled a bowl of grapes out.

She couldn't pluck them from the stems fast enough. Sometimes, she didn't even manage to do it — she could feel the dry, chewy stems in her mouth, along with the sweet, tart juice of the grapes, and she couldn't even make herself slow down. Within moments, the grapes were gone, and she started tearing open packages of string cheese, losing track of how many she ate.

She had another one in her hand when she forced herself to slow down, to stop, to think. Some of her hunger was vanquished, though she knew from experience that she could easily keep going. She placed it carefully back on the shelf in the refrigerator, closed the door, then held her hands out as if signaling to herself that it was time to stop.

Eyes closed, deep breaths, one after another. Instinctively, she reached for Shadow, and it responded.

Stop fighting, it seemed to whisper in her soul.

Sophie ignored it, but she was willing to let it fill her, let it fill the emptiness that had come with Calder's curse. It didn't erase the emptiness, and it didn't make her feel any less insane, but it numbed everything, like a dark veil settling over everything she was feeling.

Sophie stood, and breathed, and let herself feel the floor beneath her feet, the warmth of her cottage around her. She could smell beeswax, the last of the dried herbs hanging from the beams in her living room. She pushed away her irritation at Calder. If he wanted to act like an ass, that was his problem.

She opened her eyes and looked out the kitchen window, which looked out over her acreage, the small pasture, the barn, the woods beyond. Merlin was in his yard. She glanced at the clock. She had forgotten that she had two more male goats arriving later that day to keep him company, which their owners were giving up because males were a pain in the ass.

"Obviously," Sophie muttered. "Doesn't even matter which species. Males are always a pain in the ass."

She opened the back door, breathing in the cool air. As soon as she stepped out, Merlin started bleating at her in his loud, grumpy-sounding way.

"Hello, you ornery old man," she greeted him. She opened the gate and stepped into his corral. She had meant to rake out the little barn where he slept. He needed new bedding, and she wanted to take a look at his hooves to see if he needed to be trimmed. He immediately came up to her and butted her hip with his head, rounded horns connecting solidly with her side.

"Don't be a jerk, Merlin," Sophie muttered, pushing him away. He gave her a crabby bleat, then bounded away and started ramming the side of the barn.

"We'll see, old man. Maybe one of these new males will teach you some manners. Though I doubt it," she added. She grabbed the large pitchfork and started shoveling hay out of the barn and into a large wheelbarrow. She'd add it all to her compost pile when she was done. She held out hope, now more than ever, maybe, that she'd eventually be able to grow a garden again, even with Shadow slithering through her.

She was just returning from dumping the hay into the compost when she saw a large man walking up her driveway. Not the large man she wanted, of course, she thought to herself.

"Sophie? Got some goats here for you," he said. "And thank the Light you're taking them off of my hands."

The words shook her to the core.

"The Light?" she asked him, wondering why he'd said the words.

He smiled kindly. "I knew Evie, girl. I know what your family is made of."

Sophie just nodded, unable to speak over the longing in her heart, longing for the Light. It hit her harder than she could have expected. She took a breath, and followed the farmer to his truck and the trailer behind it.

CHAPTER TEN

Once the farmer, Stephen, had left after shaking her hand one last time, Sophie glanced across the street to see Calder standing in his driveway, arms crossed over his chest, watching her. She barely thought before raising her middle finger toward him and turning on her heel and heading back up her driveway. She wasn't sure, but she thought she heard a deep chuckle, a sound she loved more than just about any other, and she wasn't sure whether she was relieved that he seemed to be getting over his pissiness or irritated that he wasn't taking her anger seriously. She headed back to the corral where the goats were. They were standing there, roughly in a circle, the three of them seeming to study one another. Merlin was the largest, a deep chocolate brown. She'd been pleased to hear the names of the other two goats; apparently Stephen's family had a sense of humor. The two pure-black goats she'd taken in were named Gandalf and Dumbledore. Her little flock of wizard goats pleased her in a stupid kind of way.

Sophie stood and watched them a bit longer. They didn't move, the three of them standing there in that small circle, eyes on one another. She'd expected bleating, butting, running. Posturing. There was none of that, and Sophie screwed up her face, wondering if there was something wrong with the goats Stephen had loaded off on her. After a few more minutes of watching them stand in that freakishly-still manner, she turned toward the house with a shrug. She'd check on them again later.

When she got back into her house, her phone was ringing, and it was Layla's number on the caller ID. She picked it up. Before she could even say a word, Layla rushed to speak.

"I'm sorry," Layla said. "I'm sorry, Soph. I was a jerk. I know it was the stupid curse. I don't know what the hell came over me. I just kept getting more irritated, more angry out of nowhere as the class went on, even though I should have been getting calmer, and then when that happened, I just lashed out like a bitch. I'm so sorry, hon."

Sophie took a breath. "I was about to call you and apologize. I hate that that happened. You know I'm not interested in him. I hate that the curse does that. I'll stay away from Bryce until I —"

"No! Screw that, Soph. You don't have to do anything. He's your friend, and I know you're not into him that way, and I trust both of you. I know better. I don't know what the deal was with me earlier. I'm sorry," she repeated. "You have enough crap going on, and then you had me acting that way."

Sophie took a breath and plopped down onto her sofa. "It's okay. Though I do wish you guys had less powerful senses of smell," she said wryly, and Layla laughed, and Sophie felt herself lighten, just a little, relieved to hear the familiar sound from her oldest friend. "Really, it's freaky."

"Well I bet it makes things interesting with Calder, though. He knows the instant you're hot for him," Layla said with a bit of a laugh. Sophie didn't answer. "What's wrong?" Layla asked after a moment.

"I'm not talking to Calder right now."

"Uh oh. What did he do?" Sophie loved her friend a little more for assuming that it was Calder who did something, not Sophie or the curse making her over-react.

"I got home later than usual. He'd already heard about the thing at yoga."

"Yeah, I think Bryce told him in case you were upset when you came home."

"Yeah. Well I was out practicing, trying to see if I could control this Shadow stuff," Sophie said. "And I managed a few things. I was pretty happy with myself. I felt less helpless than I have in a long time."

"That's good!"

"I know. So I came home, and Calder wasn't talking to me. Moody. I was gone a long time, and apparently I smell sorta smoky or something when I use the Shadow magic, and that's how Marshall smells...."

"Ugh. So he assumed you were with Marshall."

"Right. And that I was somehow hiding whatever I'd done with Marshall. By then I was so annoyed I didn't even bother telling him what I was actually doing."

"He needs to get punched again," Layla said, and Sophie laughed a little.

"I mean, I can't blame him entirely. I know this is rough on him, too."

"Yeah, but it's much rougher on you and he needs to grow the hell up and give you the support you deserve."

"I love you. You know this, right?" Sophie asked with a laugh.

"Of course. And I love you too, Soph. Do you want some company?"

"Do you even need to ask?"

Less than a half hour later, Layla and Cara were in Sophie's living room sprawled across sofas and chairs like the old days. "Powerpuff Girls. Let's watch em," Cara said, pressing the button on the remote. They'd brought pizza and garlic bread, and the three of them sat and ate and watched cartoons and laughed harder than they probably should have.

"Your goats are weird," Cara said after coming in from the kitchen to get another Coke. "They're just standing there staring at one another."

"Still?" Sophie asked. She got up and headed into the kitchen. It was after sunset, getting dark, and still her three goats stood in their little circle, exactly as they had been earlier. "What the hell?"

"Maybe it's a dominance thing," Layla said, looking out the window over Sophie's shoulder. "Whoever looks away first loses, or something like that?"

Sophie shrugged. "Weird."

Talk turned to weddings and jokes about ugly bridesmaids dresses. After a while, Sophie got up to grab a tray of cookies she'd bought from the bakery in town for Calder the day before.

"Your boyfriend keeps looking over here from his driveway," Cara said from the living room.

"I told him to stay on his side of the road tonight," Sophie said, and Layla laughed. "He can look all he wants."

"Poor grumpy bear," Cara said with a laugh, and Sophie rolled her eyes. They settled in again, and by the time Layla and Cara left, hugging Sophie goodbye, Sophie felt a million times better. A glance over at Calder's house showed the light on in the living room. He'd finally left the driveway, Sophie thought with some humor. She shook her head, closed the front door, and locked it. As much as she wanted him, as much as she wanted him sleeping beside her, his strong arms around her, he needed to understand that the jealous bullshit didn't fly with her. She understood: he knew the curse better than anyone, and what it made you want to do. But if he knew Sophie at all, he should have known that she'd never let herself fall into it. If he had that little faith in her, then he didn't actually know a damn thing about her.

Sophie took a quick shower, then changed into her pajamas, wrapped her hair in a towel, and headed back out into the kitchen. She glanced out the window one more time to see the goats still standing there, staring at one another.

"Freaks," she muttered. "What the hell kind of goats did you give me, Stephen?" She shook her head and padded over to the daybed in the living room, shutting lights off as she went.

She was just snuggling into bed when her phone rang. She picked it up, saw Calder's number. She looked at it for a second, then answered.

"Hey," he said, his deep voice warming her immediately.

"Hey."

"Um. So I'm a complete asshole. Complete, total, absolute asshole, and I'm sorry. You didn't need that shit, and I don't even know what the hell is wrong with me. I trust you. I know better. I didn't even stop to think that you would smell that way when you use the Shadow magic. So far, you've only smelled like that when he's been around you.... And so what? I still had no excuse to act like that."

Sophie didn't answer for a moment. "If this is going to work, you need to trust me."

"I know. I do. I don't know what the hell is wrong with me lately. I want to fight, all the time. I'm on edge, and I'm pissed off. Restless. After Layla and Cara showed up at your place, I ran as my bear for a while."

"Did it help?"

"Some. But you know how it is when I shift. It makes everything more... more, you know?"

"Yeah."

"And I was already pissed off, so there was still that, but more. And I was already horny, because you're completely gorgeous when you're pissed off, and it didn't help with that either."

"Is that a hint?"

"Maybe."

She didn't answer for several moments as she tried to get her body under control at the tone in his voice. "Can

COLLEEN VANDERLINDEN

you give me tonight alone? I need sleep, and I think maybe a night apart will help us both get back on more solid footing. It's so easy to lose myself in you, Calder. I'm in a fog when we're together."

"I know. It's the same for me," he said quietly. "It's always been like that."

"I know," she whispered. "And I love it, but I need to master myself a little. And I can't do that when I'm wrapped up in you. We can't spend every second together. It's messing us up."

The line was silent for a few moments. "I know. We're both independent people. And Bryce told me the other night that I'm probably driving you nuts, watching you all the time for signs that you might need me."

"And it can't be good for you, either, to be waiting on edge for something to go wrong," she said gently. "I don't need to be saved." And there it was, she realized. That was what had had her off-kilter with Calder the past few weeks: he was always there, waiting to save her. She'd never had that in her life, and though she'd at times wished for it, she realized she didn't want it.

"No, you don't," he said firmly. "I know that. I just keep forgetting it. I blame the fact that I love you more than I've ever loved anyone in my life." The straightforward tone of his voice warmed her, as if he was stating a fact, like water is wet or the sun is hot. She smiled a little.

"I love you more than I ever thought it was possible to love anyone. And it means a lot that you want to protect me. But I don't want that. And I don't need it."

"Duly noted," he said. "I'll try to rein the caveman thing in."

She laughed. "Not all the time, though. I rather like the caveman at times."

He groaned. "You can't say something like that after telling me I'm sleeping alone tonight."

"Well, keep it in mind for tomorrow night, maybe," she said quietly.

"Oh, I will," he said in a low voice that sent pleasant shivers up her spine. "I love you, Sophie."

"I love you, too," she answered.

They hung up, and she rolled over and snuggled under the covers. Sleep. She needed sleep, and she rarely got enough of that when Calder was with her.

Outside her cottage, the three goats stood in the yard, still staring one another down. Beyond, in the woods, Marshall stood, looking toward her house, the way he had every night since arriving in Copper Falls, the same way he had every night of her life through her teenage years and early twenties, watching the house she lived in. She was aware of it, at some level, but drifted off to sleep nonetheless.

CHAPTER ELEVEN

Sophie was at work, trying to stay away from everyone. Keeping herself away from Calder the night before she had to go to work maybe hadn't been among her smartest ideas. Her body was going haywire, one endless void of needing, hunger, anger. She gritted her teeth and snapped her wrists, making the sheet she was laying over one of the beds on her floor snap in a satisfying way. It floated down to the bed, and she started making the bed, focusing on making neat, perfect hospital corners, smoothing the soft white sheet perfectly over the mattress.

"Having a rough day, kitten?"

Her hands stilled, and she closed her eyes. Marshall. This was one goddamn thing she didn't need today. And she hated the way he used Calder's endearment for her, twisting it, fouling it, using it in that derisive way that told her he thought it was appropriate: she was a cute, weak little thing whose claws couldn't really hurt anyone. She hated it. Calder never said it that way, but it was already happening that, when Calder murmured it to her, she heard Marshall's snide tone layered over it.

There wasn't a single thing he didn't try to take from her.

She steeled herself and took a breath, and turned to him. He stood there, looking calm and cool as always. Tall and muscled, with piercing dark eyes, she could remember, with more than a little embarrassment, thinking he was handsome the first time he'd shown up at her after-school job in high school. How she'd been flattered by the way those dark eyes had watched her. If only she'd known. Though, in truth, it had instilled a nearly lifelong distrust of men who looked at her that way. Precisely two men had gotten through it. The first had married her and ended up dead for it.

"Nothing better to do, Marshall?" she asked, happy that her voice came out strong and steady. She grabbed a pillow and slid it into a fresh pillowcase.

"You were doing something yesterday," he said. "I could feel it."

She didn't answer, instead focusing on slipping the second pillow into its new pillowcase.

"What were you doing?"

"I have no idea what you're talking about," she said with a shrug. She pulled the bedspread up and smoothed it, then walked past him to smooth the other side.

"You were doing something."

Maybe it was the anger running through her. Maybe it was the memory of her first husband, dead at Marshall's hands. Maybe it was everything, but in that moment, for the first time in years, she wasn't afraid of Marshall. Her disdain of him was greater than her fear, and she welcomed the sensation. So when she spoke, she knew he expected her to be meek, and she gave him something else entirely.

"I thought you were all-knowing when it came to me, Marshall. What's wrong? Things not going quite the way you'd expected?"

And she saw it, in the briefest of flashes of his eyes: they weren't. She didn't understand it. She had wondered why he wasn't making her do more, why he wasn't spending all of his time terrorizing her. And she realized, in that instant, that for some reason, he couldn't.

"Don't get smart," he snarled. "Just another crazy bitch from your line. That's all you are."

She crossed her arms. "That's the thing about crazy bitches though, isn't it? You never quite know what we're going to do."

His mouth dropped open, and if anything, he became more ill at ease than he'd been a moment before. "You think you're anything against me? I could crush you without a thought."

"You could," she agreed with a slow nod. Then she met his eyes. "But you haven't. Haven't you learned anything about me by now, Marshall? You think you'll break me. You think that given enough time scaring me, ruining my life, that I'll just fold. We've been at this for almost twenty years," she said with some surprise. Most of her life. She could barely remember a time beforeMarshall had been the thing she'd had to arrange her life around. "When, in that entire time, have I ever just given in?"

"You came to me. You're Shadow now," he said.

She shrugged. "I came to you knowing it was what needed to be done. It wasn't an act of defeat."

He stared at her. "I could kill him, you know. Kill him the way I killed honey number one. It wouldn't even take any effort."

Ice cold fear shot through her, but she focused on keeping herself calm. "If you do that, you lose me. We both know that. I won't survive it with any sanity left."

An odd expression crossed his face, and he looked away. "Its surprising, sometimes, what we can live through."

"Yes. You've already shown me that. But I'm tied to him. You destroy him, you destroy me."

He growled, and ran a hand through his dark hair.

"I'm not going to let you run my life anymore, Marshall," she said, watching him.

He glared at her. "I could do anything I wanted to you right now. Anything," he added for emphasis.

"You could try," she said with a shrug. "But you won't."

With one last enraged look, he disappeared, and she knew he was gone. She didn't yet understand how he did that, and in that moment, she didn't particularly care. She fell to her knees and sent a short prayer of thanks to the Light, that he'd not actually done anything to her. And then, after a moment, she thanked Shadow as well, because she suspected that it was the reason he hadn't been able to. Her hands shook now, but not as badly as they once had. He would always scare her. She knew that. Too much history, too much evidence of the evil he could do. She would be a fool not to fear him. But she also knew that playing meek would be her destruction. She'd almost been there, when both curses had first hit her. She wouldn't fall under the curses, and she wouldn't fall to Marshall, either.

She knew it was easy for him to underestimate her. He wasn't the only one. She didn't look like a fighter. She was girly, and a bit on the chubby side, and she loved her garden and goats and chickens. She swooned at paperback romances and loved that her man called her "kitten." Hippie chick, Layla had once jokingly called her, and it was truer than she knew. If Lightwitches were anything, they were all about peace and love.

The mistake was thinking that peace and love equalled weakness, or that the girly-girl was unlikely to stand her ground. After all, every kitten believes, in its heart, that it is the biggest, baddest thing in existence.

And when the mood strikes, it acts like it.

She finished her tasks in that room, gritting her teeth against the feel of Calder's curse running through her. Hunger. Thirst. Need. Always, the need. It was like a million tiny splinters digging into her body, and combined with the oily feel of Shadow slithering through her soul, she felt like she was about to lose her mind.

"I'm gong to take a quick break," she managed to mutter to Janice at the front desk, then she pushed open the door and started, quickly, down the path toward the woods trails. After she'd gone about a mile, she stopped and looked around. There. Fallen tree, something that wouldn't suffer from her powers, though the trees it was bending would benefit from having it removed. She focused, and with a wave, the large oak exploded, then fell into a neat pile of wood chips. She took a breath and looked up into the gray sky.

It was crazy, the way it felt. The pressure building in her, the edginess she felt, that need to use her Shadow magic for something, just seemed to disappear with a "pop" once she finally let go and used it. It was as if she'd fall apart under the pressure, and then, all of a sudden, it was gone and she was left wondering why she'd resisted, why she'd let it get to that point. Of course, she knew why. It was Shadow. The fact that Marshall had worked so hard to lure her to Shadow told her all she needed to know about how good it was. The fact that Light had turned its back on her as Shadow began to take over was the final, absolute judgment of Shadow's worth.

But it was what she had. And she'd have to use it, or risk losing so much more than she already had. She glanced at what was left of the tree again, then turned and started walking down the trail back toward the resort. She felt Shadow within her, satisfied for the moment, but luring her, beckoning her, to use it again, to fully immerse herself in what it was. It was attractive, seductive, even.

She neared the resort, and saw Calder's truck. He was leaning against the front of it, arms crossed, watching her with a little half-smile that made her heart skip a little. She smiled back at him, then walked to him and grabbed him, pulling him into a hug. He laughed at her obvious enthusiasm and hugged her back, hard.

"What are you doing here?" she asked.

"I was at the post office picking up the fender for the Barracuda," he said. "I swung by hoping for a glimpse of you."

She smiled. "I'm glad you did. I missed you."

The way his face lit up at the words went straight to her heart. And this was why, no matter how seductive Shadow was, she knew what real seduction was. It was the curve of his lips, the way his eyes sparkled when he was being mischievous. She reached up and ran her fingers along his jawline, the scruffy hairs there tickling her fingertips. He leaned into her touch, eyes on hers.

"Your goats got out of your yard," he said with a chuckle after a few moments.

"Are you serious?" she asked. She was about to pull back when he took her hand in his and kissed her palm gently. "Are they at your place?"

He shook his head. "I took them back to your house."

"That must have been a pain," she said.

"Not really. It's surprising how easily goats move when they're being chased by a bear. Even Merlin ran back into his pen without acting like his usual asshole self."

Sophie laughed. "I wonder how they got out?"

He shrugged. "I checked the fencing and couldn't figure out where, but you'll have to look at it later because I probably missed something. I pounded in a few more of those fence stakes. By the way, kitten, those are some creepy-ass goats."

"You too, huh? Cara and Layla said the same thing."

"Well, they are. I had pulled Bryce's car into the garage to start finishing it, and I turned and looked out the door, and the three of them are standing there, right outside the garage door."

"Were they watching you? Maybe they're stalker goats," she joked.

"No. They were looking across the road, at the woods next to your house. They pretty much ignored me until I started trying to pull them back to your house."

Sophie stood there, her hand clasped warmly in his, her body snuggled close to his. It was the perfect, heavenly combination of warmth and coolness. Between the two of them, comforting, protective warmth, while the air around them had the cold bite of October. Sophie looked up and met his eyes again. "So... my shift's over in an hour and a half. Can I buy you dinner, sexy?"

"Are you going to take advantage of me afterward?"

"God, yes," she murmured, her need for him, spurred by their closeness and the joy she felt with him, nearly obliterating everything else.

He cleared his throat. "That's a date, then."

"Want to meet me at Bayle's in a bit?" she asked as she let her hand run over his chest, her palm skimming the contours of muscles she knew well, abs she'd licked and nibbled, the flesh around his navel that she found herself drawn to again and again. She could hear his breathing becoming labored, and she smiled up at him.

"If you don't stop touching me, we're not going to make it through dinner," he said, and it sent shivers up her spine, that strain and need in his voice.

Sophie stood on her tiptoes and planted a firm kiss on his lips. "I'll see you in a bit," she said against his mouth before pulling away.

He let her go reluctantly. "Looking forward to it, kitten," he said, that mischievous glint in his eyes that she loved so much. She threw him one more smile, then headed into the resort to finish her shift. Marshall's sliminess was forgotten, at least for a little while, and now that she'd used her powers, she felt calmer as well. She could do this, she realized with a jolt of hopefulness. She could keep Marshall at bay, and hold it together. She could make it all work, because she had too much to lose otherwise.

Calder waited in Bayle's, which was one of the newer little restaurants in Copper Falls. They specialized in local offerings, in-season. As he looked over the menu, there was a lot of venison available, lots of fall vegetables and greens. Potatoes. Fish and duck. He guessed the decor was nice. He didn't really care. His stomach growled as he perused the menu, and his body was still reacting to the way Sophie had been touching him, that sultry look in her eyes. As much as he was looking forward to their dinner together, what he really wanted was something only Sophie could give him.

Really, he was surprised he was still hungry at all. He'd been eating almost non-stop, taking frequent snack breaks between working on Bryce's car and the Barracuda. His stomach growled nonetheless, and he grimaced. Fall. Bear. An actual bear would be stuffing itself in preparation to hibernate. He hated this feeling. It was way too close to what he'd lived with during his time with the curse, endless hunger, restlessness. He hadn't had an autumn since he was a teenager where he hadn't had the double-whammy of bear plus curse. He hadn't had any idea how much of the craziness was his bear.

Basically, his bear was an asshole, he thought to himself as he took a gulp of the beer the waiter had set before him. His bear wanted Sophie all the time. Every second. It wanted to keep her barricaded, protected, with him. It was happiest with her beneath him. It wanted to fight everyone and everything, and it was a gluttonous bastard.

He grimaced again. Maybe that was just him.

He glanced at the door again, and there she was. One look, and he was ready to forego dinner completely. She'd pulled up her masses of dark curls, exposing the graceful curve of her neck. She'd shrugged off the polo shirt that she wore as her work uniform, and was wearing a top that gave him a mouthwatering view of her ample cleavage. She wore a long sweater over that, belted at her waist, emphasizing that lush curve from her waist, over her hips, and down her thighs.

He'd licked his way down that curve dozens of times, and he knew she loved it.

She was walking toward him, one of those gorgeous half smiles on her lips. He stood up and pulled her chair out for her.

"You're staring," she whispered when she was close to him.

"Always," he murmured. He bent his head and pressed an open-mouthed kiss to the side of her neck, and was rewarded with a small gasp, the feel of her pulse jumping beneath his lips. He pulled back before he did the so much more he wanted to do. He sat down with some relief, shielding the raging hard-on he had just from the sight of her, her scent, that moment of his mouth on her silky skin. "I'll always stare at you. You're the single most gorgeous thing in the world."

He was rewarded with a pleased blush, a shy smile as she looked down at her menu. He knew she wasn't used to hearing things like that. She'd spent most of her adult living as a hermit, hiding from the fucking warlock who'd eventually turned her to the Shadow. A brief marriage that had ended in her husband's death at Marshall's hands. Part of him wondered if he should be jealous of that guy, that he'd had her first, that he'd lived by her side, that she'd promised herself to him. Instead, all he felt for him, may he rest in peace, was gratitude. For a time, Sophie hadn't been completely alone. Not that she needed anyone. Not that. But he'd spent enough time alone to know that, at some point, you almost start questioning your own existence. You start to forget what it's like to talk to people, and you realize that you have no one to turn to. In his craziest moments with the curse, he'd locked himself away from the world. Usually, it was Jon or Bryce who'd show up and remind him that he didn't have to face it alone.

Sophie hadn't had any of that. And she hadn't had anyone to tell her how amazing she was. He wanted to make damn sure she never went without that again.

"Let me guess. You're having the venison," she said, glancing up at him with a smile.

"Of course. Did you see they have a roasted root vegetable thing? It looks pretty good."

"I saw that. I think I'm going to try that. Ooh, do you want to try this cheese plate after?"

He nodded. "Look at the desserts, too. That apple galette thing looks good."

He watched as she looked over the menu. "Oh, heck yes. That and coffee, I think."

"Yep. And then actual dessert," he said.

She glanced up at him questioningly, and he cleared his throat and gave his eyebrows a lascivious wiggle, and was rewarded with another blush as she glanced down.

"Very bad," she murmured.

He grinned. "Actually, I wouldn't mind eating some of that apple thing from y—"

"Do. Not. Say it," she said, blushing even brighter as she glanced around to see if anyone had overheard. He could smell her though, her arousal since the moment he'd kissed her neck making him feel practically drunk.

"You keep blushing like that, and we're going to end up pulling over on the side of the road again. Remember last time?" he asked. He could see her pulse jumping at the base of her throat, and she swallowed, took a deep breath. He knew it was a little evil. The curse made it so that she was already insane with lust anyway, and he did things like that. But, oh, the reward of having Sophie out of her mind with lust for him...

"I—" she began, and then she spun in her seat. He followed her gaze, to the front door.

"Son of a bitch," Calder growled, preparing to stand up. The warlock asshole, Marshall, stood just inside the entry of the restaurant, gaze solidly on Sophie.

"Calder, sit down," Sophie said. "Not here. Not now."

"Do you want to leave?" he asked, eyes still on the warlock as he sat back down. The smirk the warlock gave him made him want to rip his throat out. Marshall took a seat at the end of the bar, far enough away that Calder couldn't leap at him, but close enough that the bastard still had a clear view of Sophie.

"No. Screw him. He's not going to control every moment of my life anymore," Sophie said, and the steel in her tone got his attention more than anything else. He met her gaze and nodded. "I'm done running," she added.

"Then we'll stay," Calder said, and she threw him a small smile. He could tell how much it bothered her having Marshall there. Her scent changed. Adrenaline. Not fear, though, and that was different. Her scent had always held that slightly acrid scent of fear when Marshall had been around before. Now… now her eyes flashed in anger as she looked at her menu without really seeing it.

"He's not going to make me run. He's not going to rule my life. He's not taking another, single, thing from me."

He watched the woman he loved, and felt his love for her expanding, growing. Jon and Bryce had been right; Sophie was the strongest person he knew. Beneath her sweetness, her quiet manner, his woman was iron. He practically swelled with pride, and glanced at the warlock. He had no idea, truly, what he was dealing with.

This stubbornness regarding Marshall was a newer thing, though. "Kitten, what were you doing that day you were so late?" he asked, guessing it was related.

She smiled then, and her entire face brightened. She gestured for him to lean in, and he did. "I made Shadow work. It did what I wanted, and I didn't hurt anything."

He sat back, shocked.

"I thought you were afraid of it," he whispered, aware that this was something she didn't want the warlock to hear.

"I was. I am. But I can't protect myself or anyone else from him if I don't use what I have. If the witch won't teach me, I'm going to have to do what I did with the Light: teach myself."

"That's why you smelled like that," he said, remembering how he'd jumped to the conclusion that she'd been with Marshall and was hiding what they'd, maybe, done together from him. His stomach knotted in shame. A waitress came and set their plates in front of them, fragrant venison and hearty root vegetables. He and Sophie thanked her, and then began digging into their food.

"It's unfortunate that it stinks. I can't really smell it," she said, taking a bite of what he guessed was parsnip.

"It doesn't stink. It just smells different from the way you usually do."

"Uh-huh," she said, a wry grin on her lips.

"Seriously. You were using it again before you saw me at the resort, weren't you?"

She nodded.

"It's a little different from him. I can smell him now, too." A realization crossed his mind.

"He came to my work today, too. You smelled him on me too."

He suppressed a growl, then nodded. "Anyway. When it's you, it's almost a smoky smell. Not sulfur, so much. Maybe that's just you. Earthy."

"Light has left me," she reminded him.

"But you're still you, babe," he said, and was rewarded with a smile. "If Light left you, then It's stupid and has no idea what It's lost."

They ate a while in silence. The restaurant hadn't been especially crowded, a few tables of locals, one of hunters who were clearly from out of town. It was always easy to tell. Him and Sophie, the warlock, and a few scattered men at the bar, watching a hockey game. Everything had been quiet, calm, but he could hear two of the guys at the bar arguing now, and he glanced that way. His gaze landed for just a moment on the warlock, who lifted his drink to Calder in a mocking way.

God, he wanted to rip the asshole's throat out.

He glanced back at Sophie, who was watching him. "Ignore him," she said quietly.

"I'm trying."

She gave him a small smile, then took another bite of her food.

He was about to say something to her, when an outburst rose from the group of out-of-towners. Two of the guys started yelling at one another, and that seemed to spur on the two guys at the bar who were arguing. One of the waiters got involved, and that seemed to draw in a couple more guys at the bar.

"What the hell?" he muttered, watching as two of the hunters stood up, still shouting at one another. There was the sound of breaking glass as one of the guys at the bar threw his glass against the wall.

The yelling got louder, more of the patrons shouting now. The rest of the hunters got involved in the fight between the first two, and the shoving started.

Sophie was dialing her phone, and then she was quietly telling someone that there was a huge fight breaking out at Bayle's.

Smart woman, he thought to himself. None of the waitstaff seemed to have the sense to do it, all of them, men and women, getting involved in the arguing. The cook came out of the kitchen and got into it with one of the guys at the bar.

It was a cacophony of shouting and rage, and his bear wanted nothing more than to get involved, to bash its way into the fray and punch it out.

"It's him. He's doing it," Sophie said, and he glanced toward the warlock, who sat, drinking his drink as if nothing was happening. He was about to respond when there was another crash from the hunters' table.

"That's it. I'm sick you you telling me what to do!" one of the out-of-towners bellowed.

Calder saw the glint of a gun as the guy reached into his coat.

"Down, Sophie," Calder said, leaping over the table and pulling Sophie down with him just as the first gunshots rang out. He pulled the table down in front of them, felt the unmistakable sensation of the shift beginning. His mate was in danger. That was all his bear knew, and it wouldn't stand for that any more than he would. He shoved his clothing off just in time.

His muscles popped. Bones lengthened, thickened, and his body became even bulkier.

Shots continued to ring out. Semi-automatic, he realized. He had no intention of leaving Sophie. He stood over her, behind the table they'd been sitting at. There were screams now, the unmistakeable click of another magazine being loaded, and then the shooting started again.

He should do something. He should....

And then he noticed Sophie peeking out from behind the table at the shooter, focusing. He butted her gently with his head, and she ignored him.

A flick of her wrist, and the shooter went flying out the front window of the restaurant. He dropped the gun as he fell through the plate glass.

The restaurant was silent for a few moments. Calder quickly shifted back and started to dress, and that's when the screaming started.

He pulled Sophie up shakily. One of the waitresses was screaming. All of the guys at the hunters' table were down, bloody. Three of the guys at the bar lay motionless, and the cook lay in a puddle of his own blood. Sophie was trembling in his arms.

"Ah, kitten. Wasn't enough in the end, was it?" Marshall sneered from his end of the bar, where he was still sitting, as if nothing at all had happened. He grinned, and met Calder's gaze. "Shadow is a powerful thing. You may think you know things, little girl. You are nothing." He took a gulp of his drink, then shrugged into his dark coat and walked out the door of the restaurant. The sounds of sirens grew louder.

Calder and Sophie spent the next couple of hours answering questions from the police, both of them leaving out the fact that Sophie had thrown the shooter out of the restaurant with her power. They both said he jumped out, crazed, and why wouldn't he? He was obviously nuts, after all. Neither of them could explain Marshall's role in it all, how he had caused the man to snap, so by some silent agreement, they left that out as well.

When they finally got into the car to drive toward home, Calder's head was swimming. Shadow. He looked at Sophie sitting silently beside him. She hadn't wanted to drive, so they'd left her car. She was clearly shaken. That was what Shadow did. That was what Sophie was, yet she'd used it to stop the carnage. Would she always? Or was she just not so seduced by it yet that she let it do what it wanted? Would she always be focused on life, rather than death?

And if not, what did that mean for him? Because he knew without a doubt that he would be by her side through anything that came up, life, death, or anything else.

CHAPTER TWELVE

August 19, 1870

Migisi lay on the floor of the little house she and Luc had built together, the place they'd loved one another, the place they'd planned to raise a family. The last light of day slanted in the window, carrying with it the scent of the forest.

Migisi found no solace in it. She panted, and whimpered. Sweat ran in rivulets down her temples, down her neck. She could feel it soaking into the cotton shirt she wore, the fabric sticking to her body as she writhed in agony.

Her child was coming. Her baby. And something was wrong. It had been hours, and she could feel her strength fading, even as her stomach undulated with her child's frenzied movements. She felt like she was being torn apart from the inside, each contraction making her erupt in wails of pain and frustration.

She would lose this child. She would lose this daughter the way she'd lost all of the others, the children she and Luc had made. Even as she cried out with the force of another contraction, her mind went back to the child she'd believed she'd successfully carried years ago, born cold and still on this very floor, Luc's devastated face as he handed the tiny body to her.

"No," she whimpered as another contraction took over. The pain...Light, the pain.

Light. She hadn't spoken to Light in years. She nearly laughed with the ridiculousness of it all, and instead, she screamed.

Blood gushed between her legs, turning the furs and blankets beneath her scarlet.

"Migisi," a voice said, a voice she knew and loved. She opened her eyes to see Luc framed in the dim light of the doorway.

She was about to answer, when another anguished scream tore from her throat. In an instant, he was there, kneeling between her thighs, in her blood.

"Please help. Oh, Light. Please don't let her die," she begged, not him specifically, but the universe in general.

"Shh," he soothed her. "I can see her. Be still a moment," he said, the French, his tone, calming her almost immediately. She forced herself to be still, tears running down her face, into her ears. She tried to calm her breathing. Luc reached between her thighs, and she felt his hands there, near her daughter.

"Her neck is wrapped in the umbilical cord," he said quietly. "Be still. Do not push, Migisi."

She nodded, bit her lip hard as another contraction tore through her. She could feel him, could see him, working to free her daughter from the death-trap that was Migisi's body.

"This might hurt," he said, meeting her eyes for a moment.

"Just save her. Please," she begged.

He nodded, and she felt it, a hard, rough push on her agonized body, his hands in her womb, maneuvering her daughter.

The pain. The pain was intolerable, worse than anything she'd ever felt. She screamed with it, heard him shout in desperation as the pain increased. The world went hazy, dark, and she felt herself slipping away.

"Migisi. Migisi," Luc said firmly. She forced herself to look at his face. "Push as soon as you're able. She's free."

Tears flowed down her face again, and with the next contraction, she pushed, and gasped in shock as her daughter came into the world, as the heaviness that had been in her womb for what had felt like an eternity left her.

"Migisi, look," Luc said. She lifted her head and looked between her legs. Her daughter lay in Luc's large hands, blood and fluid everywhere. He gently turned the baby over, patted her gently on the bottom, and then Migisi heard the most glorious sound on the face of the planet: the cries of her daughter.

Migisi wept, and Luc lay the girl on Migisi's chest, at her breast. He helped her pull her shirt open, and in an instant, the beautiful girl, her little miracle, was feeding hungrily.

Luc sat beside her and supported her body as she watched her daughter, his hand brushing Migisi's wild hair back from her sweaty face.

"You saved her," she said hoarsely. "You saved my daughter, Luc."

His eyes met hers. "I have no idea why. I should have left both of you to die."

"But you didn't," she said quietly.

His ice-blue eyes met hers. "I could not. I hate the fact that some part of me loves you still, Migisi. Do you have any idea what that is like?

"You have married," she said softly.

He nodded. "And I will be faithful to my wife," he said. "She deserves that my body will be faithful, even if my heart is not." He paused. "It is likely witchcraft anyway. There is no sensible reason I should still care for you."

"I love you," she whispered.

He nodded. "So you say. We'll see how much you love me when you see what I become, thanks to you. Because that's why I came to see you tonight. That is the one thing you can do for me, Migisi. I can protect my family from what I become. It's you who will bear that burden, which is as it should be."

"I don't—"

"No. You don't understand. But you will." He stood up, looked down at her for another moment. "Do you want me to cut the cord?"

She nodded, and he did it, quickly, and she knotted the remainder of the cord, then settled her sleepy daughter against her chest again.

"How did you know to do all of that?" Migisi asked. She couldn't take her eyes from her child, spellbound.

"The same happened with my son. The midwife wasn't strong enough to move him, so stood by and told me what to do," he said. "I could go without having to do that ever again."

"There are no words, Luc. No words for how grateful I am that you came by here tonight," she said, searching his eyes. He looked away.

"I need to get back home," he finally said.

Migisi nodded and let Luc pull her up. She bit back a cry at the pain that came with standing, her body ruined, bloody, and sore. Blood ran down her thighs.

"Do you need anything more before I leave?" he asked, watching her, and she hated for him to see her as the sweaty, bloody, sagging mess she was.

"No. You have done more than I ever could have dreamed," she said. "Thank you."

He looked at her for several long moments without saying a word. "I will see you at the full moon, Migisi. You can thank me then by making sure I don't kill anyone." He turned toward the door and opened it without looking back. "Congratulations on the birth of your daughter," he said before stepping out and closing the door firmly behind him.

Migisi slowly carried her daughter over to the pile of furs that served as her bed, in the corner of the room nearest the hearth. It was dark now, and she took a moment to light one of the lanterns. She lay on the bed and covered herself and her sleeping daughter with the light cotton blanket. She tried not to think about how badly she hurt. In honesty, it wasn't too hard to forget about it. Every time she looked at her daughter, the pain became nothing. She slept, curled against Migisi's breast, dark curls plastered against her tiny head. After a rest, Migisi would bathe her. For the time being, she lay, and tried to regain her strength, and marveled at the miracle that Luc helped her bring into the world. He may not be the one who planted his seed in her, but he was this child's father just as much as her true father as far as Migisi was concerned. He had brought her into the world. The fact that he had done so stunned Migisi and filled her with wonder. He'd shown up just when she needed him most, and he hadn't turned away from her.

"It is an honor to meet you, little one. I have waited so long for you, my love."

She lay there, and watched her daughter sleep, and thanked the Mother, the Light, the Shadow, and anything else, for the man who had created this child with her, a wizard of the Light who had fallen for her at first sight. He had been a healer, and had since moved on, needed elsewhere. She would miss him, but he'd given her the most beautiful gift imaginable. And he had not shunned her for being Shadow. He'd been truly good, truly caring, and had reminded her what it was to be alive, to see the beauty in life instead of the darkness. She had changed when she was with him. Still Shadow. Still death and destruction incarnate. Still someone who could not be around others without violence happening, simply because of her presence. For a while, she had delighted in the chaos and pain she'd caused, so full of pain herself that all she wanted, all she understood, was more pain. This child's father had made her remember what she'd once been.

She traced her fingertips along her child's tiny arm, down to the fist curled on her chest. She marveled at the tiny knuckles, the delicate thumbnail, the soft dimples on the back of that impossibly small hand.

Light.

Migisi started, nearly jumped in shock. This child was of the Light. She was like her father. She hadn't been able to feel that when the child was inside of her because of the way Migisi's own power obscured everything. But now, she could feel her daughter, and she was pure, beautiful Light.

"Oh, thank you," she said into the air. "Thank the Light," she said as tears streamed down her face again. "Thank you." She looked at her daughter again. "I shall name you Claire," she said, thinking of the child's two French-speaking father figures and wanting to honor them. "You are hope and Light and goodness," she whispered.

Then she looked up at the ceiling again. "Thank you Luc. Thank you for saving her."

Morning's light dawned with Migisi bathing her daughter, washing the remainders of birth from her tiny body even as her own body contracted and bled. She wrapped Claire in a blanket, secured to Migisi's own body and she walked into the woods. She knelt on the forest floor, and she prayed.

She prayed to the Light, and knew that somewhere, somehow, it heard her.

CHAPTER THIRTEEN

Sophie stood in the kitchen looking out at the goat yard without really seeing it. Her three goats seemed to be standing in conference again, but she thought nothing of it. She listened to the local news station on the kitchen radio as she drank her tea.

"Returning to a developing story, there was a deadly shooting at Bayle's Restaurant in Copper Falls last night," the female newscaster said in a tired voice. "After an argument, one male opened fire on other customers. Two dead, five injured. The suspect, Jason Allen, has been taken into custody by Copper Falls Police. Allen, thirty-nine, was in town on a hunting trip with four of his friends, two of whom he is alleged to have murdered last night. The group hailed from Warren, near Detroit, where Allen worked as a car salesman…"

Sophie's mind wandered. She'd heard the details of the shooting too many times already. She knew the names of the dead, their ages, occupations. She knew more about the shooter than she wanted to. She knew that five others were in the hospital, two of them barely clinging to life. She knew that the owners of Bayle's had already said they were closing indefinitely, shaken by the violence that had erupted in the restaurant that had been their dream in the making.

She knew that the violence that had occurred was because of her. Two people were dead, five gravely injured, because Marshall had wanted to teach her a lesson. She'd defied him, refused to be properly afraid and compliant. This was his way of reminding her that he would always have the upper hand.

She'd let herself forget how utterly evil, how deranged and terrible he was. Bile rose in her throat again, and she swallowed hard. Their deaths… she shook her head and leaned against the kitchen sink. She was there again, reliving other deaths.

Her mother's death in a "car crash." On an empty road. The police had guessed she'd maybe crashed into a large deer or something, the way the front of the Chevette had been bashed in. Sophie's only tie to the world of the Light, gone in an instant. Marshall had taunted her with it, even going as far as attending the funeral and extending his condolences to her father. She'd sat through her mother's funeral with her murderer watching her every move with satisfaction.

Her father's death, when his big rig had mysteriously gone over the side of the Zilwaukee Bridge, killing him instantly. "Those truckers, always on one kind of drug or another," Marshall had smugly said at her father's funeral. "Such a shame, leaving a daughter behind." She'd gone to the police then, as she had before over Marshall's stalking. Nothing had ever been done, her complaints forgotten almost as soon as she'd voiced them. By the time her father's body was in the ground, she knew it was hopeless.

She'd stopped leaving the house. Until David. Until she'd been foolish enough to let herself believe she could have something good for herself. Until he'd drawn her out and made her feel beautiful and safe. He'd married her, and she'd been foolish enough to believe that the worst was past.

Her parents' deaths had been nothing compared to David's. A suicide that wasn't. Marshall's pleased, smug face at yet another funeral. The knowledge that he'd died for one reason, and one reason only: she'd allowed him into her life. She'd let him in, and he'd been murdered by Marshall because of it. She decided then never to let anyone else in, that she wouldn't risk anyone else. And she'd tried to die, and the Light had saved her, and she'd eventually made her way back from the brink, and the lure of death stopped filling her every moment. The letter from Aunt Evie's lawyers had felt like a sign, a new beginning, a chance for life in the place she'd been born.

And it was happening again. He wouldn't hurt her. He wouldn't risk hurting Calder directly, because they were connected in some weird way by the curse and he wouldn't risk losing Sophie if he killed Calder.

But he had no problem hurting anyone else she came into contact with. He'd demonstrated that perfectly the night before. He'd done it without a thought.

She set her teacup down on the counter, clasped her shaking hands together. She still stared out the window. She could hear Calder snoring in her bed. They'd been up late, held tightly in one another's arms in silence, each lost in their own thoughts.

She wouldn't let him fall to Marshall, she told herself. She knew the inherent threat Marshall was making: he might not kill Calder, but he sure the hell could hurt him if Sophie pissed him off enough. The fact that he'd told her that once she became Shadow, those she cared about would be safe from him had been something she'd foolishly held onto. She was beginning to believe she'd been played for a fool. Nothing was sacred to Marshall. Nothing but getting his own way.

She glanced into the living room, at the nook where the daybed was tucked between two large bookcases. Calder lay there, snoring lightly, chest bare, legs tangled in the white sheets. One hand rested on his stomach, the other stretched across her side of the bed, as if he was reaching for her. Unexpected, angry tears came to her eyes, Shadow was rising, Calder's curse was eating at her sanity, and she was reliving too many deaths on top of seeing innocent people die in front of her. She felt like she was crawling out of her skin, filthy, wriggling madness making her feel full and nauseous.

She grabbed a piece of chalk and left a note for Calder on the small chalkboard on the refrigerator: "Going for a run. Love you." With one more glance at him, she walked out the back door, past her freaky goats, then toward the woods.

When she was there, she ran. She wasn't foolish enough to believe she could out-run the craziness inside her. But she'd rather be distracted by her lungs burning, her side aching, her legs screaming, than by everything going on in her head. Her feet pounded the soil, and the cold air stung her lungs. Her mind raced. She was aware that she was being pushed into a corner, having her options taken from her. Marshall had made his move, revealing his strategy. He'd take, and he'd destroy, and he'd stalk until she did what he wanted. Until she agreed to be his mindless servant, until it wouldn't require threatening anything she cared about to make her do his bidding, because Shadow would be in control, because she'd finally given up on trying to keep herself together, on getting back to the Light.

That may well be an impossibility anyway, she told herself as she ran. She could hear the falls in the distance. She'd been going to them more often, letting the sound of water rushing, bubbling, soothe her.

Impossible, Shadow seemed to hiss deep inside her, rising again as if trying to force her to accept it.

She let out a loud, enraged shout, and she released the stupid amount of power that had been building in her since the night before. She hadn't focused it, hadn't really tried to do anything in particular. The soil around her blew out in a wave, away from her, leaving her standing in a dead crater, all of the late wildflowers and fallen leaves gone along with at least a foot of soil.

She bowed her head and tried to breathe.

"You'll kill yourself that way," a wry voice said to her right. Her gaze shot up, and her stomach twisted in dread. Through the dusty air, she saw a person, features becoming clearer as the air cleared. Long red hair, that same black sweater held tightly around her. The witch from the Victorian house stood before Sophie, looking amused. "Unless that was what you were trying to do?"

"N-no," Sophie managed through gritted teeth. She felt dizzy. She closed her eyes for a moment, then opened them again, trying to re-focus herself. The witch was still standing there, looking bored. "Why are you here?"

"What? Don't you like it when people show up at your home unannounced?" the witch shot back.

Sophie just watched her, and after a moment the witch gave a derisive laugh. "You want to tell me what happened at that restaurant last night?"

"Why?"

"Because I have the feeling it was more than just some gun nut going off. You were there."

"How do you know that?"

"Word spreads."

"It wasn't me."

"Yeah, no kidding," the witch said, rolling her eyes. "I never said it was. But you should know that you could definitely make that happen. I've made that happen," she added. "Though not to that extent. It used to be fun to see how many fights I could inspire in a night. Quite a few, to be honest." She studied Sophie for a moment. "You're not strong enough to cause that much violence in such a short amount of time. Your level of power would cause general irritation, maybe a fist-fight or two over time. But it would take a while."

"Well, that's a relief," Sophie said, taking a deep breath.

"So who else was there?"

"The warlock who turned me to Shadow," Sophie said quietly.

"Why did he do it?"

"He was making a point," Sophie said in disgust, and the witch nodded. "Why? Looking to join forces with another Shadow?"

"Hell, no. I just wanted to verify my suspicions. This is the one you want to learn to fight against?"

Sophie nodded.

"Little girl, you don't have a chance in hell."

Sophie crossed her arms. "You don't know me."

"I don't need to know you. All that matters is power, and yours is shit. Like I said before, probably best to put your affairs in order."

"He's not going to kill me. He wants to completely corrupt me. End my line and make sure we're all Shadow... it's a whole long thing," she said with a grimace. "He's nuts, basically."

"Of course he is. Anyone who'd go as far as he went last night is fucking insane." The witch studied Sophie. "I'm guessing that's not the first time, either."

Sophie shook her head. "I'm not just going to cower and let him have his way."

"Then more people are going to die while you posture and try to prove a point," the witch said. "Is that what you want?"

"No. It's not, and I'm not going to let him do it again."

The witch laughed. "Let him? If he did that, there's no 'letting' him do anything. Are you delusional?"

"If you don't plan on helping me, then leave. I don't need you."

"That's a lie, and we both know it. Even with as little power as you have, you could kill yourself or someone else, out of sheer stupidity."

"I figured out some of it," Sophie argued.

The witch was studying her. Then she blew out a breath. "The only thing I like less than having to deal with other Shadow, are men who don't know the meaning of the word 'no.' And I rather like my house and I'm not in any mood for a bunch of crazies following the same stories you did in some witch hunt if he keeps doing this." She was so tense, so angry, that Sophie was caught off guard. Then it hit her.

"Has that happened before?"

The witch gave a terse nod. "Years ago... I'm very old, little girl," the witch added, and Sophie nodded. She knew that was possible from Marshall. Long life, extending your life through Shadow. "Years ago, I came here, and I unfortunately came across another—" She broke off, then narrowed her eyes and stared at Sophie, then looked toward the house, as if fully realizing where she was. "Oh, hell no," she said, turning on her heel and stalking away. Sophie started following her before she realized what she was doing.

"What?" she asked the witch.

"Nope. Hell no. I am not getting involved in your line's particular brand of crazy again." She spun and glared at Sophie, then snarled. "I knew you fucking looked familiar. You're Migisi's."

Sophie stopped, frozen. "You knew her?"

The witch stopped walking, and pointed toward Sophie's house. "That bitch is the reason the lovely people of Copper Falls came after me in the first place. She was fucking off her rocker, but they couldn't hurt her. Too scared. And they knew what I was, so they came after me to make themselves feel better. Burned my house to the ground, tried to burn me with it."

Sophie stared at her, open-mouthed. "I... wow."

The witch gave a derisive snort. "Are you telling me it's Marshall who caused that?"

Sophie nodded numbly, head spinning.

"Then I'll say it again: you don't have a chance. Migisi was strong, and he turned her, and she caused so much destruction that it became necessary for any witch, Shadow or Light, to hide what they were. People lived in fear of her and those like her." She paused. "She settled down after a few years, but by then the damage had been done."

"She was turned from the light by Marshall. Same as me," Sophie said.

"Then you're fucked, my dear." And with those words, she spun and started walking away again.

"Did you know Luc?" Sophie asked, and the witch paused. She did not turn, though something changed in her posture. "Did you?" Sophie pressed.

"Luc was just another in the long line of people she destroyed in her own special way," she said in a tight voice, still turned away from Sophie.

"So you knew him?"

The witch finally turned. "How do you know about Luc?"

"His descendants still live here. Still living with the curse she put on Luc... sort of," she said, looking away. "I'm in love with one of them."

After a moment of tense silence, the witch shook her head. "You all sure are good at repeating your mistakes," she said. "You'd think he would know enough to stay away from your line."

"He came to me to see if I could break the curse."

"And?"

Sophie shook her head. "I let Marshall turn me so I could take the curse from him. So I have it now, but it's messing me up."

The witch watched her closely. "So you're telling me that you have Shadow magic, you don't know how to use it, and you're slowly but surely losing your mind thanks to Migisi's curse."

Sophie nodded.

The woods were silent around them, Sophie realized. No bird calls, no rustles of animals running through the underbrush. Two Shadow witches. Of course. Life shied away, protecting itself from what they were. Not her, so much, yet. Her magic wasn't powerful enough. But this witch… she could give Marshall a run for his money, Sophie realized.

"What were you thinking, taking that curse?" the witch asked, vibrant green eyes searching Sophie's.

"I was thinking that I couldn't watch him get worse. I saw his father at the end…" she trailed off and shook her head. "And I knew I'd cause less damage with it than he would. Shifter, you know."

The witch nodded, still watching Sophie.

"I hoped it would buy me time. I didn't count on it making me lose it so quickly. This, today, what you saw… that was what happens when I'm feeling nuts. The curse gets Shadow all excited, and then I have to take off and try to get some release. I feel like I'm this close to losing it completely," Sophie said, holding her thumb and forefinger up, barely any light showing between them. "And I can't lose it. If I lose it, he wins and Calder will never forgive himself for the fact that I took the curse from him. I have to win. You understand?"

The witch silently watched Sophie for a while, as if trying to come to some kind of conclusion. "I'm Esme. And I'm not doing this for you. I'm doing it for me. And for Luc's memory. Maybe his line can finally have peace."

Sophie nodded, a combination of relief and dread swirling within her. "Thank you, Esme."

"Not for you," Esme repeated, and Sophie nodded.

"What was so special about Luc?" Sophie asked quietly.

Esme's expression closed up completely, but not before Sophie caught what might have been regret in her eyes.

"What wasn't?" Esme said in a barely perceptible voice. Then, in a her more usual, commanding tone, "come to my house tomorrow morning. Know that this will hurt, and I may very well enjoy it, little witch." This time, when she walked away, Sophie did not follow.

CHAPTER FOURTEEN

Sophie pulled into the driveway that meandered toward Esme's big creepy Victorian house. She was edgy, not just from nerves over whatever would happen when Esme started "teaching" her, but because of the argument she'd just had with Calder. He was not happy about her coming to Esme, to put it mildly. They'd argued about it most of the previous night, taken one another when they woke up that morning in a frenzy of need and anger, then promptly went their separate ways, him to work on Bryce's car, and her for her shift at the resort. They hadn't said a word to one another. She wasn't budging on it, and he couldn't understand why in the hell she would go to someone who clearly had a chip on her shoulder about Sophie's family. A Shadow witch, no less. She didn't disagree with him, but she also counted on whatever history Esme had with Luc to make her want to help for his descendants' sake. She also didn't tell Calder that the clock was ticking; she was having more and more time, every day, when she felt out of control and crazy.

She got out of her car and straightened her back, steeling herself against the desire to run away. The witch in the creepy house was her chance. Didn't matter if Esme hated her and her ancestors. Didn't matter that she didn't seem to believe Sophie could manage to protect herself or anyone else from Marshall. All that mattered was that Esme was Shadow, and she knew things, and Sophie had way too much to learn and, as always, not enough time.

Never enough time.

She climbed the front steps to the huge wraparound porch, her sneakers making a "thud" sound on the wooden treads that practically echoed in the silence around Esme's house. She lifted her hand and knocked twice on the old-fashioned wood screen door, and Esme opened the door wordlessly, waving Sophie in. Sophie took one more steadying breath, and then walked through the door feeling as if she was willingly stepping into a dragon's lair. The front door closed behind her with a loud slam, and Sophie jumped.

"There are rules here, little girl," Esme began, stalking past Sophie and into another room, and Sophie followed. The rooms they passed through were stark. White walls, uncomfortable looking furniture. It looked more like a department store or furniture store, arranged in ways that suggested no one actually lived there. She followed Esme up a narrow stairway, and Esme kept talking. "You do what I tell you. I don't give a shit if you get hurt. I don't care if you're tired, or if I hurt your delicate little feelings. If you can't focus, I won't teach you. I'm not wasting my time here. If you breathe a word of me to anyone else, I will destroy you."

"I told Calder already," Sophie said quietly.

Esme turned and glared at her. "He's okay. Tell him to keep his mouth shut, too."

Sophie nodded. They walked down a long, narrow hallway. More white walls, doors closed on either side. Finally, at the end of the hallway, Esme opened a door and stepped into a room. Sophie followed her in and looked around.

She realized they were in the large turret at the western corner of Esme's house. The room was round, with soaring ceilings, and unlike the rest of the house, this room felt lived in. Tall narrow windows were spaced around the round room at regular intervals, looking out at the dismal scenery outside. But where there weren't windows, there were bookshelves; tall, floor-to-ceiling bookshelves, gleaming wood, with brass rails to which there was an actual ladder attached so you could reach the books on the highest shelves. Sophie had only ever seen library ladders like that in movies. The shelves themselves were packed with books, wooden and stone boxes, small works of art, sculptures, and enough other bric-a-brac that Sophie could have spent all day just looking through Esme's bookshelves. In one half of the large room, there was an enormous desk that matched the gleaming wood of the shelves, its surface covered with books. A computer sat on the desk, looking out of place in the timelessness of the rest of the room. A large leather chair sat behind the desk, and the window behind it was the only stained glass window in the room. Sophie's breath caught when she realized what it was: a large bear against a backdrop of fall forest. She tore her eyes away from it to see Esme studying her with an irritated expression on her face. Sophie began looking around the room again, her gaze landing once more on the stained glass. She appreciated the fact that Esme was letting her get her bearings, seeming to understand that she needed it if she was going to focus. The other side of the room was mostly empty, just an overstuffed sofa and large leather ottoman.

Sophie looked at the window again, then glanced at Esme, raising her eyebrows.

"Let's not jump to conclusions, eh? I'm Finnish. Bears are sacred to my people."

Sophie nodded, though she had a nagging feeling that there was more to the story than that.

"Lots of Finns in this area," Sophie said, trying to make conversation.

Esme nodded, a small smile on her lips. "None quite like me, though. Let's begin." She paused, and looked around. "We'll train here," she said. "I don't know how much good it'll do you. I still think you're screwed, but I hope for your sake and your man's that I'm wrong."

Sophie nodded. "Thank you for teaching me."

Esme smirked. "We'll see how much you're thanking me in an hour or so." She walked across the room. "Okay. Give me your best shot," she said.

"Uh…"

"Now. I need to see what I'm dealing with. Show me."

"You want me to hit you with it?" Sophie asked.

"Did you think this would be a fucking sewing circle, little girl? You're talking about protecting yourself against one of the most vile Shadow warlocks I've ever heard of. Now hit me, or it's time to go. I could be reading right now."

Sophie tamped down her irritation and focused. She gathered her magic, felt it slithering through her, ready. She gritted her teeth, then flicked her wrist and sent power hurtling toward Esme. With a whispered word and a graceful wave of her hand, Esme constructed what seemed to be an invisible shield against the magic. Sophie's spell hit it, and, after a moment, Esme dropped her arm.

"Again."

Sophie went through it all again, and Esme shielded herself easily.

"Again."

Her head was starting to ache, her stomach turning, her mouth dry with thirst. She shook her head, trying to rid herself of the distractions, and gathered her power again, throwing it at Esme with another flick of her wrist. Esme blocked it in an almost bored way.

"Damn, you're weak," Esme muttered. "I barely even needed the shield."

"Thanks," Sophie said irritably.

"You got stronger as you went on, though," Esme said as if she hadn't heard her. "What changed?"

"Calder's curse is messing with me."

Esme nodded slowly. "You said you were practicing with your magic. What were you able to do?"

Sophie told her about the trees, the moss she'd made grow. Her theory that she could use the magic well only when it matched up with her beliefs as a Lightwitch. She had expected derision, mocking. She knew Marshall had no respect at all for the Light, and assumed that was a general attitude among Shadow witches and warlocks.

Esme looked thoughtful. "Who taught you how to use your Light magic?"

"I did."

Esme watched her closely. "Self-taught?"

"My mom had no magic at all. I mean, it was there, but not enough to actually do anything with. She said that I was the first one in our line in a very long time to actually be able to use my magic for anything. It's dying out in our line. I guess it has, now, thanks to Marshall."

"Did he ever go after your mom? Didn't your aunt live around here?"

Sophie nodded. "Both of them were pretty much powerless. Once he knew that, he didn't bother with them. You can't turn someone when there's nothing there to turn, I guess."

Esme nodded. "Is your mom still around?"

"She's dead," Sophie said, aware of her clipped tone. She was about to start clawing at herself to get some relief from the wriggling feeling of Shadow and the curse crawling beneath her flesh.

"What happened?"

"Marshall killed her," she said, starting to pace. "Can we get back to work now?"

"So is this about revenge or protection?"

"Why does it matter?" Sophie asked as she paced. She felt like she was moving in a weird, jerky fashion, like a marionette, almost, as if her legs and arms refused to move in calm, easy motions. Her heart was pounding, that weird pressure building inside of her.

"You've already figured this out, and I'm starting to get the picture, too. It has to be about protection for you. You try to use your magic to destroy, and it's useless. Honestly, you may as well have been tickling me."

Sophie threw her a dirty look. "Protection isn't going to do a lot if it comes down to a face-off against Marshall. I need to make this work."

"There's no 'making' Shadow work," Esme sneered.

"I made Light work," Sophie shrugged.

Esme narrowed her eyes. "You assume a level of control. Most likely, you stumbled into figuring out how to let Light work."

Sophie didn't reply. She didn't feel like arguing, or like explaining to someone she barely knew, how she'd eventually come to work with the Light.

"No matter what you think you know, you don't know a damn thing," Esme said after a moment. "And I don't know. Maybe that is the way Light works. But it's not the way Shadow works. Shadow is wild. Uncontrollable. It is bigger than all of us. You would do well to remember that." She stood up. "Again."

"That's pretty much it. How many times can you watch me do the same thing?" Sophie asked. "I need you to teach me something new."

"And I need to get a good sense of your power before I can do that. So shut it and hit me."

Sophie focused, drawing Shadow together within her, and threw it at Esme.

"Again."

Sophie groaned, but did what Esme told her to do. They went through the routine several more times, Sophie gathering Shadow to throw at Esme, and Esme acting for the most part as of she barely felt what Sophie was throwing at her.

"Okay. Let's try something else," Esme said.

"Thank you," Sophie muttered, and Esme smirked.

"I'm so sorry you're not entertained, your Highness," Esme said. "You've watched me make my shield several times now. It's your turn. I'm going to hit you now. Try to block it."

"I—" before Sophie could utter another syllable, Esme's power hit her, sending her crashing back into the bookshelves behind her.

"Oh, I forgot to mention: you're going to pick up every book you knock off my shelves. They're in a specific order, and I want them put back just the way they were."

Sophie glared at Esme, wincing a little. She would definitely have a bruise on her back from that one. She noticed Esme raise her hand, getting ready to hit Sophie with Shadow, and Sophie hurriedly tried to ready herself. She could see, again, how to make a protective shield. Light knew she'd done it for most of her life, shielding her home and herself from Marshall and his power. The spell was still there, as if it was waiting to be filled so she could use it. She tried to force Shadow into the spell she knew, and was rewarded by another trip crashing back into Esme's bookshelves.

"Again," Esme said, and now she was smiling.

"You're enjoying this," Sophie said in disbelief.

"Oh, it helps that you look so much like Migisi. Again." And without any further warning, Esme hit her with Shadow again, and, just as before, Sophie went flying back into the bookcases.

"You are pathetic," Esme said, shaking her head. "Pick those books up. I need to think." She sat behind the large desk and wordlessly watched as Sophie started picking up books and putting them back on shelves. Every time she bent, Sophie winced. She was going to be feeling this lovely little training session for a while.

"That's not where that one goes," Esme said, and Sophie glared at her. "It goes between *Aphrodisiacs in Shadow* and *Vanity Curses*."

Still glaring at Esme, Sophie put the book in the place she'd indicated. "Yeah, Shadow is a lovely thing," she muttered. "I feel dirty just holding these books."

"Oh. Well I'm so sorry you've fouled yourself, princess," Esme said. "Remember that you asked me for help."

"I know," Sophie said quietly, finishing putting the books back. The room was silent for several moments as Sophie finished picking up the mess and Esme sat, watching Sophie with a thoughtful look on her face. There wasn't a sound in the room other than the ticking of the ornate black clock on the wall near Esme's desk and the sound of books sliding onto their shelves. "And I appreciate the fact that you're even helping me. Light knows you have no reason to," Sophie continued, crossing her arms and studying Esme once she finished cleaning up the books she'd dislodged. "But you need to understand that as much as I want to learn to protect myself from Marshall, I also have every intention of working my way back to the Light."

"And I think you should know that in all my years, I've never heard of such a thing. The Light is fickle. It leaves its champions for the slightest mistake. And every one of you eventually wishes it would come back."

"Did Migisi wish for it?"

"Of course. She was as obsessed with the idea as you seem to be. And I can tell you, without a single doubt, that she never made it back to the Light. She died a Shadow witch."

"How did you meet her?"

Esme visibly stiffened. "Through a family member," she said, her face like stone.

"Well. I'm not Migisi. I'll find a way to make it back. So I won't be doing anything that's going to corrupt me further. And thank you for reminding me of what I am. I think you were right—"

"There's a shock," Esme said, and Sophie shook her head.

"—I can't use my power to cause pain, or it won't work. I kind of got that when I was practicing with the trees. I can't just cause outright destruction, even though that's what Shadow wants. I have to have a Light-worthy reason, or nothing happens. So, yes, you're right. All I want to do with Shadow is learn to protect myself. I just need to learn how to shield, maybe."

"Do you really think shielding, even if you are able to learn it, will matter against Marshall? Hasn't he already proven that he won't hurt you by going after you directly? He'll go after those around you, because he knows that'll hurt you the most," Esme said, steepling her fingers in front of her mouth. "From what I know of him, he's not above hurting women. He did some awful things to Migisi, especially once she seemed like she was trying to get out from under his control. And sometimes, even before then. He got off on that kind of thing."

"He mostly just seems to like seeing me afraid of him. He seemed like he wanted to hurt me the other day, but he couldn't do it. I remind him of someone he cared for."

"That won't protect you forever," Esme said.

"I need to do this my own way."

Esme sighed and shook her head. "Then I hope you're prepared for those around you to suffer while you try to keep your hands clean. Marshall doesn't have a speck of nobility in him."

"I know," Sophie said.

"That's all for today. Come back on Friday, same time."

Sophie nodded, knowing it would be easier to just ask her boss to switch her shift, especially now that it was the off-season, than it would be to get Esme to reschedule.

"You can see yourself out. Just close the front door behind you."

"Thanks, Esme."

Esme opened a book, acting as if she hadn't heard Sophie. Apparently, she was dismissed. She walked down the stairs, through the stark white hallway, past all of those empty rooms again, and sighed with relief once she stepped out the front door. She closed it, then practically ran to her car, more than ready to be away from Esme and her anger and her creepy empty house.

CHAPTER FIFTEEN

Sophie got out of her car and immediately felt the calmness of being home settle over her like a blanket. No matter what else was happening, her little piece of the wilderness never failed to make her feel as if all was not lost.

Of course, if she didn't get herself figured out, she could very likely see it disappear, just as the forest had died around Esme's house. Life and Shadow. The two didn't exactly go together.

Sophie got out of her car and glanced toward Calder's house. He wasn't in his driveway, which was a surprise. He kept very regular work hours for someone who worked for himself, in his driveway. In the past several weeks, they'd established a pattern: wake up together, run, eat breakfast, then Calder would head to his garage to start working. Sophie would start her day, and, if she was home, they would get together again for lunch. He'd go back to work for a few hours, and then they'd make dinner together. If Sophie was working, the schedule was a little different, but she knew that whether she was there or not, Calder was always in his driveway between nine and four.

His car was still in the driveway, and she could see his motorcycle near the side of the house. Sophie bit her lip, then shrugged and headed around her house to check on her goats, wondering if maybe they'd gotten out again and Calder was dealing with them. When she got there, though, the three goats were standing in their pen, and they all looked toward Sophie with that bored, disdainful look that certain goats just seemed to have nailed. She gave them fresh water, and went around re-checking their fencing. Wherever she went, Merlin shadowed her, trying to headbutt her through the fence.

"You are an asshole, goat," Sophie muttered. "Go butt your weirdo friends." One of the other goats bleated at her disapprovingly, and she moved on to the next side of the goat pen. She heard a car on the road, and looked up to see a big white truck pulling into her driveway. She smiled and waved as her friend Thea climbed out of the truck, and jogged toward the driveway.

"Hope you don't mind my stopping by," Thea said as she and Sophie hugged.

"Of course not," Sophie said. "I meant to come by and see you this week."

"Come by anyway. I have a new pizza dough recipe I'm trying out. You can taste-test it for me." Not only was Thea the local Ojibwe historian and record-keeper, a retired teacher, and a youth counsellor, she was also the best cook Sophie had ever known, and she considered herself lucky to be the recipient of so many of Thea's culinary experiments.

Sophie grinned. "Deal."

"Though, really, I don't know how much use I'll be to you, kiddo. Want to walk?" Thea asked, gesturing toward the woods, and Sophie nodded. They began walking toward the trees, toward the path that Sophie ran every day. "I brought the last of the files I could find about Migisi." She handed Sophie a manila envelope, and Sophie accepted it gratefully. "There really wasn't much left."

Sophie and Thea had continued to work together to put together the pieces of her ancestor's life after the curse. Sophie had enlisted Thea's help on the off-chance that, as a local historian and member of the Ojibwa tribe, as Migisi had been, she would be able to shed some light on her crazy ancestor and the things she'd done. They'd found bits and pieces of Migisi's story all over Michigan's upper peninsula, and even down in Detroit. What had emerged was the story of someone who had clearly lost her damn mind, and, maybe, somewhere along the way, found it again. Reports of Migisi right after the time in which she'd cursed Luc had been terrifying, a witch who had spread violence and discord wherever she went. Not only had her mere presence caused riots in some cities and small towns, but Migisi herself had at times gotten right in the middle of the violence, injuring and cursing people. Of course, most of the stories of curses were written off in the local media at the time as hysteria and superstition, but Sophie had a feeling they were much more than that.

And then, a few years later, mentions of Migisi in the media had pretty much ceased. They'd started looking for anything that may have been an allusion to her, though it had often felt like grabbing at straws, and their meetings had become less regular in the past few weeks, partially because of the fact that there was little to talk about as far as Migisi was concerned, and partially because Sophie was finding it hard to sit still and study old newspaper articles.

"It looks like she ended up settling back here, in your house, which we already knew because she died here in Copper Falls," Thea said, and Sophie nodded. Oddly enough, Migisi and Luc had died on the same day, and were buried side-by-side in the local cemetery, just down the highway. Reports of each of their deaths listed separate, unrelated reasons: illness and an accident. The story Calder's family had was that Luc had jumped off one of the

Rockway cliffs in a desperate attempt to end his suffering, cursing Migisi as he did.

One thing seemed clear to Sophie: if they'd hated one another so much, they wouldn't have been buried together. Not when Luc had a wife and child who were later buried in a separate plot elsewhere in the cemetery. She held onto that fact, that maybe they'd somehow managed to find their way back to one another. It made the worst days, those days when the curse she'd taken from Calder had her teetering on the edge of madness, a little less desperate. It wasn't much to hold onto, but she'd take it.

Thea continued. "Even so, any reports about her after she got back here are sparse. There's an article in there about her saving a child in the tribe from a bear attack. I assume we both know who the 'bear' was, yes?" she asked, raising her eyebrows. Sophie nodded. "And later, there's a small mention of her daughter. It was after Migisi's death, but the article talks about how she was a healer, but too many remembered what her mother had become and few trusted her. Apparently she went to live with the rest of the tribe when she was a teenager, but I didn't find any mention of why, or where Migisi was at the time."

They walked in silence for a while. The crisp fall leaves crunched under their shoes. Sophie could smell woodsmoke in the air, the scent of decaying leaves and, underneath it all, the clean, refreshing scent of the stream at the back of her property, which she and Thea strolled toward. She could hear the falls from where they were. She was hit, all at once, with how much she loved this place, while also envisioning what the land around Esme's house had become. This, as much as the curse, as much as her own sense of her self, was why she had to find her way back to the Light. She had the weirdest sense that her own well-being was tied to the health of the place she'd come to see as her sanctuary. If it failed, so would she. But to save it, she had to find a way to keep Shadow from overtaking everything and everyone around her.

She had no clue how to do that. Which was another reason she clung to that tiny, impossible hope that Migisi had figured it out.

If she had, it would have been super if she'd have written it down somewhere, Sophie mused irritably. No chance of it being that easy; Sophie had looked through everything Migisi may have touched, scoured the journals she'd left for hidden messages... nothing. Other than those later watercolors of Luc, there had been nothing.

"Have you run across anything about Luc?" Sophie asked Thea. They reached the stream, coming out of the woods near the boulder. Her and Calder's boulder, Sophie thought to herself with a smile. They'd first kissed on it as teenagers. They'd done a heck of a lot more on it in the time since they'd found their way back to one another.

Thea shook her head. "No. Other than his death notice, there's no mention. In his obituary, they mentioned his wife and son, but there's no mention at all any of his ancestors after that." That made sense. Sophie knew from what Calder had said, from what she'd seen with Calder's own father, that the men in their line usually died at home. There were no obituaries; the family tried hard not to draw attention to itself, for obvious reasons. Thea continued. "In fact, the next mention I found of the Turcotte line was Calder, and that's because he started getting attention for his car restorations. A couple of papers in the area have written about him." She paused, then smiled at Sophie. "Those are in there, too. I thought you might like to see them."

Sophie smiled. "Thank you."

Thea nodded, and they stopped and looked at the stream, and the falls beyond, a little way down the stream. "Good lord, it's beautiful here," Thea murmured.

"It is," Sophie agreed.

"No wonder you were so desperate to save it." Sophie had confided in Thea about Calder and his curse and how he'd used her house to try to force her to help him. He'd given the house back to her; it was in her name again, as it should be. He hadn't accepted any offer of repaying him for the money he'd spent on her house at the auction, waving it off and saying that she'd held up her part of the deal. The curse wasn't in his line anymore. Of course, now, Sophie had it, so it wasn't *gone*, exactly. She still had to try to find a way to destroy it completely, now that she had it contained in herself instead of in Calder. The key was managing it before she completely lost her sanity.

"This area, especially along the river and near the falls is steeped in folklore," Thea said. She grinned at Sophie. "It was one of the things I used to bore my students with when I taught."

"You were never boring, Thea."

"Not many ten year olds are interested in stories about wise women and *windigoo*."

"I always liked it when you shared those stories," Sophie said.

Thea looked out over the river. "Do you remember the story of the falls?"

Sophie smiled. "The forest loved the lake, yet neither could live where the other reigned. Forests drown, and water dries on land. So lake came to forest in her own way, and twist and turns through it, and gives it life even in the driest seasons, and the falls are lake's overflowing love for forest."

Thea beamed. "You remember!"

"I loved that story."

Thea went over to the boulder and looked up at the two enormous oaks that flanked it. She put her hand on the rough bark of the one nearest to her.

"Funny story about these trees, too," she said, still looking up at the branches with their rattling, dry leaves. "Have you heard that one?"

Sophie shook her head.

"This came from one of the old timers, who said that one day, a group of youths was fishing in this area. The fish were plentiful here, the water cool and clean. They played on this boulder, and leaned against it when they were resting. And they left, vowing to come back the next day." Thea kept looking up at the tree, her hands on the bark. "So they came back the next day, and they swore to everyone they knew that these two trees had not been there the day before, but had appeared out of nowhere, as enormous and majestic as they stand today."

Sophie looked up at the trees. "These were teenage boys?"

Thea transferred her gaze from the trees to Sophie. "Yes."

Sophie let out a small laugh. "They probably were screwing off and didn't notice the trees the first time around. It's a forest full of trees. Something probably just drew their attention to them that second day."

"You are no fun at all, Sophie Turner," Thea chided, stepping away from the tree after giving the bark a gentle pat. "So logical."

"Yeah, logical. That's me," Sophie said with a smile. "Obviously."

Thea shook her head, and they started walking back toward Sophie's house. "Thanks for walking with me. It was a long day and it's been too long since I've given the old legs a good stretch."

"Anytime. Thank you for coming out. And for this," Sophie said, holding up the manila envelope.

"My pleasure. Make sure you come and see me, though!"

"I can stop by on Thursday if you like," Sophie said as they reached Thea's truck.

"That would be fabulous. We'll try the new pizza recipe and you can take a look at the new art on display in the community center."

"It's a date," Sophie said with a nod. "Oh, hey," she said, a thought coming to her. "One of the guests at the resort had one of those supernatural Michigan books, and there was a story in there about a witch in the woods. Do you know anything about that?"

Thea laughed. "I've read that book. The place doesn't exist. You can keep driving down South Mine road and see nothing but forest. That road curves out onto another highway, and nowhere along it are the woods dead," she said with a roll of her brown eyes.

Sophie tried to hide her surprise. One more thing to ask Esme about. "Oh. Well, yeah, I figured that," she said. "She was going to try to find it, and I told her it probably wasn't worth bothering."

Thea nodded. "Tourists," she said with a grin, and Sophie forced herself to smile back.

"I—" Thea began, but whatever she'd been about to say was interrupted by an earth-shaking, terrifying roar from the forest. Sophie and Thea both spun, looking toward where the sound had come from. Sophie recognized the sound immediately; Calder had roared just like that the night of the first full moon after he'd made the deal with her about the house. The sound echoed through the forest again, loud, enraged.

"What the hell?" Thea asked.

Sophie shrugged. "Bears, maybe. They're settling in for winter, right? Maybe fighting over food."

Thea gave Sophie a look that suggested she knew exactly what kind of bear it was that had made the sound, but Sophie didn't feel like talking about it. "You should get back to town before it gets dark. I hate driving these roads at night."

"Me too. All right. If you're sure?" Thea asked, looking closely at Sophie.

"I am. I'm in no danger," she said, trying to reassure the older woman.

"Sweetheart, the biggest danger to any of us is the one we love most. They're the only one who can truly break us. That's what makes love such a damn terrifying thing. And it's even more so, in your case."

"I'll be fine," Sophie said, pulling Thea's truck door open for her. "I'm going to go in, and have some tea, and look through these files."

Thea gave her a nod, then got into the truck. Sophie closed the door once she was in, and, within moments, Thea was turning down the highway, heading back toward town.

Another angry roar thundered through the woods, this time sounding farther away. Sophie rubbed her arms against the sudden chill in the air. She went to the front of her house and sat on the stone steps outside her front door, looking at the woods across the road, waiting for some sign of Calder. She waited for a few minutes, then went inside, lit a fire in the fireplace, and grabbed a thick wool sweater, pulling it around her tightly. Then she went back outside and sat on the front steps again. She was starving, thirsty. She wanted to run. She wanted to find Calder and reassure herself that the crazed sound wasn't really coming from him.

Another roar pulled her back from her own desperation. In truth, the roars were angry, mournful sounds. Unhinged, she thought. Too much like the sounds he'd made the night of the full moon.

Sophie lost track of how long she sat there. Darkness settled in around her, millions of stars and a sliver of moon bright in the sky above. The roars continued, sometimes sounding near, sometimes farther away. She heard another crazed, angry roar, and made up her mind. He could be hurt, and she was sitting around hoping everything would be okay, Sophie chided herself. She went into her house, grabbed the big, heavy Maglite flashlight she kept near the door, then jogged down her driveway. She'd start with the woods around his house, she planned. And then go out further if she didn't catch any sign of him.

Just as she stepped onto his side of the road, she notice a light come on in his kitchen. She paused for a second, then ran toward his house. Her heart pounded, and her nerves were a wreck. She felt like she was on the verge of snapping, after having listened to his insane roars for so long, not knowing what was going on, only knowing that those roars should not have sounded the way they did. Not if everything was okay.

She knocked on the front door, waited a few seconds, then knocked again, louder. She chided herself for not getting a set of keys to Calder's house, the way he did for hers. He'd offered to have them made, and she'd brushed it off, saying they usually spent the night at her place, anyway.

"Stupid, stupid, stupid," she muttered to herself as she ran around to the back door, past Calder's motorcycle, past Bryce's ugly car. Her feet pounded up the wooden stairs and she tried the knob. Locked.

She knocked, loud, and called Calder's name. "Calder, open the goddamn door," she shouted, pounding on the door again.

She glanced down at the handle, wondering if she could break it, when she saw something that made her even more determined to get inside: a smear of blood.

"Calder!" she shouted, knowing, in some sense, that she was probably looking and sounding completely insane, knowing that her curse was making her even more obsessive about getting to him, but, for once, not caring. She glanced at the kitchen window, which she could get to by standing on the railing of the back porch. She knocked one more time, called Calder's name, then went over to the garage and grabbed a piece of wood that was leaning against the side of it. She ran onto the porch, climbed up onto the railing, and hit the kitchen window with the short piece of wood. It shattered, the sound seeming to echo through the night. She used the wood to clear away as many shards of glass as she could, then she pulled herself up into the window.

Inside, she jumped off of the kitchen counter and listened. She could hear the shower running upstairs.

155

Her face heated. If she'd just broken Calder's window, and the only reason he hadn't answered was because he'd been in the shower, she was going to feel like a complete ass. And maybe her curse was making her more nuts than she realized.

But her mind went back to that smear of blood, and she ran up the stairs. On the wall of the stairway, there was another long smear of dark blood, and, in the hallway, another. The bathroom door stood open, steam pouring out of it.

Sophie stepped into the bathroom, then let out a strangled sound and ran to the bathtub. The shower was on full blast, hot, and Calder lay unconscious in the clawfoot tub under the spray. Several long cuts along his side turned the water in the tub red before it swirled down the drain.

He was so still, Sophie had a moment of frozen panic, then she snapped herself out of it and bent over him. The water scalded as it hit her arm, and she quickly turned it off, noting the angry red tone of his skin from the too-hot water.

But those cuts... three down the side she could see, another three on his shoulder. She wondered if there were more on his other side. He was on his side, head on the side of the tub, body laying in the tub. Naked, which sickeningly enough had her body aching in need thanks to the vile, stupid, asshole curse Migisi had put on his family.

"Calder, honey," she said, patting his face gently. "Honey, wake up," she said. Terror rose in her, the fear that she'd been too late, that she shouldn't have waited on the porch for so long, that she shouldn't have spent so much time trying to get him to come to the door. She flashed back to the day she'd found her young husband, David, cut and bleeding in a bathtub, and a strangled cry came from her throat as she started shaking. "Calder," she sobbed. She put her hand to his throat, where she could feel his pulse, thankfully. It seemed slow, and she lifted a shaking hand from him. He couldn't keep bleeding like that.

She had to call an ambulance, she realized. She dug her phone out of her pocket and nearly hit 911 before realizing that that would raise too many questions. How had it happened? Why was he healing so fast? Shifters healed unnaturally quickly, and there as no way to explain it well to a non-magical person.

If she didn't do something, she'd lose him. Even though he'd heal fast, it needed help. The cuts down his side definitely needed to be stitched up, and she knew she could do it, but there were too many and he was bleeding heavily. There's no way she'd be fast enough, she realized, and she screamed in frustration. She could have healed him with her Light magic. Now, she was without it. She hit Jon's number instead.

He answered on the first ring, and she gave him the whole story, barely stopping to breathe.

"Okay, Sophie, listen to me. Listen," Jon said in a calm, steady voice over the phone. "Sophie."

"Okay," she said, staring at Calder.

"Okay. He got into a fight with something. Probably another bear. Good job not calling 911. He'll be okay, and we don't want any goddamn questions. Okay?"

"He needs stitches."

"He doesn't. He needs someone to put pressure on the cuts until they knit back together. I'd come, but I'm in Iron Mountain right now."

"Why?"

"Calder sent me here to pick up a car he's going to be working on. Sophie, you can do this. Okay?"

"Just put pressure on it? You should see these things," she said, grabbing a towel off of the rack and kneeling next to the tub. She put the towel on his side, on the worst of the cuts, and held her hands down, hard, on it. "They're deep. Long. Are you sure?"

"We had stuff like this happen all the time with my dad," he said, his voice kind of trailing off. "Shifters get into fights all the time," he said. "He'll heal. Can you stay with him and keep pressure on the cuts?"

"Of course."

"Okay. That's all he needs, Soph. He'll be okay."

"He's bleeding a lot," She said, looking at the way the blood was already beginning to soak through the towel.

"I don't doubt it. Trust me on this, Soph. Calder and I went through all kinds of shit with dad, and with each other. He'll heal, but you need to keep an eye on him. Keep pressure on his cuts, clean them as soon as you're able so he doesn't get infected."

"I found him under a scalding hot shower," she said.

"Well, that's Calder. He knows what he's doing. Just keep pressure on them, then. He's going to be cold from all the blood loss. I doubt you'll be able to move him, but try to keep him warm."

"Okay."

"Okay. It'll be all right, Soph. I was going to stay the night here, but I'll head out now."

"No, you don't have to do that. You're sure he'll heal?"

"I'm sure."

"Okay. Well, no need to drive all that way in the dark, then. I'll take care of him."

"You're sure?"

"Yeah." She pulled another towel off of the rack, replacing the first, blood-soaked one, and put pressure on it again.

"Okay. I'll be by in the morning then. Call me if you need anything."

"Okay." She let the phone drop from her shoulder onto the floor, her focus completely on Calder. "You hear that, Calder? He says this is all you need. Don't prove him wrong, okay?" she asked, and her voice caught. Tears sprung to her eyes, that first flash of remembering her first husband, the fact that the scene in Calder's bathroom had been too similar, still making her tremble. She was still raw, all these years later, still able to see every detail from the day she'd lost David. Because of Marshall.

She blinked back the tears that wee threatening to spill over, and looked at Calder's face. "Did he do this?" she whispered, knowing there would be no answer. He'd threatened that he'd take Calder from her, just as he'd taken David from her. She'd thought he was convinced that she was tied to Calder, but maybe he wasn't. Maybe he didn't care. "I won't let him destroy you," she promised Calder. "I don't care what it takes. I'll do anything." She knew she as babbling. She was trembling, her teeth chattering so hard she clamped her jaw to try to keep them still.

She shook her head, tried to force herself to focus. All she really wanted to do was run. Destroy something. Eat until she burst. Scream. All at the same time, and all because of Migisi's stupid curse. She let out a frustrated, angry shout, then took several deep breaths, trying to get herself under control. She'd never felt so close to the edge, barely holding onto reality and what she knew she was supposed to do.

"Not now," she pleaded. "Not now," she said, more strongly, more to herself. Through the insanity and fear, a glimmer of sense: her fear was making her crazy. She needed to focus on something other than the fear. She made herself take a slow, deep breath, still feeling completely nuts. Another deep breath.

"Take care of Calder," she muttered to herself. "Focus on that, you crazy bitch."

She kept one hand on the towel on Calder's side and reached around him, trying to gently feel his other side. There was no blood coming from that side that she was able to see, so she took that as a good sign that the worst of his injuries were the ones she could see: the cuts in his side, on his shoulder, and another on his chest. She grabbed another towel and tied it tightly over and around his shoulder, putting pressure on the cut there. The one on his chest was not as deep as the others, and it was already bleeding less. Sophie held a washcloth to that in one hand while she kept pressure on his side with the other. After a while, the towels were soaked with less and less blood, though large, angry red gashes still marred the side of his body. Sophie rooted through the cabinet under his bathroom sink, and found a first aid kit. She rubbed antiseptic ointment gently over the cuts, feeling the rough, raised edges of his wounds under her fingertips. That done, she placed gauze pads over the cuts, then wound a roll of Ace bandages around his body, keeping the gauze pads in place and pressure on the wounds.

As she worked, she felt the insanity of the curse receding. She noted it thankfully, but didn't really give it much thought. She was just grateful that he wasn't dying.

She placed another gauze pad on his chest and taped it down. She left the towel tied around his shoulder. It seemed to be working well enough.

"I'm supposed to keep you warm," she said to Calder, noting the occasional shiver. There was no chance in hell of moving him into a bed or anywhere else; he outweighed her by at least a hundred pounds, and she was no lightweight herself. She grabbed a clean towel and dried him off, then wiped out the tub, trying to get the tub as dry as she could under his body as well. She quickly went to his bedroom and grabbed the thick blue comforter off of his bed and brought it back to the bathroom with her.

He was shivering violently now, and she knew that though the worst of it was over, he would need time to recover. She was exhausted.

Sophie kicked her shoes off and climbed into the clawfoot tub beside Calder, wrapping herself around his body. She pulled the comforter over both of them, making sure he was covered. She put her arms around him, and tried to get comfortable.

"Not our sexiest night, Calder," she murmured. She rested her face against the firm muscles of his back and closed her eyes.

She came awake with a start what may have been seconds later when she felt Calder moving. She sat up with a grimace. Her neck was stiff from sleeping in the tub with him.

"Hey," she said quietly, patting his hip. He started to stand, and she stopped him. "Hold on. You lost a lot of blood."

"You can't sleep in the bathtub," he said stiffly.

"I had to keep you warm," she said. His face had been like stone, and his expression softened just a little.

"You did. Thank you. I can walk to bed now."

He gently pushed her hand away and stood up, carefully, and though he tried to hide his grimace from her, she saw it. He stepped out of the tub and held a hand out to her. She took it, and he pulled her up. She stepped out of the tub, and he let go of her and removed the towel from his shoulder. The cut there was still red, but looked like it had scabbed over.

"Leave the others on. They were deeper," Sophie said, and he nodded. He wouldn't look at her, and Sophie's heart ached. "Calder…"

"I'm tired, kitten," he said.

"Then let's sleep. Can I stay with you, or do you want to be alone?" she asked, hoping like hell he would ask her to stay.

"Don't leave me, Sophie,' he said, finally meeting her eyes.

"Never," she promised. He took her hand and led her down the hallway to his bedroom. She took her bloody clothing off, and settled herself into bed beside him. Calder pulled the comforter over them and gathered her into his arms.

Sophie sighed contentedly and snuggled closer to Calder. She could barely keep her eyes open.

"What happened, Calder?" she asked sleepily.

"We're both exhausted. We'll talk about it tomorrow," he said, and she rubbed his back and kissed his chest.

"I love you," she murmured.

After a moment, he squeezed her tightly against him. "I love you too, Sophie. There aren't enough words to tell you how much."

Calder lay awake for a long time, long after Sophie's breathing slowed and her body became relaxed and still in his arms. He held her, and admired her as she slept. Everything he'd put her through since he'd come back into her life, and she still held him like she never wanted to let him go, still looked at him like he was the best thing she'd ever seen. And what had he done to deserve it? Blackmailed her, terrorized her, stressed her out. She carried his curse, for fuck's sake.

Yeah, some catch he'd turned out to be, he thought with disgust. How this gorgeous, sweet, sexy, warm woman could look at him the way she did was still a mystery to him. Every second he spent with her, he felt like it was a precious moment stolen, because one day she'd wake up and realize that she could do so much better. Sophie Turner had always been too good for him. Had been when they were kids, and still was, as far as he was concerned.

He was a selfish asshole. He hoped the day never came when her face didn't light up when he entered a room, when she didn't realize how much better she could do. But it was coming. He knew it. And for her own safety and sanity, it would probably be better if it was sooner rather than later. Tonight's insanity had proven what he'd suspected for a couple of weeks now.

His curse wasn't gone.

It felt like it was coming back. It felt the same way it had the first time he had started feeling the effects of his family's curse. The hunger, the thirst, the need to keep moving. The need for the satisfaction only Sophie's body could give him. And then what had happened earlier that night…

He looked at Sophie again, wishing he could drift off to sleep for a while. He had just closed his eyes when he heard a soft knock at the front door. He gently pulled away from Sophie and got out of bed, tucking the blankets around her to keep out the cool night air.

Calder pulled on some pants and headed downstairs, and the knock at the front door sounded again. He scented the air, and groaned.

He pulled the front door open. "What in the hell are you doing here in the middle of the night?" he asked Jon, who stood there, bleary-eyed.

"You're welcome. It was totally worth driving from Iron Mountain for," Jon said, shoving past him. "Glad to see you're okay."

"What?"

"Sophie called me. She was in a panic. She wanted to know if she should call 911."

Calder groaned and rubbed his hands over his face. Jon closed the front door behind him.

"So you're okay?"

"Shh." Calder said.

Jon raised an eyebrow, and Calder pointed up the stairs.

"Sophie's asleep now."

Jon nodded, and they went into the kitchen where they could talk without waking Sophie up. There was a lot he wanted to say to his brother, and he wasn't ready for her to hear any of it.

CHAPTER SIXTEEN

In the kitchen, Jon grabbed a beer out of the fridge. He held one up, wordlessly asking if Calder wanted one, and Calder shook his head and sat at the small, scuffed table.

"What happened to your window?" Jon asked as he dug the bottle opener out of the kitchen drawer. Calder glanced that way.

"Sophie must have broken it getting in earlier," Calder said, hating himself again for what he'd put her through.

"She doesn't have a key?"

"I keep forgetting to make one for her."

"She can have mine," Jon said, pulling out the other chair at the kitchen table and settling into it.

"You might need yours. I'll have one made for her," Calder said. He got up and started pacing across the kitchen. "The curse isn't gone. It's coming back," he said quietly as he paced. He glanced at his brother out of the corner of his eye. Jon had been about to take a gulp of beer, and he froze with the bottle lifted partway to his mouth.

"What?" Jon finally asked. "What the hell are you talking about? Soph took it."

"She took it," Calder agreed woodenly. "But it's coming back."

The look on Jon's face was enough to make Calder want to storm into the woods and fight something. A mix of fear, confusion, and anger. Helplessness. "So, she doesn't have it anymore?" Jon finally asked.

Calder looked away. "She does. She's getting worse, man. I look at her sometimes, and I know she's not really there, you know? She gets this blank, weird look in her eyes. She wanders, and she doesn't know she's doing it. Mostly at night. I'll wake up and she's gone, and I'll find her pacing crazily in the woods."

"That must have her freaked out," Jon said.

"She doesn't know about it. Doesn't remember it happening. She blacks out completely when it's going on, and she has no idea it even happened. I'm this close to tying our wrists together or something before we go to sleep at night, because most nights, now, she's wandering. I'm losing her," he said, and the words hurt more than he thought they could.

"But you said the curse is coming back for you, too," Jon said, watching him closely.

"It is. Constant thirst, hunger. I can't sit still. I want to fight all the time, unless Sophie's around, then all I can think about is doing something else."

"What happened tonight?" Jon asked quietly, resignation in his voice. They'd both known, it seemed, that it was too good to be true. That the Turcotte curse could just be taken, transferred to someone else. It would have been all right, if Sophie was improving, if the curse was just transferring itself back to Calder, to its rightful prisoner. But that didn't seem to be what was happening.

Calder sighed. "I was working and waiting for Sophie to get home. And I just got more and more edgy. Couldn't be still, couldn't calm down. So I decided to go for a run. I didn't trust my bear, so I ran in my human form," Calder said. Jon waited, and after a few moments, Calder continued. "I could smell that fucking warlock in Sophie's woods. Strong, like he'd just been there. It was like that was all it took. I must have shifted. I don't remember doing it or deciding to do it. All I knew was, the next time I was coherent enough to focus on anything other than my rage, I wasn't in my human form." He crossed his arms over his chest. "Anyway, I was running then as my bear, and clearly, I was in a fighting mood. I stumbled into the path of a great big, pretty pissed off black bear. I think I was a little too close to its den."

"So you fought," Jon said, putting it together.

Calder nodded. "At first it was all instinct. Male bullshit. I felt all bear. Saw things like a bear."

"Fuck," Jon said, scraping his fingers through his hair.

"Yeah." They both knew what it meant. Shifters keep their humanity, even in their animal forms. They think like humans, reason like humans, just in the body of a bear, or a wolf. The curse and the madness it entailed made it so that the men in Calder's family lost their humanity. The first sign of that, they knew from generations of the first-born male dealing with the curse, was that in their bear form, they began feeling more animal than man. Eventually, that would be their default state, and they'd lose their humanity forever.

Calder and Jon had both watched it happen to their father. They both knew what it looked like, and, from his time with the curse before Sophie took it, Calder knew damn well what it felt like. And it was happening again.

"But it doesn't make any sense. How?" Jon asked, and Calder's stomach twisted at the desperation in his voice. He'd hoped to save his brother from having to babysit him the way he'd had to care for their father at the end.

"I don't know," Calder said quietly. "All I know is that Sophie's slowly losing herself, and so am I. And she's the only one who can save us."

"She can't save you, Calder," Jon said. "Not now. Shadow," he said, and the hatred in his voice grated on Calder.

"Shadow has nothing to do with it. The fact that she can't remember shit she did a few minutes ago is the issue here. My curse, which she never should have taken. Migisi's going to have the last laugh, because we're both going to end up raging lunatics, and the fucking curse is going to go on forever."

Neither of them spoke for a long time. The clock on the wall ticked the seconds by, echoing emptily in the dim kitchen.

"I need you to lock me up if I get too bad. The first person I'd hurt would be her, and I'd rather put a bullet through my head than do that," Calder said quietly.

"You should break it off with her now," Jon said. "As much as you don't want to… it would be better for both of you."

"I know," Calder said. "I know."

Jon sighed. "Look, I know there's something between the two of you that most people can only dream of having. You two are drawn together in a way that everyone around you can see. It's been that way since we were kids. I don't understand it, but damn if I don't want something like it for myself someday. I know walking away from her isn't something you want to do. And I know that your bear makes it even harder, because it definitely doesn't want to let her go. But you need to think, while you still can, about what's best for Soph. We both know she won't leave you. She's not the type to walk away."

Calder didn't answer. They sat in silence, and after a while, he said, "you know what she'd say if she heard you right now?"

"What?"

"That she can decide for herself what's best for her."

"You're trying to use that as an out, man, and you know it. Love is blind, and you two are more blind about one another than most."

"That's bullshit. She sees me better than anyone ever has. She knows me."

"And I'll repeat it: the two of you are blind. She knows damn well that she'd be putting herself in danger staying with you. You're a ticking time bomb, and she's too stubborn to walk, even once she does realize what's happening."

"We have a little more time."

"So you say," Jon said doubtfully. "You lost yourself tonight, Calder. Luckily, the only one who suffered from it was a bear. What if it's Sophie next time?" he asked, meeting Calder's eyes. Calder looked away. He knew Jon was right. He knew it, and the idea of breaking things off with Sophie was something he couldn't even imagine doing.

"She could still figure it all out. I believe in her."

"And that's great. But she's also losing her mind, man. How much of her is really left?"

"A lot. She's still mostly together."

"As far as you know. She goes to work. You don't think things happen there? Or when she's driving? Or when she's alone at home?"

"Just... we'll figure something out," Calder said, holding his hand up to halt his brother's speech. "She'll do it. I know she will. This is Sophie, and she doesn't know the meaning of the word surrender. Okay? We'll help one another through this, and she'll figure it out—"

"Yeah. And we'll all live happily ever after. The end," Jon said. He got up and poured the rest of his beer down the kitchen drain and set his beer bottle on the counter. "Like I said, you two are blind. Or stupid."

"Just promise me that if I get too bad you'll take care of it so she doesn't have to. I don't plan on letting it get that far. If I get bad, I'll lock my own ass up rather than put her through that."

Jon just glared at him, then gave a terse nod. "I'll come back tomorrow to help with the window," he said as he walked toward the back door.

"And check on me," Calder said. "You don't have to."

"I know. It'll make me feel better, though," Jon said, and Calder clapped him on the shoulder.

"I'll be okay," Calder said.

"You can put your faith in Sophie if you want to. I prefer to live in the real world," Jon said, and without another word, he walked to his truck and drove back down the driveway. Calder watched his taillights until he turned off of the highway onto the road that led to the house they'd grown up in. He glanced at the driveway, where Jon had left the great big old Studebaker he'd gone to pick up for Calder. His next restoration project. Calder looked it over, for no other reason than because it gave him something else to think about for a minute. He made a mental list of parts he'd have to order based on what he could see at first glance. There would be more once he started pulling things apart.

"Hey, you. Aren't you cold?"

Calder glanced up at the front porch to see Sophie there, wearing one of his ugly old sweatshirts as a nightgown. Her hair was in disarray, and she had that bleary-eyed look she got when she could use a little more sleep.

He'd never loved anyone as much as he loved her.

"I'm fine. We should get you inside though," he told her.

She held her hand out, beckoning him, and he went. He'd expected her to lead him back upstairs, but instead she gently pulled him into the living room, toward the recliner where he usually sat when he was watching TV. She gently shoved him, urging him to sit down, and as soon as he did, she settled herself onto his lap. He folded her into his arms, the motion coming as naturally to him as breathing. She rested her head on his shoulder, and he could smell the herbal shampoo she used.

They sat in silence for a while. The only light came from the weak under-cabinet fluorescent light in the kitchen, bathing the opposite side of the room in a bluish glow.

"Are you feeling better?" Sophie finally asked him.

"I am. Thank you for everything. I'm sorry I put you though that."

She took a breath, and then sat up so she could look at his face. "You didn't 'put me through' anything, Calder. I came to look for you, and I took care of you, because I love you."

"You love me. But you took care of me because it's what you do," he said, rubbing his hand over her hip.

"Are you going to tell me what happened?"

He looked away, and she gently placed a hand on his face and turned him to look at her again. "Calder."

"I ran across a bear getting ready for winter. I think I must have been too close to its den. Anyway, it went after me, and I had to fight it off. I was afraid it would be a fight to the death for a while there, but he eventually turned tail and ran into one of those little caves not too far from the falls."

Sophie was watching him, skepticism plain on her face. "I heard you roaring," she said. "It's been a while since I heard you sounding like that."

She shifted a little, and he groaned when she brushed against him. He was already having a hard time focusing with her on his lap, nothing between him and her lush curves but the sweatshirt.

"Sorry," she murmured, looking into his eyes. He felt, more than saw, the way her body flushed. "Stop looking at me like that when I'm trying to talk to you," she said, and the touch of breathlessness in her voice was enough to nearly drive him insane.

"There's nothing to talk about. I'm fine, thanks to you. And I'll avoid any bear dens in the future. I should have been paying attention." He ran his hand over her hip, then lower, down her silky, shapely thigh. She trembled a bit against him. "I think we should go back upstairs so I can thank you properly," he said. He leaned down and kissed her neck, sucking the delicate skin just a little bit, her scent surrounding him. He could feel her heart pounding, the pulse point beneath his lips racing. He reached under the sweatshirt, trailing his fingers up her stomach before cupping one perfect, heavy breast in his hand. She let out a little moan, and he rubbed his thumb over the hard peak of her nipple. The cry of frustrated need she gave had him ready to lay her out on the living room floor and have his way with her right there.

The last time he'd done that, she'd gotten rug burns on her gorgeous ass. Can't have that, he reminded himself.

"Upstairs, before I lose my mind," he growled.

"Have I ever told you how much I love the growly voice?" she murmured as she kissed his throat.

"How about if you show me?"

She stood up and walked toward the stairs, and the devilish grin she shot him over her shoulder told him he wouldn't be getting any more sleep that night. Not that he was complaining.

He followed her, and as he ran up the stairs behind Sophie, he told himself this was why everything would be okay. Everything else could fall apart, but they kept each other sane.

It had to be enough.

CHAPTER SEVENTEEN

September 17, 1870

She was not surprised to see him walking out of the forest. Luc's appearance, as always, never failed to warm Migisi. His broad, muscled body, those icy blue eyes. Blond beard, his blond curls peeking from beneath the wide-brimmed hat he wore. His jaw was clenched, his movements stiff. As he drew near, she could see a wild look in his eyes.

A wave of guilt washed over her. He seemed to be nearly in pain.

"It's the full moon," he said in greeting, and Migisi nodded, understanding. She unconsciously put a hand on Claire, who slept, strapped snugly to Migisi's body. "One day every month, I hate you more than usual, Migisi," he continued. "And it gets worse, every. damned. month."

"I will do what I can to help," she said, meeting hie eyes. "There is no point in apologizing. I was not sorry when I did it, and apologizing now does not change a thing."

"I don't want or need your apologies," he said, a snarl in his voice. "Just keep me from hurting anyone. Keep me away from my family, so they don't have to see me like this anymore. I'll be well enough by tomorrow night. Until then, you get to witness firsthand what you did to me."

Migisi simply watched him. "I will protect them," she said. "I do not want to hurt you."

He gave s short, bitter laugh. "You can't do any worse than you've already done. It's a little late to worry about that now." He turned away from her and sat on the low stone wall she'd begun building around the garden. To her shock, the moment Claire had been born, plants had started to grow again. Not as well as they had before, but well enough to ensure that next spring, the squash and beans she planted would actually grow. Another gift from her daughter.

It was as close as she'd ever get to the Light again. She was grateful for it. Her daughter would not be a powerful witch, not the way she would be had she been born to two Light parents, or even a non-witch and the Light her father had been. But there would be enough to ensure that she would never starve, that she would be able to heal the small things, that the things she did, as long as they were good and Light-worthy, would succeed. It was a gift, and she thanked the Light daily for bestowing it on her daughter, despite the things Migisi had done. Despite what she'd become.

Migisi sat down on a log nearby. Claire was beginning to fuss, and Migisi opened the front of her dress. That was another fear she'd had, that her body would not be able to sustain her child. Thankfully, so far they had managed well enough.

She didn't know what to say to him, doubted that he actually wanted her to say anything. He wasn't there because he wanted to be, she reminded herself. No matter how much she still loved him, no matter how her heart seemed to swell at the sight of him… she knew they were long past the point where those feelings would ever be returned again. Not the way they once had been. He'd admitted that he still cared. Cared, but didn't trust. Cared, but would never, ever let himself become caught up with her again.

And she couldn't blame him. She knew it must rankle him to have to come to her for help, after she had put him in the situation in the first place.

"Tell me what I can expect," she said, her attention mostly focused on her daughter.

There were a few moments of silence. "Do you even know what you did?" he asked, disbelief in his tone.

"I was not thinking clearly. All I knew was that I wanted you to hurt as much as I did at that moment." She paused. "I was already falling into Shadow."

"I remember," he said.

"Seeing... what I saw that night, I lost all sense. It was as if Shadow flooded into me, all at once, and all I craved was vengeance. All I wanted was to make you hurt. The darkness gathered for months."

"That warlock," Luc said. "I should have killed him as soon as we realized what was going on. You should have told me about him."

"He'd already cursed you, to turn me. Curses do not die with those who cast them. Besides, he would have killed you."

"It would have been better than this," he said, and the anger and desperation in his voice was like a stab to the heart.

It had taken Migisi a while to work it out, as blind in love as she had been with Luc. The more time she'd spent with him, the more she felt herself being drawn into Shadow. And the intensity of her feelings for him just made it all the more powerful. The warlock, Marshall, he was calling himself now, had gloated after it was all said and done, once he'd realized she'd fully succumbed to Shadow. The only way she could have avoided becoming Shadow would have been to avoid Luc. In the end, he'd been cursed twice: once, by Marshall, so that the more time she spent with him, the deeper she was drawn into Shadow, and later, by herself, to punish him for the pain she'd felt. Pain caused by, what she now realized, was a scene set up by Marshall to finally push her over the edge. In all of it, Luc had been an innocent, a tool used by Marshall. And of all of them, he'd suffered the most for it.

"Tell me about it," she said, shaking off her anger, her desire to destroy the warlock who had done this to them. One day, she promised herself. "What does it do?"

She heard Luc take a breath. "I am starving, dying of thirst, unsatisfied every moment of the day. Did you purposely give me a *windigoo* curse, or was that just luck?"

"I did not intend that. I felt empty, and I wanted you to feel the same."

He snorted. "Well, you succeeded marvelously. You must be so proud."

She didn't answer. He had every right to give her barbs.

"I spend every day, every moment of my life feeling empty. No amount of food, or drink, or sex, or activity can fill the need or distract me from it. It is like a never ending irritation, like I'm about to crawl out of my skin. I can't relax. There is no rest. My wife has long tired of trying to sate my needs. My child, our one and only, is our last," he added.

Migisi did not feel the slightest sorry about that.

"So that's bad enough, and is a decent enough curse if you wanted to punish me. But in your insanity, you forgot the fact that I have another side to my being."

"Your bear," Migisi said softly. She shivered as icy fear slid down her spine.

"My bear," he repeated. "When you combine painful, unending hunger with an enormous bear, it does not end well. I try to run far enough away in the days before the full moon that I will be unlikely to bother any villages, far enough away from my family that they don't have to see what I become. But recently, it is never far enough. Last month, I spent hours roaring outside of my home. My child was terrified. My wife looks at me like the monster I am.

She had her cousin come to live with us, because she's a witch and she hopes that, if it comes to that, her cousin's magic will protect them." He paused, the angry, feral look on his face transforming him into something fearsome, something that lacked the care and warmth she knew Luc to have. "So the joke appears to be on me: I have a witch living in my house, protecting my family from the curse a witch put on me," he finished, and his voice was raised, the final words shouted into the emptiness around them.

"If she is there, then why come to me?" Migisi asked after a few tense moments of silence.

"Because I want you to experience firsthand what you did to me. And you're stronger than she is. But mostly because if anyone deserves sleepless nights over this, it's you."

He stalked away and sat on the ground against a tree at the edge of the forest, away from her. She finished feeding Claire, and held her, gently patting her back until she settled back to sleep. Migisi gently tightened the ends of the fabric that held Claire tied to her body and went inside, coming back out moments later with a blanket. She lit a fire in the small ring of stones behind her house, and kept an eye on Luc as the sun began to set. She transferred Claire from the sling she wore around her body to a cradleboard, which she wore on her back. It would keep Claire safer than having her in front of her, should Luc actually manage to strike her somehow.

As soon as day bled into night, she heard the first painful growls from the edge of the forest. Luc was already shifting. She watched it happen, man to beast. It was a process she'd always been fascinated by, because she knew that Luc enjoyed it so. This night, there was none of that joy. There was desperation on his face warring with the rage that was his curse. It had once been his joy, and she'd managed to take that from him as well.

"Don't let me hurt anyone, Migisi," he said in a strangled voice just before the shift completed.

And it began. It began with a roar that sent ice into her veins. It began with Luc, his beast, charging toward her with hatred in its eyes. Before he could reach her, she waved her hand, creating a force that knocked him back a bit and shielded both herself and Claire from his advance. He shook his head, charged again, and met the same invisible wall.

Again and again, Luc charged toward Migisi, and though she fully expected her shields to hold, she feared for Claire, sobbing quietly on the cradleboard Migisi had hastily strapped to her back. She knew she couldn't set the baby down and still be able to maintain any focus, worried as she would be that Luc would somehow harm her.

The rage, the pain, the confusion... every roar, every pained growl was filled with it, and Migisi wept even as she threw up shield after shield, keeping him away from her and her daughter. Tears flowed down Migisi's face, dripping in frozen rivulets down her neck, and still she forced him back and away from her.

After what felt like an eternity, Luc turned and charged in the opposite direction. That would take him toward the small village that had grown around the copper mines, Migisi realized. She let out a frustrated cry and formed another invisible wall, this one keeping him from continuing east as he was. He bellowed in rage.

He was getting smarter, she realized as she formed yet another invisible wall. No longer was he simply bashing the same shield over and over again. Instead, he walked a bit, tested the barrier, then walked some more. The key was staying one step ahead of him, putting up shields before he could charge further away.

Silently, she crept closer to him so she'd be able to act quickly if he gave any indication of trying to get around the shields. Claire had stopped sobbing, and Migisi hoped that she slept. She could already feel her own exhaustion, the stress of watching Luc deal with what she'd done to him. The guilt was crushing.

It was nearly impossible to breathe over the way her chest twisted at each pained sound he made. Her magic was still there, ready when she needed it, but she wondered if she would be able to keep this up all night.

"No time for doubt now," she whispered to herself, and for Claire's benefit, knowing that if she was still awake, she would be soothed by her mother's voice. She formed another shield as Luc charged again, and he hit it, hard, and fell back shaking his enormous, shaggy head.

His bear. How in the Light had she been foolish enough to do this to him and not take his bear into account? How had she been so blind, so stupid, so evil? And she knew she could easily blame it all on Shadow, that Marshall's plan to turn her, to force her to be the thing she swore she'd never be was at the root of why she'd done it. But it was a lie. All she'd felt in that moment when she'd seen Luc kissing that woman was rage. Pain. Emptiness, as if her entire world had just been taken from her. She'd wanted to hurt him.

And she had. And she swore to the Light and the Shadow and anything else that she would do everything she could to make the rest of his life as peaceful as she could. She would find a way to break the curse, she hoped. There had to be a way.

She swore she could hear something laugh on the cold wind that whipped through the woods near her home. She formed another shield, and Luc gave a desperate roar, turning and charging her again in rage.

Another shield. Another enraged roar.

It went on all night, as the full moon rose high into the clear sky, the millions of stars above making her feel insignificant as she warded Luc off over and over again. Her head ached. Her heart ached.

She began talking to Luc as he raged.

"Do you remember the day we met?" she murmured. He grunted and tried to ram through the shield she'd created around her and her daughter yet again. "Do you remember how you trailed me? How in that first moment our eyes met, it felt as if the entire world changed?"

She hated the way her voice shook, but, to her surprise, Luc stopped trying to break through to her. He stood, breathing hard, watching her with those ice blue eyes that she would remember until the day she ceased to draw breath. "Do you remember the first time we kissed? The way we never seemed to stop touching one another?" She stood, watching him. They must make quite a scene, she thought to herself, tiny woman and enormous bear, staring one another down beneath the vast, cold sky. "Light, how I loved you," she whispered, and he stared. "How I still love you, though I know we are well past the time when that matters." She kept her eyes on his, knowing that the eye contact, which had so often connected them as lovers and friends, seemed to soothe him even now, even after so much had gone wrong. "You enjoyed it when I sang to you. Remember?"

And so, she sang. She sang of the wind and the trees and the falls, of death and rebirth, of light and darkness. She sang, and she laced her words with magic, calling Shadow, forcing it to do her bidding, forcing it to do something good and decent, despite itself.

By the time she'd sung her voice hoarse, Luc had slumped to the ground, still in his bear form, breathing deeply, the occasional rumble issuing from his bulky form. Her child slept soundly on her back. Migisi gently took off the cradleboard, then picked Claire up and held her closely, needing the comfort of her daughter's sweet scent, her calm, pure sleep. She wrapped herself and Claire up in a large wool blanket, and together, they sat near the dwindling fire as she watched Luc sleep.

As dawn whispered into the world, she watched Luc's body reforming itself, shaggy fur disappearing, giving way to muscled flesh. The pain of the shift finally woke him. He stood with a pained expression, and Migisi watched him silently.

He pulled on the pants and shirt he'd shed the night before, met her eyes for the briefest of moments, and trudged away without a word.

After a moment, it felt as if he'd never really been there at all.

Luc stalked through the morning mist toward the home he'd built for his wife and child. Thoughts of Migisi, of her voice, of her eyes, threatened to invade the cold, hard shell he'd built around his heart.

Of course. Of course, of everything he'd tried, she would be the one able to soothe him. Of course. He shook his head in anger. The damnable woman had probably planned it that way, that when he needed help most, she would be the only one who could save him.

Even as he thought it, he knew better. He believed her when she'd said that she didn't know what she'd done, that she hadn't meant for it to go so far. He believed her, but it hardly mattered.

He walked up to the clapboard house he'd built for his family. The boards, from trees he'd felled and sawn with his own hands, were beginning to gray, ever so slightly, after a handful of years exposed to the elements. Smoke wafted from the stone chimney, which meant that someone was up. He could guess who. Certainly not his wife, who would spend every moment of her day sleeping if she was able, an escape from the life she'd never envisioned.

He could hardly blame her. If he could sleep his way through it all, he would as well.

No, it would be her cousin. Another witch, which immediately made him dislike her, whether it was deserved or not. She lived there to protect his wife and child from him.

He hated her for that as well.

She ran his home and family because, as more time went on, he was less and less able to do so. She sold potions, spells, palm readings to bring in the cash to support her cousin and her child, money that Luc was less and less able to earn, thanks to the curse.

He hated her for that, too. And he knew he was wrong. He knew he should be grateful.

He paused near the rough-hewn gate that led up the front walk to their home, and the object of his irritation stepped onto the slanted front porch. Thick red hair haloed her face and covered her back and shoulders like a shawl. She met his gaze briefly, then quickly looked away.

"So your witch kept you from killing anyone, eh? Unless you managed to kill her as is her due," she said, more of a question than a statement, her eyebrow arched as she waited for his answer. She was quiet in general, and didn't speak much, but when she did, it was with such outright authority, such confidence that he wondered how it was that she and his wife could have been raised in the same family.

She watched him for a moment. "Ah. So she lives yet."

He gave a brief nod.

"It was peaceful here without you last night, though I would rather you trust me than run off to her."

Her cheeks reddened with the words, and she looked away again. She was alway on edge with him, angry and frazzled. He knew she despised him for what he put her cousin through. He imagined that she hated him for causing her life to be disrupted as well, as she came to care for the family he could not.

"She should be forced to clean up her own messes," Luc said. "And she managed, and I am glad you were all saved from another bout of my insanity."

"I would love to destroy her. It would take so little effort," she said, her voice a feral snarl. "Maybe it would break the curse."

"We both know better than that," he said, crossing his arms. He caught sight of his wife, her pale face peeking out of the upstairs window at him before she quickly pulled the curtain back as if hiding from him. His cousin-in-law caught the movement as well. "She fears me," Luc said to her.

"She is hurt. It is one thing to know there was someone before her. It is something else entirely to know that you run to her when you need help." She was flushed again, and Luc wondered at her volatile moods. "It would be better, maybe, if you'd just stay gone. It's only going to get harder on… on her," she finished.

"I will have to eventually," he conceded. "I will not put them in undue danger."

She nodded. "Be sure that you do." She kept her eyes trained to a spot somewhere over his shoulder, as if she was unable to look directly at him. "I will take care of my cousin."

"I know you will," he said with a sigh, tamping down his anger, his frustration that he would not be capable of doing even that much. "Thank you, Esme."

She gave a brief, haughty nod, and turned and walked back into the house, closing the door firmly behind her.

CHAPTER EIGHTEEN

Sophie pushed her cleaning cart down the carpeted hallway and used her key to unlock the next room on her floor. She picked up the travel mug of tea she kept on her cart, taking a quick gulp. She grimaced; it had cooled. Lukewarm tea was a sad, disappointing thing. She chided herself for not drinking it sooner. She definitely needed the caffeine.

The elevator dinged, and Sophie glanced that way. Her boss, Sherry, stepped out, looked in one direction down the hallway, then the other. She spotted Sophie, and walked in her direction. Sophie watched with some amusement as Sherry walked toward her. Sherry, in her early sixties, reminded Sophie of a bird with her quick movements and large eyes. The tiny woman practically swam in the large sweaters she often wore, and her white hair was piled high on top of her head.

"Hey, Sherry," Sophie said. "I'm just about done here, and then I can help with the linens if you need me to." The smile on her face froze as she noticed that Sherry wasn't smiling back. Her boss's gaze was down, as if she was inspecting Sophie's cart. "What's wrong?"

Sherry sighed, then finally looked up at Sophie. "I'm going to have to let you go, Sophie," she said.

Sophie closed her eyes, then looked at her boss again, sure she'd heard her wrong.

"It's just not working. You're freaking everyone out. When it was just us, it was fine, but we're hearing more complaints, and this morning, one of the guests came to me, concerned that there was something wrong with you."

Sophie stared at her. "What in the world are you talking about? I've been up here cleaning for the last hour and a half."

"You started this floor three hours ago."

"No—" Sophie stopped and pulled her phone out of her back pocket. It was well after lunch time, and she'd started cleaning the second floor just after she'd come in at nine. She glanced at her tepid cup of tea, then looked back up at her boss in confusion.

"Don't you know what you've been doing? It's been happening for a few weeks now," Sherry said softly, concern on her face.

"I don't understand."

"You wander, Sophie. Sometimes down into the lobby, sometimes outside and onto the trails. You get this strange, blank expression on your face, and you don't hear or see anybody."

Sophie shook her head, as if doing so would make the words untrue. "That's not possible. I'd remember."

"Isn't it happening at home?"

"No. Calder would have said something if it was. I mean, I know I'm a little scatter-brained lately, but I think you're blowing this out of proportion."

"Sweetie, if it was just us, I'd let it go. Right? We've worked together for a long time now, and your work is as good as it always was. But I've gotten comments from guests, and one of them apparently emailed the big boss, and he wants you gone, at least until you get some help. This morning's episode was just the final straw. I'm sorry."

Sophie's pulse thundered her ears. Everything seemed to be in slow motion, as if she was having a nightmare. She forced herself to nod, then handed her master key to Sherry. She unclipped the employee ID from her shirt and woodenly handed that over as well.

"I am sorry. Really, you shouldn't even be driving if you're having these fits, sweetie. It could be so much worse."

Sophie nodded and turned toward the elevator. She grabbed her purse from the employee locker room, then made her way to her car in a fog. Once inside, she locked her doors and sat in the driver's seat, frozen by exhaustion and fear and anger and the never-ending hunger that haunted her every waking hour.

She hadn't known. She thought back to the past week or two. She knew she'd lost track of time a few times, but she figured it was because she was fighting the curse so hard or lost in daydreams of Calder. She'd glance at her phone, and it would be a half hour or so later than she'd expected, and she'd work faster to catch up. She didn't recall ever being out in the woods unless it was on one of her breaks, and she remembered those times because she worked with her paltry Shadow magic when she went out there.

She'd remember, she told herself. Sherry had to be mistaken.

But in her heart, she knew Sherry wasn't. The woman was sharp, organized, and seemed to know everything that happened at the resort, down to which guests were celebrating a birthday or anniversary.

She sat, hands gripping the steering wheel. If she hadn't been so freaked out about what Sherry had told her, she might have panicked over the fact that she was now officially unemployed with no soap business to back her up. She knew she could depend on Calder. But she didn't want to.

"I'll figure something out," she murmured to herself, shaking her head a little to clear it. The first step would be trying to get a handle on the blackouts. She guessed that was related to the curse. She'd have to ask Calder. She knew he said he'd had times like that.

She wrinkled her brow as she turned the key in the ignition. He would have told her, right? If she was wandering away or blanking out when they were together, he would have told her.

She put the car in "drive" and maneuvered though the parking lot, around the front of the resort, and made her way toward the highway. She tried to enjoy the view of the lake peeking through the bare trees, but it didn't bring her the peace or joy it usually did.

If she was losing entire chunks of time, not only did it mean the curse was getting worse than she realized, but it also meant that she was much more vulnerable to Marshall and his crap than she thought she was. What if he'd already made her do things?

No, she'd know, she told herself, abandoning the thought even as she had it. Marshall was Marshall. He'd be sure to gloat about it if he had her doing his bidding. It was what he'd been working toward, for some convoluted reason, since she was a teenager. His admission about her ancestor, Micaela, and the love he'd had for her made her uneasy. First of all, the idea that Marshall could truly love anyone was laughable. But that, plus the way he'd gone on and on about how she looked like Micaela, the way he'd looked at her the last time he'd forced her to come to him... that look had been there for years. Possessiveness. Terrifying focus. And if it was just her, she'd deal with it. She had been for most of her life. She worried more about Calder and what Marshall might try to do to him if he got tired of waiting for Sophie to be Micaela part two. Because she wasn't going to become that, and she knew from experience that Marshall didn't let anyone or anything stand in his way for long. So far, she'd been the only one in his life to continually thwart him, though those around her had suffered for it.

She was so lost in thought that she barely saw the deer bound out onto the highway in front of her. She had a split second to slam on the brakes, even as her heart sank. She knew it wouldn't be enough. Her car hit the deer with a stomach-turning crunch, a screech of her brakes, and the thick, acrid smell of her airbags inflating. The airbag punched into her, jolting her back into her seat. Her windshield shattered, and her car careened to a shaky halt. Sophie gripped the steering wheel tightly, even after the car stopped moving, trying to catch her breath.

She opened her car door with some trepidation. The deer hadn't gotten up, which meant she'd seriously hurt it. She walked around the side of the car, and the deer lay there, its side bloody, legs helplessly thrashing as it tried, and failed, to stand. In the few moments she stood there, its movements slowed, as if it had worn itself out. Its eyes rolled, whites showing in its pain and fear.

"I'm sorry," Sophie whispered, hating herself again not only for what she'd done, but for what she'd become. She remembered the day she'd healed a doe, just a few months ago. She remembered Light flowing through her, the deer bounding off as if nothing had ever happened.

And now she was this... thing. Useless to help, too wrapped up in the insanity of her curse to freaking watch the road ahead of her. She knew deer-related accidents were common; it didn't make her feel any better. She let out a frustrated, angry shriek that she knew very well sounded insane, but there was no one there to hear her.

She went back to her car and tried to back it away from the deer, for no other reason than the fact that it was the only thing she could do. Her car refused to move, and she lay her head back against her head rest, gritting her teeth against the frustration and anger inside her.

She pulled her phone out and hit Calder's number as she got out of the car again. She'd need a ride home, and honestly, not leaving the house for a very long time sounded pretty good just then. The phone rang for a long time, and then she got kicked to voicemail. She listened to Calder's warm, deep voice telling her to leave a message, and she did. She went back to the front of the car. The deer still lay there, looking around helplessly.

She dialed Calder again. No answer. She was just considering calling Layla or Cara when a big silver truck pulled up alongside her.

"Hey. You okay?" She glanced in the window to see Jack, the alpha of the local shifter pack, looking at her with concern.

She nodded, unable to say anything, because she knew if she talked, she'd start crying like an idiot and she didn't know Jack well enough to feel okay about crying in front of him. He pulled over onto the side of the road, then she heard his door slam as he got out of his truck.

"Sophie, are you hurt?"

She shook her head. "I'm fine," she managed. "He's not, unfortunately," she said, ashamed again at the pain she'd caused the animal. She glanced up to see Jack studying her closely. She'd seen him around town, and the times she'd visited the bar he owned on the outskirts of town. He was what she would have expected of an alpha wolf: tall, muscular, gruff. Dark, wavy hair, dark stubble across his chin and jaw. He had the tawny eyes of a wolf, a cross between brown and gold. He was loud and rough, usually. Not exactly who she would have picked to find her stranded on the side of the road.

"I can end his suffering," he said quietly, and she nodded. She turned away, looking toward the rear of her car. She heard the unmistakeable sounds of him shifting, then a wet sound she'd rather not have heard. A few minutes later, she heard Jack on his phone.

"Marcie? Yeah, it's Jack. I have a fresh deer out here on the one-forty-four if your brothers want to come get it. It's a big one," he added, and Sophie stayed looking down the highway. She tried Calder again. No answer, which was only stressing her out more. The first thing she thought of was that Marshall had done something. Her hands shook, and her stomach twisted.

She heard footsteps crunching on the gravel and broken glass on the road's shoulder behind her, and Jack came around so he could look at her.

"Okay. That's taken care of. If it makes it any better, that deer will feed a family who sorely needs it this winter."

"That does make it a bit better. Thanks," she added, and Jack nodded.

"Is Calder on his way? Or Layla?"

"Calder's not picking up. I was just about to call Layla, but I figured I'd give him a chance."

"I'm heading that way. I can drop you off at your place." He glanced at her car. "And I can give my cousin a call about towing this. You gonna have Calder look at it?"

She nodded. "You don't have to do all that," she said.

He waved it off. "It's nothing. Come on. Let's get out of here."

Sophie reached into her car and took the keys from the ignition and grabbed her bag from the passenger seat.

"Thanks again," she said. Jack nodded and led her toward his truck. She tried not to look at the deer as she walked past. Jack opened the passenger side door for her, and Sophie climbed in, thanking him again. As he was walking around the front of the truck, another pickup truck pulled up, and a young man got out. He and Jack spoke for a few moments, then Jack helped him load the deer into the back of the truck.

Within moments, the other truck was driving away and Jack opened the driver's side door and climbed in. He started the engine and pulled onto the highway, driving toward her house.

It was then that Sophie remembered that Bryce had told her the reason Calder had fought Jack a couple of weeks back was because Jack had said something lewd about her. She blushed a little, then looked out the window.

"You don't have to be afraid of me," he said.

"I'm not."

Of course, it was her luck that the curse didn't care that he was apparently an asshole. She heard him scenting the air.

"That has nothing to do with you," she said sharply.

"Okay," he said, and the innocence in his voice made her look at him. "Look, I guess you heard what I said that night with Calder."

She didn't answer, but crossed her arms over her chest.

"I was trying to rile him up. The boy came into my place itching for a fight, so I gave him one. Not that I don't find you pretty. You ever get tired of Calder, you know where I am," he said with a roguish wink. Sophie rolled her eyes.

"So you were being a humanitarian by making lewd comments about his girlfriend?" she asked, happy to focus her ire on Jack for a while.

"I didn't say I was a *good* humanitarian," he said, and, despite her discomfort, she had to laugh.

Jack rolled his window down all the way. "Damn, do I wish that had something to do with me, though," he said, the low growl in his voice only adding to the stupid need roaring through Sophie. She hated shifters, and the way they could smell everything from fear to arousal. She rolled her window down, too.

"You can drop me off here. It's not far," Sophie said.

"Then we can drive it even faster. Calder would tear my guts out if he heard I left you on the side of the road."

She didn't answer, looking out the window instead. She tried Calder's number again, and when she got voicemail, she told him that she was on her way home, and Jack was dropping her off.

"His battery probably died or something," Jack said, as if seeming to sense that she needed some kind of reassurance.

"Maybe. He's usually really good about that kind of thing," she said, looking at her phone, as if looking hard enough at his name could make him call her back. Her hands were shaking.

Jack cleared his throat. "Calder's a good guy. Uh. I knew his dad, too."

"Oh? Did you know him well?"

Jack glanced over at her. "I knew him well enough to know what happened to him at the end. I knew him well enough to have him confide in me that his son would go down the same way."

Sophie shook her head. "He won't."

"So you know," Jack said.

Sophie took a breath. "I know. And I also know that it's not going to happen. Not to Calder, and not to Jon."

"Why?"

She didn't answer.

"Well, whatever you think you know, know that old man Turcotte confided in me about the fact that he nearly killed his wife and that's why she left. Be careful, Sophie."

She snorted. "You'll forgive me if this doesn't seem a little self-serving on your part."

"Darlin', I have my pick of women. That's the benefit of being an alpha. I don't need to connive and scheme to get one, and as happy as I'd be to be the one you run to, I hope it never comes to that. He loves you."

"I know he does. And I love him. And he's not going to end up like his father."

They drove in silence for a while, and Sophie was relieved to see the enormous white pines that lined her driveway.

"Just promise you'll ask if you ever need help. No strings attached, I promise," Jack said, and Sophie nodded. As they got near Calder's house, she glanced at the driveway. He was there, sanding the rusted side of the Barracuda in a methodical, focused way that reminded her of the way he so often looked when he worked, as if he was a million miles away.

Calder glanced up at the sound of tires crunching on gravel to see a silver F-250 pulling up in Sophie's driveway. He stood up, grimacing a little at the stiffness in his shoulders and back. He'd lost track of how much time he'd spent sanding down the Barracuda. He pulled the respirator off of his face and watched as Jack got out of the truck and quickly went to the other side, where Sophie was already climbing out of the truck. Jack took her elbow to help her down, even though she clearly didn't need it.

Jealousy slithered though Calder. Anger. His first instinct seeing Jack touch what was his was to rip the alpha's throat out. His second instinct was confusion. Why was she with him? Where was her car?

If she needed a ride, why hadn't she called him?

He watched as Sophie and Jack exchanged a few words. Jack gave him a small wave, then climbed into his truck and took off down the road. Calder watched Sophie. The fact that he could smell her adrenaline and need even from across the road definitely didn't help his mood.

She started walking across the road, and, just like every time he looked at Sophie, he was mesmerized by the way her long, thick cascade of curls flowed over her shoulders, the soft curve of her hips and the way they moved when she walked.

She came to him, and without a word, threw her arms around him and held him tightly.

He hated himself, but the first thing he did was smell her. If he smelled Jack on her skin, he'd kill him.

"Calm down," she murmured against him. "He just gave me a ride home."

"Where's your car?" he asked, wrapping his arms around her.

"I ran into a deer on the way home. It's at the side of the road. Jake's having his cousin tow it to you, but it might be a lost cause."

He pulled back a little so he could look at her, inspecting her face for any signs of injury. "Are you okay, kitten?"

"I'm fine. The deer's not, though."

"I'll take that, any day. Why didn't you call me?"

"I did. I called like five times and it went to voicemail."

Calder furrowed his brow and dug into his jeans pocket with one hand while still holding her in his other arm. The fact that she could have been hurt only made him feel more on edge. His phone showed two messages and five missed calls, all from Sophie's number.

"I had it on me the whole time," he said, looking at the phone.

"Maybe you had the ringer off? I sometimes turn mine off by mistake," she said, and he pulled her closer to him again.

"I'm sorry, honey," he said.

"Nothing to be sorry about," she said, resting her head against his shoulder. Then she sighed. "I got fired today."

"What?"

She nodded, still resting against him, and he led her to the front porch. He settled onto the porch swing and held her on his lap. "What happened?" he asked, trying to ignore the desire that shot through him when she shifted a little on his lap. The desire to obliterate any scent of Jack from her body still lingered, despite the fact that he knew she was telling the truth. It was stupid, and he hated himself for it. He trusted Sophie, but he didn't trust the curse, and he sure the hell didn't trust Jack.

"Sherry said I keep wandering off and it's freaking everyone out. The big boss heard about it and demanded she let me go," she said softly, and Calder winced.

Damn it.

She sat up so she could look at his face. "Have I been doing that around you, Calder? Blacking out? Wandering off?"

He didn't answer immediately, and he saw the moment she realized the truth.

"Damn it, Calder! How long has it been going on?"

"A couple of weeks. Mostly at night," he said quietly, meeting her eyes.

She got up and stalked away. Then she turned back to him. "And you didn't tell me... *why*, exactly?"

Internally, he was warring with himself over being worried that his woman was pissed at him and the curse was being more of a problem, or admiring how gorgeous she was when she was pissed.

"Calder Turcotte," she said sharply. "Stop looking at me like that and goddamn answer me. Why didn't you tell me?"

"I hoped it was only happening at night. You don't wander off when you're awake with me."

"We're usually doing something else when I'm awake with you," she muttered, crossing her arms over her chest, and he bit back a groan at the way her breasts flowed up over her arms when she did that. He shook his head a little.

"I really did think it was only happening during sleep. I would have said something if I thought otherwise."

"You should have told me it was happening," she said, glaring at him.

"I didn't want you to have one more thing to worry about. It was happening at night, and I'd go and get you and bring you back. It wasn't a big deal."

"But it was, Calder. We both know that's not normal. Damn it," she muttered. She pushed her hair back from her face and started pacing.

"Do you need to run?"

"Don't change the subject. I don't need you to protect me, Calder," she said, meeting this eyes again. "I'm not helpless, and I have every damn right to know what's happening, especially when I'm the one it's happening to. How am I supposed to fight it if I don't even know it 's happening?"

"You can't fight a blackout, kitten."

"The hell I can't. If I know it's coming, I can try to head it off. I can make sure I secure myself...I can't believe you didn't tell me," she said, and the way her voice shook had his stomach turning. She was more pissed than he'd ever seen her, and he knew that beneath that, she was scared. They both knew what the blackouts meant: the curse was getting worse. He hadn't wanted to admit it to himself. That had been part of it, of course. If he didn't say it out loud, then it wasn't true.

"You're right. I'm sorry, Sophie. I should have said something."

"Stop trying to protect me," she said.

"I'll never stop doing that," he said. "But I won't keep shit from you anymore. Okay?"

She sighed, and shook her head. "What was I doing when you found me?"

He wanted to go to her. He wanted to hold her, pick her up, take her to bed and make her forget everything but the two of them. And he could, too. He knew how well he could distract her by now. He pushed the thought away.

"Usually, you were just kind of standing there. Always in the woods behind your house. Just stood there with this blank look on your face. You didn't recognize me when I came for you."

"I wasn't doing anything? Just standing there?"

He nodded. "Apparently you'd get up and walk out there. But it seems like you usually let your goats out, too."

"What?" she asked, wrinkling her nose in a way he still found ridiculously cute. Just as cute as when they'd been kids.

"Yeah. Every time I found you, your three weirdo goats were there, standing with you."

She scrunched up her face even more. "So you'd have to bring me back home and a then go track down the goats, too? I'm surprised you didn't just leave their creepy asses out there."

"I would have. They followed us back and jumped into their pen every time."

Sophie shook her head again, a lost, confused look on her face that he wanted to kiss away. He was about to suggest letting him take her mind off of things for a while when a tow truck pulled up in his driveway.

"Can you take a look at it for me? I think it's ruined now, though," Sophie asked.

"I will."

"I need to go feed the goats," she said, and then she was crossing the street. He knew that tone, too. It was her "I want to be alone right now and if you don't give me a few minutes here I'm going to lose my mind" voice. So he went to the tow truck instead, kicking himself the entire way for keeping her blackouts from her.

One look at the car told him she was probably right. It wouldn't be worth it to fix it. After signing for it and trying to pay Jack's cousin, Ryan, who refused payment on Jack's orders, he popped the hood and looked at the engine. If there was a way to salvage it, he would. He knew Sophie had a bit of a sentimental attachment to the little Chevy. It wasn't a great car, but it had apparently gotten her back to Copper Falls.

For the first time, he wondered if that had really been such a good thing, as far as she was concerned.

CHAPTER NINETEEN

Sophie rounded the back corner of her house and went to the small barn where she kept the goat's feed. She carried a bucket of it to their pen, let herself in, and dumped it into the hopper. All three of them stood there, watching her, their square-pupiled goat eyes following her every move. She leaned down to turn on the tap to give them fresh water, and was nearly knocked flat when something butted her thigh. She turned to see Merlin standing there.

"Creepy goats," she muttered. She finished filling the water, then scratched Merlin behind his ear. "So, what? I have guard goats?" she asked Merlin as she scratched him. She patted his neck one more time, then let herself out of their pen. "You three are like big ugly dogs," she said, and Merlin bleated at her irritably. She let out a small laugh. "Stupid goats. Just because I open your gate when I'm zoned out doesn't mean I actually expect you to come with me," she said. She knew she was rambling, talking nonsense to creatures who couldn't answer her. Somehow, though, it made everything feel a little less terrifying.

She rested her arms on the top of the fence and watched as they began eating. The goats stood, munching hay, occasionally head butting one another if one of the others happened to get in the way. Normal, ordinary, stupid goats, she thought to herself, laughing at the way Calder's words had had her wondering about the bad-natured animals she shared her land with. They still, even after being in the pen together for several days, seemed to stand in silent conversation with one another. She glanced toward the woods, at the sun beginning to set behind the pines. She could finally feel herself starting to relax a bit after the crazy day she'd had, when all three goats gave angry, deafening bleats. She jumped, and looked in the direction they faced, their necks stretched, eyes rolling in what looked to her like rage.

Marshall strode out of the woods.

Sophie started drawing her meager amount of Shadow magic to her. Not that she actually expected much, but she knew from experience that she could throw him back with her power if she needed to. She'd done it once before, and honestly with the mood she was in, she almost hoped he'd give her a reason to try it again.

"It's time to earn the gift I gave you, little girl," Marshall said in his smooth voice, and the gleam in his nearly-black eyes made her stomach twist. "Come to me. Now."

She felt his power rolling over her, enticing her, pulling her.

"You've been resisting, Sophie. I've called you twice in the past few days. You don't want to anger me by ignoring my summons," he said, and she felt more of his power roaring over her. "Now come to me."

She stood, letting his power wash over her, even as she held her own power at the ready.

She heard him growl. "If I have to come over there and get you, you're going to regret it. Kitten," he added snidely. "Your little boyfriend is busy with your car. Anyone who can spend that much time staring at metal has some kind of mental deficiency," he said, and she felt his power increase.

It pulled. It slithered, and enticed, frightening yet seductive, and part of her wanted to follow it. Part of her, the part he owned, wanted to give into its dark promises, that all she had to do was come to him, do his bidding, and all of her pain would end. He never said those things with words, but now, his power spoke, and it said one thing: he wanted her to be his creature completely. And he'd expected it to be easy once he'd turned her to Shadow.

"This isn't working out quite the way you expected, huh?" Sophie asked quietly. She didn't understand it, but she would sure the heck take it. He couldn't make her do what he wanted. He'd managed once, and he'd failed since. Her heart leapt at the thought.

He snarled and charged toward her. She threw her arms up, hoping it would work the way it had before.

Marshall flew threw the air, back toward the woods, where he landed on his back. He was up an instant later, hand raised. There was no finesse now. As his hands tightened at his sides, she felt the first signs of pain, as if she was being pummeled by large, invisible fists. She cried out through the pain, threw her hands up and tossed him back one more time.

The pummeling stopped, but he was up again as if nothing had happened, and she readied another shield, even though she knew she was reaching the limit of how much she could actually do. This time, he waved his hand, and she went flying back, hard, as if she'd been slapped. Her face ached, and bright light exploded behind her eyes with the pain. She forced herself to get up, and when she could see straight again, she saw the goats leaping high over the fence and charging the warlock.

They ran at him, and though his hands worked as if he was doing spells, nothing seemed to phase the goats. First Merlin charged him, knocking him back. He got up and tried to throw a spell at them. She could feel his magic filling the air, but it had no effect on the three goats. Gandalf butted him, hard, knocking him into the trunk of an oak, and then Dumbledore did it, slamming his dark, curled horns directly into Marshall's face.

Even from where she stood, Sophie could hear Marshall's nose break. She stood at the ready. Marshall stood up slowly.

"How did you get familiars, bitch?" he asked. His voice was thick, gurgling, and blood from his broken nose ran down his face.

She didn't answer, mostly because she didn't know how. She stood at the ready instead as the goats advanced on Marshall.

He straightened, wiped the blood pouring from his nose, then smirked at her, gave her a sarcastic salute, and disappeared.

The malice in his eyes told her one thing: she'd hear from him again, and next time, he wouldn't be caught unaware.

Sophie watch listlessly as the goats leapt back into the pen as if nothing had happened. She watched them for a few long while, confusion warring with hope.

He'd called them familiars. She'd read about familiars often, wishing for one, begging the Light to send one her way for most of her teenage years. Mostly because she wanted a companion so she wouldn't feel so alone. She'd gone through her "can I please have a familiar" phase before Marshall had come into her life.

Familiars were rare things. Animals, usually goats, cats, or owls, who served witches, who protected them and their home from harm. A very rare gift, indeed.

And one only ever bestowed upon those of the Light.

She stared at them in disbelief for a while longer, then closed her eyes and sent a silent thanks to the Light. She was on the verge of weeping with gratitude. The fact that they were there was so much more than protection from Marshall. They were a sign.

If they were there, then she was not a lost cause.

Sophie opened her eyes again, smiled at her three weird, wonderful, magical, bad-natured goats, and walked away. She felt like she could fly.

She walked around her house and across the road, to where Calder was bent over her car.

"I think it's a goner, kitten," he said apologetically as he stood up.

She didn't say anything, just went to him and pulled his head down to her, kissed him relentlessly, hungrily, as if kissing Calder, as if being in his arms, was the only thing in the world that mattered. Because right at that moment, it was.

"I need you," she murmured against him, and that seemed to be all he needed, too.

Later, as she lay in his arms, she reflected on the fact that what they had was actual magic, because against all odds, everything else fell away when they were together.

"Sophie," he said sleepily.

"Hm?"

"I messed up. I'm sorry for not telling you about the blackouts."

She held him tighter. "It's okay. I get why you didn't. But don't do it again."

He smiled in that lazy way she loved when he was halfway between sleep and wakefulness. She saw everything in it: the boy she'd sworn she'd love forever, and the man who had made it impossible not to. "Yes, ma'am." He opened his eyes again. "I want to spend the rest of my life with you," he said.

She was warmed again by the tone in his voice, that certain, straightforward way he had of telling her he loved her. "I want that, too."

"Seeing Bryce… it's like he's fully alive now that he has Layla, you know?"

Sophie nodded.

"And I know I'm the same way since you came into my life again. I want to wake up with you every morning, and fall asleep like this every night. I want to spend every possible moment loving you, and it still won't be enough," he said. "Marry me?"

Tears flooded her eyes, and she took a breath. "There are things we need to take care of first," she said. "I want our happily ever after to actually be happy. I don't want this curse hanging over us. I don't want Marshall stalking us."

"We can deal with that stuff together."

"And we are," Sophie said, running her hand over his muscular arm. "I love you so much. I want to enjoy planning our wedding. I want to know that if we decide to start a family someday, it'll be safe from all of the crap Marshall and Migisi caused. Don't you?"

"Of course. Yes—"

"I want to remember planning our wedding," she said quietly, needing him to understand. His face softened. "I'm watching Layla plan her and Bryce's wedding, and she's… she glows," she said with a smile. "The way I am now, I'd forget that feeling. I don't want to."

He lead toward her and kissed her gently, then lay, his forehead against hers. "I'll wait as long as you need me to," Calder promised. "I'll wait."

Sophie kissed him again, and they loved each other until they fell asleep, limbs tangled, breath mingling, bodies pressed tightly to one another, as if there was no way to get close enough.

And there wasn't.

CHAPTER TWENTY

November 17, 1870

Migisi watched as Luc pulled his wool sweater back on, covering an expanse of muscled flesh, that line of golden hair that led from his navel down into the waist of his pants. She suppressed a sigh and looked away.

Claire was snuggled close to her body, the two of them wrapped in a heavy fur Migisi had carried outside with them as they sat through another full moon with Luc. The singing had worked every month since they'd began, and though Migisi's voice was hoarse and her throat burned, she was grateful that, in this one small way, she could be a comfort to him.

How she would love to comfort him another way, she thought as she looked at him again. She knew he wanted her as much as she wanted him. The way he looked at her brooked no doubt about his desire for her. But she also knew that he would be faithful to his wife, and she was torn between admiration and frustration over his loyalty.

"We both know you should just live here with me," she said. "It is what we both want, and I can watch you. The full moon is not the only time you need my supervision." It was true. In the past several weeks, he had come to her often, usually when the curse was wearing too heavily on him, when he felt as if his control was at the breaking point. Luc had gotten quite adept at reading his moods and the curse's effect on them. When he'd been sure his control would snap, it usually did. And, thankfully, she was there to shield and protect the world from Luc.

"We're not discussing this now," he said, turning away from her as he buttoned his coat.

"Your wife doesn't want you. You said so yourself," she said.

"And I was wrong to speak of my wife to you. It is none of your business."

"I want you," Migisi said softly, so softly that anyone who was not a shifter, with a shifter's preternatural senses, would not have heard her. "I always have."

"You are a worthless whore," an enraged voice said. Migisi and Luc both looked toward the house. Migisi groaned in disgust.

Esme.

How she despised the woman. If it were not for Luc telling her to leave Esme alone for his wife's sake, she would have destroyed her already. Always coming to check on Luc when he was with her, always reminding her of everything she'd done wrong. Shadow upon Shadow, Migisi thought when she looked at Esme. The Shadow witch's soul was even darker than her own. Though they did have at least a few things in common.

"Shouldn't you be running your cousin's household right now?" Migisi said, and Luc spoke to her sharply in French, telling her to be quiet. "Let me guess, she's in bed. Asleep. Too much of a wastrel to bother raising her child and caring for her home."

"You are vile," Esme spat, and she raised her hands.

"Esme, stop. She holds a baby," Luc said loudly.

"What do you care?" Esme cried, glaring at Luc. "You should want to take every bit of happiness she has. It's what she deserves!"

"But the baby is innocent. And whether you like it or not, Migisi is the only way I'm able to support my wife." Since their arrangement had begun, Luc had managed to go back to trapping more regularly. Migisi knew it helped, that he felt some pride again. It had worn on him even more that he had to count on Esme for financial help in addition to the running of his household and the fact that she protected his wife and child from him when the curse was at its worst. Between Migisi and Esme, Luc's family had not suffered seeing him in the throes of the curse in months, and Migisi was even less fond of Esme for it. She could care for Luc on her own.

"She is the entire reason you are this thing," Esme said, and Migisi watched placidly, observing the fire in the other woman's eyes, the desperation in her voice. Her lip curled in anger.

"Esme, go home," Luc said tiredly. "I know what you're doing."

"What?" the redheaded witch demanded. Migisi watched her closely.

"You're trying to make sure I don't bed Migisi. You want to make sure I stay faithful to your cousin. I can promise you, without a single doubt in my mind, that I would never allow myself to fall in with Migisi again."

"Your curse may say otherwise," Esme said. A look passed between Esme and Luc, one that made Migisi want to end the infuriating woman on the spot.

"My curse is the never-ending reminder of what she did to me. Trust me, I'd rather die than touch her again."

The words were a blade to her heart, and Esme's smug look was like a twist of the knife.

"Go home," Luc repeated.

"You will return soon?" Esme asked, and Migisi hid a roll of her eyes.

"I want to check my traps, and then I will be home."

"Michael will be so happy to see you. He has been asking after Papa," Esme said, and the gentle smile on Luc's face was enough to make Migisi want to claw his eyes out.

"Tell him I will be home soon. Go now, it is cold out."

Esme nodded, cheeks flushed with something other than the frigid air. She didn't spare a glance for Migisi, but turned and headed back through the woods in the direction of the land Luc had claimed as his own.

Luc pulled his gloves on, which meant he would be leaving any moment now. Migisi had to do everything she could to keep from begging him to stay. Especially after what he had just said, she knew her pleas would be met with derision.

"You know that her interest in what happens here has nothing to do with your wife, do you not?" she asked instead.

"She doesn't trust you," Luc said. "Can you blame her?"

"It has nothing to do with that, either," Migisi said.

Luc heaved a deep, weary sigh. "I'm tired, Migisi. If you have some nonsense to spew, then go ahead and say it. I have work to do, and then I want to see my son."

His son. Resentment burned within her. "She wants you for herself. Obviously," Migisi said.

Luc shook his head. "I forget sometimes that you are insane. And then you say something like that to remind me."

"She does. She wants you to bed her. She has no interest in making sure you're faithful to your wife. She just doesn't want you with me. She'd welcome you to her bed in a minute."

"You are a fool, and you're just as vile as she says you are." Luc said, anger evident in his voice.

"Would she walk miles through the woods, truly, to ensure you remain loyal to a woman who doesn't want you?

No, Luc. That obsessive need to know what you do with me is the act of someone who covets you for herself."

He didn't answer, but stormed off into the woods, and Migisi looked after him, hating the way she felt when she watched him walk away, as if her entire reason for being was leaving. A few moments later, she turned, and started in surprise. Esme was standing behind her, red hair like flames against the snowy backdrop around them.

"Ah. Is this the part where we fight, Esme? Because that will not go well for you," Migisi said, adjusting Claire slightly.

"I hate you. You sicken me, you worthless, sickening piece of trash," Esme seethed.

Migisi laughed. "Oh. You heard what I told him, hm?"

"I will make you pay for what you've done to him, Migisi," Esme said, as if she had not even heard Migisi's taunt. "Whether it's you, your daughter, or someone else, your family will pay for what you've done to his. I swear it on Shadow and everything I am."

Migisi affected a bored look, though the vehemence in Esme's words unsettled her a bit. Esme was not as powerful as Migisi, but she was no weakling, either. She could actually do things, if she meant what she said. "Go, run back home to greet Luc. He will show just as little interest in you as he always has."

Esme watched Migisi wordlessly for a moment, then a slow smile spread over her shapely lips. "Yours will pay for what you've done to mine, Migisi. I will not rest until your family suffers for your actions the way mine has. The way he has." And in the next instant, she was gone.

CHAPTER TWENTY-ONE

"This is the ugliest dress I've ever worn. If you even think of making us wear these, so help me I will hurt you," Cara said. Sophie hid a smile and nodded as she stood beside Cara. They studied their reflections in the large floor-to-ceiling mirrors in the dressing room of the bridal shop. They'd started the day early, driving an hour and a half to get to the boutique, and they'd been trying on dresses for nearly an hour.

The latest abomination, a coral number with enough ruffles to make Sophie think she looked like a badly-decorated cupcake, was just the latest in a long list of bridesmaid dress failures.

Layla sat in one of the chairs, hiding what Sophie knew would be a laugh behind her hand. "I love them," she said, and Cara threw her twin a disgusted look.

"The blue ones were better than these," Sophie said, and after a moment of hesitation, Cara nodded.

"That's not saying much, though," Cara said, and Sophie laughed.

Sophie knew they were getting on the nerves of the poor attendant who'd been helping them. The woman stood with her arms crossed, watching the shenanigans with a stony expression.

"It sounds like you ladies want something a little simpler, perhaps," she said.

"Yes. It's going to be a small wedding. Simple would be better," Layla said, trying to keep a straight face. The original dresses the attendant had brought out for them had been enormous puffy monstrosities of a style Sophie didn't even realize they made anymore. This third round of dresses had been better, but not by much. The attendant left in a huff, and the friends exchanged amused glances.

"Is it my fault she didn't hear me the first three times I said it?" Layla said after the woman left.

"I have the feeling they're desperate to get rid of some of these," Cara said, and Sophie chuckled. On the long car drive over, Sophie had filled her friends in on everything that had been happening, including her firing, the blackouts, and Calder's fight with the bear. She'd finished with the story of Marshall versus her goats, and the twins had sat in silence for a while, taking it all in. It had felt good to confide in them, to have them call Marshall every name under the sun, to know that others despised him just as much as she did.

The day with her friends was exactly what she needed, she realized.

"Just think. You and Calder will be planning one of these soon," Layla teased, and Sophie felt a blush warm her face.

"Hopefully," Sophie said.

"You'll find a way. You always do, and you have us to back you up," Cara said. Sophie wriggled out of the flouncy dress and pulled on the robe she'd brought with her at Layla's suggestion. She was glad now that she had. Unlike Cara, she wasn't comfortable sitting around in her underclothes.

"Are you seeing that witch again soon? Esme?" Cara asked.

Sophie nodded. "I'm supposed to go for another round of her beating me up this weekend. I swear, the woman does not like me."

"Well, from what you said, she didn't seem to like Migisi much, either. Maybe she just doesn't like you on principle," Layla said, and Sophie shrugged.

"I don't really care if she likes me. I'd just like her to not be quite so enthusiastic about showing me how weak I am," she said wryly, and the twins nodded.

The attendant came back with another armload of dresses, and Sophie and Cara began trying them on. The eleventh style was the charm: long, simple gowns with sheer sleeves and fitted bodices. Cara and Sophie sat around as Layla put in an order for both dresses in dark purple. Sophie spent a few minutes messaging with Calder. She'd found herself checking in on him more since the bear thing, and she knew he was checking in on her more, too, since they'd brought her blackouts into the open. The first few days after she'd been fired, they'd spent mostly in Calder's bed, or in hers. It reminded her a bit of the days right after she'd taken his curse, when they'd stayed together in much the same way, being comforted just by being in one another's presence.

Layla finally stepped away from the counter after shaking the attendant's hand, and she turned to Sophie and Cara with a smile. "I am starving. Want to head over to the mall to grab something to eat?"

"Don't have to ask me twice. I could eat a deer," Cara said

"Yuck," Sophie said, and the twins laughed. Old jokes, her two wolf friends teasing the vegetarian over differences in their choices of diet. It all made Sophie feel normal, for just a while.

At the mall, they headed for the food court.
"Chinese sounds good to me," Sophie said.
"Long line, though," Layla said.

"It probably won't take too long."

"I need a burger," Cara said, and Layla nodded. The twins headed for the burger place as Sophie got in line at the Chinese place. The line moved pretty quickly, and Sophie had just decided on veggie stir-fry when she heard a loud shout from the opposite direction. She turned that way, and heard another shout. Two men, not much older than teenagers, were shouting at one another, their tone angry even though Sophie couldn't understand the words. Their shouts got louder, and then one punched the other in the stomach. They began wrestling.

Sophie heard some of the people in line with her start arguing with one another, and her heart sank.

"You cut in front of me, asshole," one man said to another.

"Are you blind? I've been here this whole time," the second guy said. The first guy shoved him, and then the other people in line, those who'd been jostled first, started shoving back.

I'm doing this, Sophie thought to herself. Shadow. Her mind flashed back to the restaurant that horrible night.

Maybe stepping away would calm them down.

She looked for a somewhat empty part of the food court. Somewhere away from crowds that would be affected by her Shadow. How foolish she'd been, letting herself forget that her and crowds were a bad combination.

Shouts started at a different part of the mall, down past the food court in front of a clothing store. A crowd there was shoving one another. She looked around in panic, looking for Cara and Layla. The original argument had happened not too far from the burger place where they'd been waiting, and in the short time since those first shouts had sounded, a large crowd had grown there, as if people had been drawn to the chaos.

She couldn't see Cara and Layla in the crowd.

Another fight broke out near her, and she moved away, trying to edge around to find Cara and Layla while also trying not to get too close to anyone. She didn't want anymore fights to start. Hopefully once she got out of there, everyone would calm down.

In the midst of the shouting, shoving crowd, she saw Layla trying to break up a fight between two women, Cara at her side, helping her sister.

Suddenly, it was as if the volume and intensity of everything around them turned up to full blast. The shoving became punching, and the shouts became screams. People started hitting, and, in one case, biting, whoever was in the nearest vicinity. She ran toward Cara and Layla, shouting, telling them it was time to go.

She was nearly to them when she saw a man pick up one of the metal stools near the burger place and just start randomly swinging it at people, full of rage, madness in his eyes.

She focused, and threw a shield up over him, blocking him from hitting anyone. He'd been far too close to her friends with that last swing, she thought.

"Guys! Let's get the hell out of here," she shouted. Cara heard her and nodded emphatically. She took Layla's arm and pulled, but Layla was in the process of going to a teenage girl who'd been taken down by the maniac and his swinging stool. She'd just bent down to check on the girl when someone hurled a small table in that direction.

Sophie watched in horror, in slow motion, as the table struck Layla. Her head snapped to the side, and her body fell to the floor.

Cara's scream was louder than anything else, and both she and Sophie rushed to where Layla lay, blood seeping from her nose and head. Sophie was about to dial 911, but then she saw police flooding into the area, around the still-growing mob of fighters.

"No," Sophie whispered, picturing what would happen if the officers became afflicted with the same insanity the rest of the crowd was. She looked around, taking in the chaos, Cara talking and crying over Layla.

There, just past the nearest mob, stood Marshall, casually leaning against a column. His gaze met Sophie's, and he smirked.

"Let this be a lesson, *kitten*," he said, and though he was nowhere near her, she could hear his voice as clearly as if he was right beside her. "I'm not a man you want as an enemy, and now you're going to suffer for your disobedience." With that, and another sickening grin, he disappeared.

Within moments of Marshall leaving, the chaos began dying down. The police got control of the crowd, and paramedics started running in with gurneys and stretchers to transport the injured. Sophie watched and listened in numb terror as Layla was secured onto a board, her head and neck secured so they didn't move anymore, her body strapped down to keep her completely still. She held Cara's hand as Cara tried to hold it together and listen to the paramedics. Cara trembled uncontrollably, her teeth chattering.

"She's going into shock," one of the paramedics working on Layla called. Another came and wrapped a gray blanket around Cara. They followed the gurney to a waiting ambulance, and Cara and Sophie climbed in the back. Once Layla was secured, the paramedic riding in back with them fitted an oxygen mask over Cara's nose and mouth and instructed her to take slow, deep breaths. She still shook, and Sophie could hear her teeth chattering.

"I've never seen anything like that," the paramedic said. She was young, maybe just out of school, Sophie guessed.

All Sophie could do was nod, and keep her arms tightly around Cara's shaking body, trying to give her some sense of comfort, but she knew it didn't do anything, really. Cara's twin, her best friend, lay still and pale in front of them. Nothing Sophie did would change that, and she had only herself to blame. Because she'd angered Marshall, and then been stupid enough to try to pretend she could have a normal life.

She flashed back to days, weeks, months on end spent hiding alone in the house her father had left her, shades pulled, only the television and its tinny voices for company. Eating stockpiled frozen dinners and scurrying to and from her crappy job a quickly as possible to avoid Marshall, even though she'd known better.

He was always there. Watching, waiting. Testing the wards she'd managed to set around her home and car to keep her safe. Now, even those were not possible.

She could too easily see being there again, alone in the dark, hoping and praying that he would't do anything else to hurt her by hurting those she loved. She knew now what she didn't know then: he'd never hurt her personally. He wouldn't kill her. What fun would there be in that? What point, when his entire goal in life was to mold her into the second coming of Micaela?

Everyone around her would suffer. Everyone. He would toy with her, like a cat with a mouse, pouncing and causing mayhem and pain when she least expected it.

Unless she gave him what he wanted. That was what he said, anyway.

But she knew Marshall. It would't end. Even once he had what he wanted, he would use those she cared for as leverage. He would hurt them anytime she irritated him, or anytime he thought she was drawing away from him. It would never, ever end. Not until she was dead and buried, or he was. Shadow ensured she had a long existence ahead of her, unless something killed her.

She shook her head a little. Her thoughts were becoming fuzzy, frenzied, her mind scrambled by her terror over what had happened, her fear for Layla, and the effects of the curse plus Shadow. She'd tried escape via ending her life once. It hadn't worked out. She'd lived, and she'd lost a good portion her already-minimal Light magic as well. It had ended up making it that much easier to succumb to Shadow, likely via the same curse that Luc had been infected with to ensnare Migisi. From what she could guess,

Calder's line had continued to carry that curse as well, except that that one didn't matter unless they began spending time with one of Migisi's descendants.

Once again, Sophie cursed the day Luc and Migisi laid eyes on one another.

The ambulance pulled into a driveway at the large hospital not too far from where they'd been shopping, and other medical staff was there waiting, likely expecting the influx of new patients due to the riots. They wheeled Layla out. Cara pulled off the oxygen mask and blanket, and she and Sophie follow the gurney as far as the hospital staff would let them.

"Wait here, please," an orderly said. "You'll be updated as soon as we can assess her condition."

Another attendant got Cara's attention, asking for Layla's information.

"I'll call your parents and Calder and Bryce," Sophie told her, and she nodded then went to the counter to get her sister registered.

Sophie went to the waiting room, finding a quiet corner. The waiting room was likely to get rather full in the next few minutes, she realized, as more ambulances with victims from the fights started showing up. She dialed the number at the diner the twins' family owned, and explained what had happened to their mother, feeling like a complete waste of space as the woman started crying, thanking her and telling her they were on their way.

Sophie dialed Calder next. Thankfully, he answered on the first ring.

"Hey," he said cheerfully. "Are you guys coming back soon? Bryce and Jon are here and Bryce is getting antsy," he said, and she heard Bryce say something in the background. Tears sprung to her eyes.

"Layla's hurt. She's in the hospital here. Mayton General."

"What?" Calder asked, and she heard Bryce again, alerted by Calder's tone.

"There was this big riot, thing, at the mall and Layla got hurt. We're in the emergency room."

"Okay. Okay. We're on our way. Does her mom know?"

"Yeah. I just called her."

She could hear Bryce in the background again, his concern evident. "We're on our way now," Calder said. "I love you."

"Love you too," Sophie said, tears springing to her eyes.

He hung up, and she was left clutching her phone, wishing they could rewind the day to that morning, to her and Calder lying in bed feeding each other slices of apple and cheese. She should have stayed home. Everyone would be safe right now, if she'd just stayed home and away from people. He hadn't gone after Calder yet, believing as she did that they were connected via the curse. She didn't know how much longer that would hold, though.

Sophie leaned forward and buried her face in her hands. "Light protect everyone from the chaos that surrounds me," she whispered. "Don't let them suffer for my mistakes," she prayed. She could only hope that Light was able to hear prayers from Shadow.

Cara came and sat beside her, and they sat, hands clasped. Within an hour, their family and friends were there: the twins' parents and grandma Faye, Bryce, Calder, and Jon. They sat, filling an entire row of chairs in the waiting room. Doctors and nurses came and went.

"She has some severe swelling of her brain. We need to operate to relieve the pressure."

"She won't be conscious for quite a while. We won't know just how severe her injuries are."

"It is likely she may have some permanent damage."

"We can't tell you how long her coma will last. We just don't know."

Bryce paced, and the twins' parents sat, staring helplessly into space. Cara sat with Jon, who occasionally talked to her in a quiet, calm voice. Sophie sat with Calder, her hand held tightly in his. It was well into the next day before the twins' parents started urging them to go home and rest. As much as Sophie wanted to stay to hear about Layla, and to be there for Cara, she also welcomed the idea of getting away from people who could be hurt if Marshall decided to strike at her again. Bryce and Cara stayed at the hospital, and, after many hugs and promises to call and murmured empty phrases meant to comfort, Sophie, Calder, and Jon left. They climbed into Calder's truck, Sophie sitting between Calder and Jon in the cab.

They drove much of the way in silence. It was early afternoon, Sophie realized when she looked at the clock. They'd been in the hospital for nearly twenty-four hours.

"What happened, Sophie?" Jon asked finally.

"A brawl broke out. Some jerk threw a table, and it hit Layla when she was trying to help a girl who'd been hurt," she said. She didn't want to share the part about Marshall causing it all, because of her. She could confide in Calder later, and she would, but she wasn't ready to have that conversation with Jon.

"That's it? A brawl just broke out out of nowhere?" Jon pressed.

"Drop it. She's tired," Calder said in a voice that made it clear he wasn't in the mood to argue. Jon clamped his mouth shut and stared out his window for the rest of the long drive home. They drove in silence, and Sophie kept going over the whole thing in her mind. No matter how she let her mind wander, it kept coming back to one thing: the people she cared about were the ones who suffered when Marshall wanted to teach her a lesson. Who would be next? Cara? Bryce?

Calder?

Her friend Thea, who had helped her discover the truth of the curse? All of them innocents, in danger because of their relationship with her.

The truth settled over her like icy death. A truth she'd known for most of her life but had tried to ignore since foolishly believing herself free of Marshall once she'd made her way to Copper Falls.

No one she cared for would ever be safe as long as Marshall was around. Even her death wouldn't end his insanity; he'd hurt them in rage if he lost her to death. Of course, she had no idea how to get rid of Marshall. All she could do was try to make herself strong enough to protect them all.

Which left her with one solution.

CHAPTER TWENTY-TWO

When Sophie and Calder got back to her house, she let them in the front door in silence. Calder closed and locked the front door behind them, then came to her and held her.

She breathed him in, determined to memorize his scent. She gently pushed him away, and it was the last thing she wanted.

She looked up at him, into those eyes that had made her tongue-tied since she was a little girl, and she tried to steel her heart against everything she was feeling.

"I think I need a little space," she said.

Calder's brow crinkled, and he recovered. "I... I'm sure you're tired. I'll go home and shower and stuff and you can rest."

She shook her head. "No. I mean, I need a break."

"From what?"

Her heart felt ripped to shreds, but she said the words anyway. "From us."

He shook his head. "Come on, kitten. I know you're upset over what happened back there, but that has nothing to do with us." He moved to hold her again, and she stepped back.

"It has everything to do with us. Marshall did that, Calder. Do you know why he did that? To punish me," she said, and when he reached for her a third time, she strode to the door.

"So we stick together. We fight, and we're ready for him the next time he comes at you."

"Don't you get it? Are you really that dumb?" Light, she hated herself. "No one in my life is safe from him. And I care about you, but I don't care enough to give myself to him to keep you safe."

His expression hardened. "And I'd never want you to do that. I don't need you to save me."

"You kind of do."

"No. I never needed you to save me, Sophie. Not when you took my curse without asking, and not now. Do you really think shutting me out will protect me from him? That dude is fucking nuts. He doesn't care if we're actually together or not. He knows you'll hate yourself if anyone who knows you gets hurt in the crossfire. You know this."

"I know that I can't focus on warding off Marshall, trying to function with this curse, and being with you all the time. I just can't. do. it. Okay?"

"Well, that's great," Calder said. "You know the curse is coming back, don't you?"

Her stomach twisted. He'd come to the same realization she had about his night with the bear.

"Which is another thing. You lied to me about that night, didn't you? You sounded insane, and I know damn well what that means. I can't trust you to be straight with me. You keep hiding things from me, like I'm some helpless little girl who can't deal with reality. What else are you keeping from me, Calder?" she asked, aware that now she was shouting. Shadow rose in her, and the curse only added to the insanity. For once, she welcomed all of it. Maybe he would see that he was better off without her.

Instead, he shook his head, a wry smile on his lips. "You're right. I keep trying to protect you. I'm new at this relationship thing." He studied her. "You need a break, I'll keep my distance for a while But don't try to pretend this is over, Sophie, because it's not. You love me, and every word you just said verifies it. You want space because you think it'll save me from Marshall. At least be honest about why you're doing this."

She didn't answer, and after several tense moments, he shook his head again and walked toward her. "Have your space, kitten. I'm done sitting around and waiting for him to come after us."

"What the hell do you mean by that?" she asked.

He met her eyes as he opened the door. "It means I hope I meet the bastard skulking around in your woods. He always takes off before I get to him. I'm going to have to be faster."

"Calder!"

He left, closing the door firmly behind him.

"Shit," she muttered. Now she had a pissed off Calder. Which was better for her heart than a sad Calder, but it put him in so much more danger when he was hot-headed. Calder confronting Marshall was the last thing she wanted.

She tried to think her way through it, but she kept zoning out, blanking out, getting distracted by her hunger and that ever-present buzzing of rage just beneath the surface.

"Getting rid of this goddamn curse would be a really good start," she muttered. She glanced at the clock. There was only one person she knew who knew curses at all.

Minutes later, she was getting into the rental car she'd borrowed while they were figuring out what to do about her crashed-up car. She drove quickly down the highway, noting that Calder was in his driveway, bent over the engine of the Barracuda. He didn't make a show of looking up, and she tried not to look directly at him, either. She made her way to the forest, to the gravel road that took her to Esme's creepy Victorian and the stone wall that surrounded it. She got out and clomped up the front steps, then pounded loudly on the front door.

The door opened, and Esme looked at her icily. "You are not scheduled to be here until Saturday," she said, and she started closing the door.

"I need to learn more. Now," Sophie said, wedging her foot into the door before Esme could close it. Before she could even ready herself for it, Esme tossed a blast of power at her that had her flying backward, off the porch. She landed on the sidewalk near the front steps, and Esme advanced on her, coming out of the house.

"Who in the hell do you think you are to demand anything of me?" Esme asked, and her voice was full of malice. "The descendent of a worthless whore, a powerless mongrel. You are nothing."

"Marshall caused a riot. My friend is in a coma. He's going to hurt someone else next, and I can't let him do that."

Esme was about to say something, but she stopped. Then she shook her head. "I've tried teaching you. You're hopeless. You manage to shield yourself, but that's it, and it's likely all you'll be able to do. You have the focus of a gnat."

"I know. That's part of why I'm here. Please. Unless you maybe want to kick Marshall's ass for me?" Sophie asked as she stood.

"Marshall and I stay out of one another's way. He can't touch me, and I can't touch him."

Sophie tilted her head. "How did that end up happening?"

"It was a deal. One that is none of your business."

Sophie watched her, and Esme sighed.

"Do you really think this is the first time Marshall has posed a threat to Migisi's loved ones? Oh, but I forget:

you're of Migisi's line. Everything about you is special," she added with a sneer.

"Are you going to explain it to me, or not?"

"Fuck off, princess," Esme said, and Sophie looked away. She knew saying much more would just ensure that Esme wouldn't help her at all.

"Fine. The curse, though. Do you know how to break curses?"

"Curses can only be broken by those who set them. Or their descendants."

"So I can break the curse," Sophie said, dread sinking into her stomach. Migisi's scrawled words hadn't been a lie.

"You think you'd look a little happier about it," Esme said.

"Can I just run this past you? Please? And then I'll leave if you want me to. I need to do something here, but I can't do the thing Migisi said I have to. There has to be another way," Sophie said.

"This is not my problem," Esme said, heading toward the front porch again.

Sophie dug her phone out of her pocket and scrolled to a photo of Calder, smiling at the camera as he stood in front of the falls. If her hunch about Esme was right, maybe it would help.

She shoved the phone in front of Esme's face. "This is Calder. This is him, and he doesn't deserve any of the crap that's happened to him because of Migisi. You think you hate her? I hate her even more. I love him, and everything I am spells his doom. If I do anything in this life, I need to save him and his family from what Migisi did to them. Okay? The curse is coming back to him, somehow, and I don't know how to stop it."

Esme had taken the phone and was staring at the screen. "Jesus, it's like seeing Luc all over again," she said softly, and for the first time, Sophie heard a note of softness in her voice.

"Really?" Sophie asked gently.

"Same eyes, same smile," Esme said, transfixed by the photo. She glanced up at Sophie. "And you look so much like Migisi. It's like being back there all over again, like having both of them haunting me in the flesh instead of just in memories."

"He's a good man, Esme. He works hard, and he's dealt with this curse, with seeing what it does, for too long. You can hate me all you want. It's fine. I don't know what happened between you and Migisi, but I don't blame you for hating any memory of her. Just help me save him."

Esme looked at the photo for a moment longer, such yearning in her eyes that Sophie practically felt it. She sighed, and then handed the phone back. "You say she left instructions for how to end it?" she asked.

Sophie's heart leapt, and she followed Esme toward the house. Once inside, they went up to her study and sat on opposite sides of the cluttered desk.

Esme was watching her. "Did you say the curse was coming back to Calder?" she asked, and Sophie nodded.

"I took it, but it seems to be affecting him again. He tries to hide it, but he forgets that I know what it looks like. He finally admitted that it's back."

"How did you know to take the curse? Because that's some super Shadow nastiness. Taking any kind of magic from another, curse or not, is simply not something that's done."

"Marshall told me to. He told me that if I turned Shadow, I could take what I wanted. And it worked. For a while."

Esme stared at her for a moment, and then she shook her head. "You are utterly clueless. You played right into his hands."

"What are you talking about? It worked, at first!"

"Did you specify which curse you took?"

Sophie looked at Esme in confusion. "I just focused on taking the curse."

"You're aware there were two curses, yes?"

Sophie didn't answer, her mind twisting, turning, just on the edge of piecing something together.

Esme sighed. "There was the curse that made him crazy, yes. But in your brilliance, you're forgetting the initial curse, the one that started it all. It was what turned Migisi to the Shadow, and what worked to turn you as well. I'm guessing you felt the darkness flowing into you long before Marshall turned you?"

Sophie nodded.

"The curse is a pretty basic one, but ingenious in its design. It makes it so, with extended contact with a cursed person, that someone becomes that which they fear most. For you and Migisi, it was Shadow. For Calder, it was…"

"His curse."

"His curse," Esme agreed. "So you took his curse, but you took the other one too. Which means that he's getting pulled back into his initial curse, because it is his nightmare. And this is why children shouldn't meddle in magic."

"I didn't know."

"Of course not. And Marshall played you beautifully and you're a complete moron for believing a single word that came out of his mouth."

"It bought me time," Sophie snapped, her face burning with shame.

"Maybe. Anyway. You were asking about breaking the curse Migisi put on Luc, which is the more worrisome of the two. If that curse is broken, Calder and his family have no reason to worry about the other one."

Sophie pulled Migisi's journal out of her bag, opened it to the page where she'd written what Sophie believed were instructions for ending the curse, and set the book in front of Esme. "This was hers. Read the words written in the backgrounds of each of the next four drawings," Sophie instructed.

Esme gave her in irritated look. "You can't just tell me what it says?"

"I may have missed something. I want to see what you think."

Esme sighed again, then began studying the drawings. She spoke, reciting words Sophie had long memorized:

"I have wronged
The one I loved above all others.
Corrupted by the Shadow,
Distraught and alone,
I became that which I disdain.
Some years hence, a son of Luc's line
Will give everything he is to a daughter of mine.
He will love her fully and absolutely.
And she will destroy him.
On that day the curse will be lifted
And Luc's line will be free
And my soul will rest in peace.
She who reads this is chosen by Migisi."

They sat in silence for a few moments. Finally, Esme sat back in her chair. "She was a really shitty poet."

Sophie groaned. "Come on," she said.

"You're making some assumptions here. First off, you're assuming that this actually means anything. She was a complete fucking psychopath at the end. Second, you're assuming that he actually does love you fully and absolutely—"

"He does," Sophie said quietly.

"Of course he does. Just like Migisi," Esme muttered. "And third, you're assuming that you're the first to have read this and the one 'chosen' by Migisi."

"The two lines have avoided one another when Luc's line hasn't been killing Migisi's. I don't think there were many of Migisi's descendants falling in love with Luc's," Sophie said. "You know as well as I do that this is something."

Esme read the words again. "So what was your takeaway from this shitty poem?" she asked.

"That I have to kill Calder to end the curse."

"You are a bloodthirsty group of bitches, I'll give you that," Esme said.

"I didn't say I *want* to kill him!" Sophie said, clenching her jaw to keep from saying more and risking angering Esme further.

"You're not all that smart, either," Esme remarked, and Sophie bit her tongue, hard. Esme smirked. "You're taking it too literally."

"How else should I take it? What do I have to go on besides what she wrote?"

"Think. It says 'destroy,' not 'kill.' What caused Migisi's destruction?"

"Shadow?"

Esme shook her head. "Shadow was the tool, as well as the punishment. What made her curse Luc?"

"I don't know!"

Esme watched Sophie. "You don't know this story?"

"I know there are stories about him cheating on her and her losing her mind. Is that the destruction you mean?"

Esme nodded. "Luc went away for a few days to meet with some of his business partners, and for some reason, Migisi decided to go to him," she said with a shrug. "When she got there, it was to find Luc plowing some camp follower against a tree. She snapped, and cursed him in that instant."

Sophie watched Esme. "So her destruction came from a broken heart?"

Esme nodded. "Sappy, huh? She watched the man she loved screw someone else, and it broke something inside of her. She cursed him without even needing to think about it. Instantaneously."

"So I need to break Calder's heart?" Sophie asked slowly, not wanting to hear it.

"If your theory about this is correct, that these are the crazy bitch's final instructions for breaking the curse, then yes. That's a big 'if,' though, and you need to do more than

227

just hurt his feelings if that's the case. You need to crush his heart so completely that he'll never want to love again."

"Well that's just great," Sophie muttered, looking at her hands folded in he lap, even as dread settled over her.

"It's better than killing him."

Sophie didn't answer. "I can't do that to him," she said after a while. "I can't kill him, and I can't do that to him."

"Then the curse will keep going," Esme said with a shrug. "You said Marshall's after everyone who matters to you? Don't worry about it, though. Soon you'll be too insane to realize it's even happening."

Sophie glared at Esme. "Do you have any heart at all?"

Esme gave her a bored look and leaned back in her chair. "Even if you manage to break Calder's curse, it doesn't rid you of Marshall."

"No. But it will make it more possible to focus what little magic I have so I can actually protect people from him. It's not much, but it's pretty much all I have."

"So you've finally realized that your powers are useless for battle," Esme said, and Sophie nodded. "We can focus on shielding now without you bitching that I'm not teaching you what you think you need to know." Sophie nodded again.

Sophie took a breath and met Esme's eyes. "You say you can't touch Marshall."

"I can't. Pacts made in magic are unbreakable. I can't harm him and he can't harm me."

Sophie nodded. "Can you protect someone from him though? Can you create some kind of spell that protects Calder from Marshall?"

Esme didn't answer.

"I don't know what Luc was to you. I don't expect you to tell me, but it's clear that you cared about him. Can you help him one more time? Can you protect Luc's grandson from Marshall? Because I've already lost one husband to Marshall's rage, and I can't lose Calder too. Even if I can't be with him anymore," she added, her heart aching as she realized what was going to happen.

Esme studied her for a while, then nodded. "I can do that."

"Can I ask you something else?"

"Your questions are annoying."

"Please?"

Esme gave a short nod.

"You've lived here all this time, and so has Luc's family. You never interacted with them?"

"Shadow magic," she reminded Sophie. "You see what the land around my home looks like. You see what happens when someone with my amount of power goes out in public. Undoubtedly, you've caused a bit of unease even with the small amount of magic you have. No, I have kept my distance, from Luc's family and everyone else. I came to your property that day, and other than that, I have not left this land in nearly a hundred years. And before that, I left it rarely," she said with a shrug.

"Is this what I have to look forward to? An empty house and dead land?" Sophie asked quietly.

"You already know the answer to that. Come on, let's work on your shields now. Then I can avoid seeing you on Saturday."

"You'll do the spell to protect Calder, right?"

"I already said I would. He'll be protected. Not for you, but for Luc, and for Calder."

"Thank you."

Esme waved it off, and they went out to the back yard. A light layer of snow covered the dead ground, outlined the branches and trunks of the twisted remains of trees. Again and again, Esme threw power at her and Sophie raised her shields to protect herself. She tried to focus, but the curse, her stress over Layla, and Marshall, and the things Esme had told her she had to do to save Calder from the curse all wore at her, and she slipped in and out of focus, sometimes being jolted back by being struck with Esme's power.

"Again. And focus this time," Esme spat, and she readied another blast of power.

Sophie had every intention of raising a shield, but she blacked out again.

When she came to, it was to hear Esme screeching in rage and throwing a considerable amount of power at her. Sophie flew across the yard, landing in a heap on the ground, and then she found herself being lifted into the air again, held there by an invisible force.

"What the hell did you think you were doing?" Esme screeched. Her face was a mask of rage.

"What are you talking about?" Sophie asked, shaking her head, keeping her eyes on Esme so she would be ready if Esme decided to throw her. Or worse.

"Did you think you were being cute? Trying to augment your measly power with mine? Give it back!" she screamed, moving her hand in such a way that Sophie was shaken around in midair like a rag doll. "Give it back!" she shouted again.

"What are you talking about?" Sophie shouted, trying not to vomit as Esme shook her again.

"You started siphoning my power, you worthless bitch," Esme shouted, shaking her again.

"I don't even know how to do that!"

"Fuck you. You do so. How do you think you took Calder's curse in the first place?" Esme shouted with another bout of shaking.

"I didn't even know what was happening. I didn't try to take anything from you."

With an enraged shout, Esme hurled Sophie through the air, and Sophie came to a bone-crunching landing on the gravel driveway.

"If I see your face again, I will kill you," Esme said, her voice full of rage. "I don't make idle threats. The only reason I'm letting you walk is to give you the chance to lift Migisi's curse so Luc can rest in peace. Do not cross my path again."

Esme stormed into the house, slamming the door behind her, and Sophie was left, bent over double in the driveway, trying to breathe again after having the air knocked from her. Her body ached, and, once she could breathe again, it hurt every time she inhaled. She slowly limped back to her car, got in, and headed back toward home, knowing she was lucky to be leaving alive, whether she'd meant to do what Esme claimed she'd done or not.

One thing was abundantly clear: no matter how much Esme had hurt her, it was nothing compared to what was coming next.

CHAPTER TWENTY-THREE

In the end, she put it off.

A week.

Two.

The first major snowfall fell on Copper Falls. Calder respected her wish for space, even though she knew from the set of his shoulders the few times they talked that he hated it. It only made her love him more, that he did the one thing he didn't want to: he stayed away from her.

Layla's condition hadn't changed, and Marshall had been suspiciously quiet since the day of the mall riot.

It lulled Sophie into the belief that she had time, that she could maybe just live out the rest of her life as long as she kept herself holed up. She thought she felt power wash over her once in her sleep, but when she woke, she didn't feel it anymore and wrote it off as a dream. She dreamt once that she'd woken to find herself in the woods, in Marshall's arms, his fingers tangled in her hair, when the goats showed up and chased him away.

She tried to practice with her Shadow magic, with the paltry things she'd managed to learn from Esme. Her life became a blur, a mix of consciousness and an increasing fuzziness that she knew was Calder's curse getting worse. And if it was getting worse for her, it was getting worse for him as well.

She spent another night dreaming of Marshall, of his arms around her, his hands on her body. Hoarse whispers in her ear, and the goats appearing as if to save her.

She woke to find the bottom of her pajama pants wet, her boots sitting in a puddle near the back door.

She ran to the bathroom mirror, remembering her dream, and when she saw the bite marks on her neck, bites she'd dreamed Marshall giving her, she bent over the toilet and vomited.

The curse. He'd figured it out, and he was using it against her. First for his own sick sense of victory and control and later, who knew? Sophie rinsed her mouth out and leaned against the bathroom vanity, trying to steady herself against the way her body shook, against the terror flooding through her, the sense of wrongness.

The knowledge that her time, time when she was still even partially in control of herself, was coming to an end. She went back into the living room and paced, because sitting still was impossible. Sitting still would drive her insane. Every time she turned, her gaze landed on the leather bound journal Migisi had left her descendants.

I want to remember planning our wedding.

I will love you for the rest of my life. I always have.

All we need is you and me, Sophie. We have those two things, and we have everything.

Beside the journal, her phone sat where she'd tossed it after she'd gotten back from Esme's house. She hesitated for another moment, dialed a number she never thought she would.

"Hey, it's Sophie. I need your help. Do you have time later today?"

CHAPTER TWENTY-FOUR

Calder walked into Jack's for his weekly meet-up with Jon. Bryce usually joined them, but he spent most of his non-work time at the hospital, waiting for a miracle to happen with Layla. He didn't even especially feel like being there, but it beat being home alone waiting to lose track of himself again. And Jon knew it, too, which was why he'd called twice making sure Calder was coming and that he was still coherent.

Persistent little shit, Calder thought to himself when he spotted his brother sitting where they usually sat, at the far end of the bar. He clapped Jon on the shoulder, and the barmaid got him his usual. He and Jon sat, looking at the hockey game on the television over the bar without really seeing it.

"How'd it go today?" Jon finally asked.

Calder glanced around. The bar was pretty busy. Jack's normal seat, at the other end of the bar, was empty. Calder was glad. He wasn't in the mood to see the alpha's obnoxious ass just then.

"It was okay. I think I came close to losing it once, but then I did the icy shower routine and it snapped me back into focus."

It was quiet for a moment. "I remember dad doing that. I remember at first, I just thought he was nuts. Why would you take a freezing shower in the middle of winter?" Jon said, and Calder nodded.

"He hid a lot from us, for as long as he could."

"Kinda wish he would have told us more before he lost it completely."

Calder nodded.

"How's things with Sophie?"

Calder didn't answer, looked at the TV instead.

"That good, huh?"

"She asked for space, and she doesn't seem to have changed her mind in the past few weeks, so I'm giving her space. And I fucking hate it, but I understand. More than anyone, I understand what she's going through. At least part of it. I'd feel a hell of a lot better if we were going through it together, but what she wants, I want to give her. She wants time and space."

"Did she find another job yet?"

Calder shook his head.

"She may as well wait out the winter now. Once tourist season hits, other resorts'll be hiring." Silence reigned after that. They both knew the likelihood of Sophie being sane enough to work by spring was slim. And Calder wasn't much better. Every day, he lost more time, more focus. Every day, he had less time when he knew he was human. If he didn't focus completely on holding it together, he lost it.

He'd been okay that day. He hadn't told Jon about the day before, when he'd spent most of it as a bear, and only remembered he was a man when he saw Sophie feeding her creepy goats.

At night, he roamed the woods. He knew he did. It was easier than spending night after night in his bed alone. He hunted the warlock, but he hadn't been lucky enough yet to come across him. He knew he smelled him sometimes, always in Sophie's woods, always as if he'd just been there. Sometimes, he thought he heard a laugh. He wasn't sure, anymore, if it was real or his own insanity closing in.

He was about to say something when something made him raise his nose, scenting the air.

Jon glanced at him. "What's up?"

Calder didn't answer, scenting the air again. Faint, but he'd know her scent anywhere.

"Is Sophie here?"

. "I kinda doubt that, man. She's not exactly the bar type," Jon said, taking a gulp of beer. "Wishful thinking, maybe."

Calder glanced around. Maybe it was wishful thinking. He missed her more than he'd ever missed anyone. Not just the time they spent in bed, though he could have done with some of Sophie's loving as well, but the times when she just sat with him. When she listened to him ramble on about old cars, or when she wasn't looking, and he could just watch her.

There it was again.

Calder got up, as if he was heading toward the men's room. He kept sniffing, scenting the air.

Her scent was stronger at the back of the bar. The restrooms were there, as was the storeroom and Jack's office.

He furrowed his brow. One of the barmaids came out of the ladies room.

"Is anyone else in there?" he asked her.

"Nope," she said, looking confused. "You looking for someone?"

Calder shook his head. He stood near the storeroom, then stepped toward Jack's office.

And he thought he heard something. Her voice. Her scent was strong there.

He looked at Jack's office door. Maybe she was talking to him about convincing his cousin to take money for towing her car. It had bothered her that they wouldn't let her pay for the tow.

Calder pushed the door open, and her scent enveloped him. Her scent, the unmistakeable, addictive scent of her desire.

Jack's scent.

It took a moment before he realized what he was looking at, before he realized that Sophie was bent over Jack's desk, moaning softly, Jack behind her, grunting and thrusting, eyes closed, cursing about how good she was.

"More," she said, her voice a plea, desperate, choked with desire.

His entire world came crashing down around him. He stood frozen for a moment, then turned and walked out. He heard a final cry from the office as he walked away.

He was on automatic.

Calder walked through the bar without seeing any of it. Past Jon, out the front door.

Fuck, it hurt. He wanted to claw his chest, anything to relieve the ache there, the heaviness. He could barely breathe.

Jon ran out after him, put a hand on his shoulder.

"Calder. Calder!" he said louder. "What the hell, man?"

"She was there."

Jon looked at him, confused.

"With Jack," Calder said.

"I'll kill him," Jon growled, and Calder was numb. Instead of the emptiness that had gnawed at him for most of his life, he felt too full. Heavy. He felt everything, and it suffocated him.

Jon seemed to sense it.

"Come on man. Stay with me for a while. You don't need to go home, not where you're gonna see her all the time."

Calder didn't answer, but he didn't argue when Jon pushed him into the front seat of his truck.

"She doesn't even like Jack," he said when they were almost to the house they'd grown up in, and even as he said it, he knew it was a lie. She'd accepted that ride from him. Been aroused by him.

That was the curse, he tried to tell himself. It was what he'd told himself that day, when he'd watched Jack help Sophie out of his truck.

It was a lie.

"He's gone," Jack said in her ear. "Remember that you promised to shield me if he comes in here to kill me."

He backed away, and Sophie sat on one of the chairs near the scarred wooden desk. They were both still fully clothed. The appearance of Jack humping her had been all they'd needed.

Sophie buried her face in her hands. Her shoulders shook silently, and she bit her lip so hard it bled to prevent herself from keening. The silent way he'd walked away, the way his breath had caught when he'd opened the door.

"Do you think that did what you hoped it would?" Jack asked, sitting behind his desk.

"I don't know. I don't feel any different," Sophie said. She swiped at her nose, and Jack handed her a tissue. She accepted it silently.

"It's a good thing he never really liked me. Even if this worked, that bastard's going to hate me forever."

"Not as much as he'll hate me, though," Sophie said quietly. "Sorry for getting you mixed up in this."

Jack shook his head. "Like I said, I knew his dad. I know what this shit does. If this little ploy managed somehow to end what happens to the Turcotte men, then it was well worth it."

"And if it didn't?" Sophie asked after a moment of silence.

"Then I just made a pretty deadly enemy. I knew that when I said I'd help you," he said with a note of finality, as if he didn't want to discuss it anymore.

Just when Sophie thought she had herself pulled together, she'd start crying again. Jack sat in silence, and she was thankful that he didn't try to comfort her.

"I'll drive you home, okay?" Jack asked, and Sophie was about to respond when her phone rang. With more than a little trepidation, she took it out of her purse and looked at the screen.

Bryce.

"What's going on?" she asked. She could hear sirens, chaos in the background.

"Christ, Sophie," Bryce said, and the first thing she thought was that something had happened with Calder.

"What is it?" she asked, standing up.

"Some guy came in and shot up Layla's family's diner."

"What?" she repeated, running toward the back door, where her car was parked.

"Sophie."

"What?" she asked, her stomach twisting at his tone.

"Their dad's gone."

"Wha... what do you mean, gone? Missing?" It became hard to breathe, and even before the words were out of his mouth, she knew what Bryce would say.

"He's gone, Soph. They'd just gotten in from their time at the hospital with Lay. Christ, she won't even get to say goodbye to him," he said, and she knew he was crying.

She fell to her knees, unable to support her own weight anymore. Memories flooded her, the twins' father giving her car a tune-up, before she knew Calder, before she had money to afford such things. The first winter she'd lived in Copper Falls, when he'd brought firewood and canned goods, figuring the city girl had no idea what she was in for. And he'd been right. Cara and Layla as little girls, being swung around by their father, happy shrieks filling the backyard.

"No," she whispered. "I'll be there soon. Cara?"

"She's talking to the police now. At the diner."

Sophie hung up.

I'm getting tired of you and your games, kitten. We were so close last night. A man can only be expected to take so much.

In her mind, surrounding her.

Marshall.

You had a chance to be a good girl. Now, you'll see what happens when you piss me off.

When she pulled up to the diner, it looked like a scene out of a TV crime drama. Yellow police tape surrounded the building and its small parking lot, and police lights flashed blue and red against the normally cheery-looking front of the diner. Crowds had gathered, and, through them, she saw Cara and Bryce standing with two police officers. She went to them, and Cara fell into her arms, sobbing.

"Did they catch the shooter?" Sophie asked Bryce over Cara's head as the two officers looked on.

"No. We saw him though. Creepy-ass guy. Dark hair, nearly black eyes, wearing a dark trench coat.

Sophie froze. She had to close her eyes to fight back the dizziness. She knew it was Marshall, of course, but she'd expected his usual manipulative methods. He'd come in person to mow down the people she had come to see as the closest thing she had to family, other than Calder.

He'd made it personal.

"I'm so sorry, Cara," Sophie whispered, holding her friend closer as Cara wept. She stood and listened to Bryce talking to the officer, and she held Cara and wished, as she had never wished in her life, that she had it in herself to end Marshall. Rage nearly swallowed her whole, her empty, shattered heart over what she'd forced Calder to see, the fact that she knew, because she knew Calder, that whether their ploy had worked or not, he wouldn't be back. The sight of so many mourners around her.

Cara's Grandma Faye made her way through the crowd. Tears made her eyes bright, but the set of her chin and her entire posture spoke of her anger. She reached them, and

Sophie put a hand on her shoulder, not knowing what else to say or do. The woman had just lost a son.

Faye patted her hand, and fixed the officer with a steely look. "You catch the bastard who did this to my family. You catch the one who took my boy from me." Her voice shook, but her posture remained tall, proud.

"We will, ma'am," the officer said. "I am sorry for your loss."

Faye looked at Cara. "Come on, girl. I finally convinced your mama to come to my house for the night. You're coming, too."

Cara nodded and went with her grandmother. Sophie and Bryce watched them walk through the thinning crowds.

"It feels like it never ends," Sophie murmured.

"Yeah," Bryce said. "You should go home. Calder's probably heard about all this by now."

That was all it took. The sound of his name, the assumption that he was still hers. She couldn't do this.

She also couldn't go home. Couldn't sleep in the bed she knew she wouldn't be sharing with him again. And the real kicker was that she felt no different. The same madness, the same hunger, the same crazed energy that she knew so well still flowed through her. The curse still lived, which meant it had all been for nothing.

She got into her car, made her way to the highway, and she drove. She didn't drive anywhere in particular, just followed the highway along Rockway, then hugging the coast. She stopped once at a gas station to get some much-needed caffeine, and then she drove more.

It reminded her of running, she realized. It reminded her of driving all night when she'd finally managed to slip away from Marshall. She'd stupidly believed at the time that he didn't know where she was going, that she would be free of him, because what were the odds of him finding her in a tiny town in the middle of the wilderness?

She laughed, and she knew it was a brittle, icy sound. Like an utter fool, she'd run to the one place he would eventually logically trail her to. He'd bided his time, letting her build a life, giving her a taste of all the things she had to lose if he decided to take it away. And he was doing just that, bit by bit, piece by piece.

It would all end so easily. Just give in. It sounded so simple. But she also knew that it wouldn't really end. He'd continue to use them against her, except maybe next time, he'd make it so that she was the one wielding the power that hurt them.

She could move again. Sneak away. It would take a little while before he found her again, and in the meantime, he'd probably hurt them out of sheer spite and vileness.

She drove, and she thought, her mind twisting and spinning. She tried her hardest not to let herself focus too long on Calder. She'd have an eternity of empty nights to cry over what she'd lost with him.

When the sun began to rise, she started making her way toward home. She'd go to Cara's later, and maybe to the hospital. She knew the family would be busy now making funeral arrangements. She drove along Rockway, along the road that wound over the cliffs that Luc had supposedly jumped from all those years ago in an effort to free himself.

"Luc and Migisi, I wish you'd never goddamn laid eyes on one another," Sophie murmured, and she turned back on the highway that would take her to her house.

CHAPTER TWENTY-FIVE

Calder lay, looking up at the cracked ceiling of his childhood bedroom. It was all too familiar, him laying in the narrow twin bed after a sleepless night, pining for Sophie Turner.

It felt like he was fourteen all over again.

He'd passed a mostly sleepless night, but when he glanced at the clock on the nightstand, he realized he must have dozed off finally. It was almost three in the afternoon.

He felt numb. Other than the ache that had lodged itself somewhere in the vicinity of his heart when he'd seen her and Jack, he didn't feel a thing. Nothing.

He guessed he could consider that a small blessing. He'd sure the hell felt it all last night. Loss, sadness, rage, embarrassment. Embarrassment, that she'd been harboring feelings like that and he'd never known. Shock and disbelief was part of it, too, because despite what he'd seen, despite those memories of Jack helping Sophie from his truck and the way she'd smelled afterward... he still couldn't believe it. And part of him wanted to put the blame solely on her curse, that she'd felt a need and given into it and Jack, being

Jack, had been more than ready to take advantage of the situation.

But he knew, too, that he'd spent plenty of time with the same curse and had managed to stay loyal to Sophie once they were back in one another's life. It hadn't even been all that hard, because they were all over one another.

Clearly, it hadn't been enough for her, he thought bitterly as he lay there. And after her whole speech about needing space. He'd stupidly believed that she wanted space just because of feeling overwhelmed by the curse and everything else. He never, ever would have imagined that she'd take the opportunity to be with someone else.

And like a fool, he'd given her everything she asked for.

The scene from when he opened Jack's office door kept flooding his mind, and he had to shove it away.

"Calder, you up?" Jon called. It sounded like he was calling from downstairs.

"Yeah."

"Come and eat something. You gotta be starving."

He wasn't. The idea of eating was the furthest thing from his mind, but he knew his brother was worried, so he pulled himself out of bed, went to the bathroom and cleaned up, then went back downstairs.

Well, he had plenty of time to restore the Barracuda now. He'd have it towed here, he though.

He walked into the kitchen. There was a plate of bacon and eggs in his spot, and Jon was digging into his own late breakfast, which Calder guessed was actually dinner. Calder poured a cup of coffee from the percolator on the stovetop, then sat at the old Formica table with his brother.

"Thanks," Calder said, and Jon nodded.

After a few minutes of eating in silence, Jon took a gulp of coffee, then pushed his plate away. "Uh. Bryce called," he said.

Calder looked up from the food he was pushing around on his plate. "Yeah? Is Layla okay?"

"Yeah. Apparently something went down at the diner last night. Lay and Cara's dad is dead."

"What?"

"Shooter. They didn't catch him. Messed up the diner pretty bad. Cara got grazed by a bullet, I guess, but their dad didn't survive it."

Calder shook his head. "Shit."

"Probably related to Sophie and Marshall, huh?" Jon said quietly. Her name was like a stab to Calder's heart.

"Probably."

Jon nodded slowly. Wisely, he didn't say anything else about Sophie. "Bryce says the funeral is the day after tomorrow."

"We'll be there. He was a good guy," Calder said quietly.

"I can go, if you want to stay here… you know she'll be there."

"It's a small town, man. I'm probably going to run into her a lot until one or the other of us moves."

"You're not moving anywhere," Jon said in a tone that brooked no argument. "Other than here, if you want, because the only reason you moved to that house was to keep an eye on her when we came up with that dumbass plan to force her to break the curse. Move back here. There's room for both of us."

Calder nodded, but didn't say anything.

Jon sighed, and Calder knew he wanted to say something, but was trying to be mindful of Calder's mood. "Spit it out, whatever it is," Calder said, taking another bite of bacon. It was like cardboard in his mouth.

"I think it's safe to say that there's a pattern to you two, you know? You're drawn to one another, you love each other madly, and then she does something to completely destroy you."

"She can hardly be blamed for her dad deciding to move them away when she was a kid," Calder said, though he felt all twisted inside.

"No. But it happens anyway. She's no good for you."

"A few weeks ago, you were telling me she was the best thing that ever happened to me."

"Well, clearly, the situation has changed," Jon said. "I didn't know then that she was the type to cheat."

Calder didn't answer. Couldn't.

"And if you didn't already have a mess thanks to the curse, I could maybe even let that shit go. That's between the two of you. But to cheat on you when she knows how you are about her... we both know this is only gonna get worse," Jon said, and the loss in his voice was clear. He was already picturing having to lock Calder up, and expected it to be sooner rather than later.

"Well. We'll deal with whatever comes up. Not like we can do much else. I'm going to call Bryce, then I'm going to stop by the house and pick up a few things and tow the Barracuda over. Can I use your truck?"

Jon nodded, and Calder got up, washed his dishes, then headed out.

As he drove, he thought about her. Of course. He'd expected it to be so much worse. He'd expected his bear to be raging to be let loose in its anger and hurt. And his bear certainly wasn't happy, but it felt like it was in mourning, just as he was. For once, the gnawing emptiness inside had nothing to do with his curse.

He ended up stopping by Bryce's when he saw the car he'd restored for Bryce in the driveway. He'd finished it in the first week of Sophie needing her "space," and had moved on to finishing the Barracuda. He went into Bryce's house, and they talked. Bryce filled him in on Layla and what had happened the night before, mentioning that he'd seen Sophie there. Calder told him, in the fewest words possible, what had happened with Sophie. It was met with shocked silence.

"That's not like her," Bryce said.

"What do we know? Maybe it was. You said she was turned on by you that day."

"Because of the curse. Don't be an asshole."

246

Calder shrugged. "I'm not exactly in the mood to be nice about it right now."

"She's not the cheating type."

"I thought so, too." They stood there for a minute. "Anyway. I'm going to be staying out at our old place for a while. Do you need any help with anything?"

Bryce shook his head. "Nah. I'm getting ready to head over to the hospital. You'll be at the funeral, right?"

Calder nodded.

They stepped out of the house, and Bryce clapped Calder on the shoulder.

"Don't give up on her so easily, man. Cut her a little slack."

"Would you be able to go back, if you saw Layla with someone else?" Calder asked.

The emptiness in Bryce's eyes, the exhaustion in them, made Calder feel like an asshole for even asking.

"Man, I would give anything right now for a second chance. People work through all kinds of shit, and if you throw this away because your pride is hurt when we both know damn well she loves you and probably only gave into the curse, then you deserve any misery you have ahead of you."

"She wanted space," Calder said quietly. "We haven't been seeing one another for the past couple of weeks," he reminded Bryce.

"Doesn't mean she meant to move on, man."

"Jon doesn't agree."

"Jon doesn't trust any witch, and he trusts Sophie even less. Just give it some thought, okay?"

Calder nodded, then got back into his truck and headed toward the house he'd lived in for the past few years. Jon was right about that much; he couldn't live across the road from her, seeing her all the time.

She wanted space, he thought bitterly. It hadn't looked like Jack was giving her a whole lot of space.

Damn it.

247

Her car was in her driveway, and before he realized what he was doing, he was storming over to her house. They would have this out, if for no other reason than that he had things he needed to say to her. He walked around the side of her house, and stopped short. She was there, near the edge of her woods. Her long curls whipped around her, and she stood in the snow wearing jeans and a gray sweater he'd always liked.

Her focus was not on him. She was focusing, moving her hands in a way that her recognized as a spell.

All of a sudden, it was as if an invisible force was shielding her from the wind. Her hair stopped blowing, and the light snowflakes that were falling seemed unable to reach her. She looked in control, calm.

She waved her arm, and the shield fell, her curls blowing wildly around her again. He watched as she looked at a tree that had fallen at the edge of her woods.

Her hands worked again, her movements calm, fluid, not at all like the jerky movements he'd so often seen from her when she tried using Shadow magic. As he watched, the tree fell into pieces, stacked neatly, the perfect shape and size to burn in a fireplace.

She smiled as she observed her work. Despite everything he was feeling, he was impressed by her control.

Whatever else had happened, she seemed to be getting a handle on herself. And she'd need it, if she had any chance against the warlock. Maybe she'd been right. Maybe space was exactly what she'd needed.

I need to master myself a little. And I can't do that when I'm wrapped up in you. Her voice echoing through his memories.

He watched her pull another dead tree apart, and then he did the one thing he definitely didn't want to do.

He turned and walked away.

CHAPTER TWENTY-SIX

February 22, 1871

"I am not going to chain you," Migisi repeated, glaring at Luc. "My magic is enough. You don't need to be treated like an animal."

"But I am that, Migisi. I am, and you made it clear last week that you aren't capable of controlling me when I need you to."

"I kept you from killing your wife," Migisi said.

"Wrong. Esme kept me from killing my wife. You seemed to be taking your time about it."

Migisi shrugged and watched Claire crawl across the large rug near the kitchen.

"You do understand that if I would have hurt her, I would hate myself even more. Tell me you understand that much, at least. Is that what you want?"

Migisi didn't answer. In all honesty, she would love to see the woman gone. She had no business wearing the title of "wife" when she clearly refused to act as one, in any way.

That title rightfully belonged to Migisi.

"Do you even care?" Luc asked, the anger in his tone forcing her to look at him.

"Of course I do."

"Clearly not. Or you would not have let it get that far. I know what you're capable of, Migisi. You could have stopped me anytime before I got back to my house."

"Well, maybe you should start running to Esme whenever you need help. She would love that," she spat.

"As if you don't love having some claim over my time," Luc muttered. "You truly are everything she says you are."

Migisi seethed. Esme. Esme this, and Esme that, and Esme keeps my household together and Esme protects my wife and child... she was utterly sick of hearing about Esme.

"Go to her, then. I certainly tire of having you here," she said.

"Liar."

She stood up and went to the window. "What do you want me to say, Luc? Yes, I'd like to make your wife disappear. Yes, I would love to rip Esme's eyeballs out. Yes, I like the fact that, a few times a month, you need me. Is that what you wanted me to say? I'm not a nice woman. Not anymore."

She turned, and he was watching her.

"Well, that may well be the first honest thing you've said to me in a very long time."

She didn't know what to say.

"Perhaps you should start looking at things in a different way, though," Luc said, crossing his arms over his chest. "My wife was there for me when no one else was. She loved me, despite seeing what the curse did to me. She married me, never expecting that it would get as bad as it has. She gave me a child, who is my light and joy. And Esme keeps them safe from me, and by doing so, saves me over and over again. So if there is any part of you that actually cares for me as you continually claim you do, maybe you should appreciate both of them a bit more. They save me, on a daily basis, from what you've done to me."

There was silence, and then he continued.

"And you seem to think that if they were gone, I would come back to you and things will be as they were before. Surely, you are smarter than that. Never again, Migisi. I won't deny that, insane as it is, I still love you, that my heart still in many ways belongs to you. But you and I will never be what we were. I cannot look at you that way, not after everything you have done. Understand that, and let go of any ideas you have to the contrary."

With those words, he clamped his hat back onto his head and opened the door, walking out into the drifts of fine snow that had fallen overnight. She watched as he trudged through the snow, his boots sinking deeply into the snow with every step.

She was about to turn away from the window when she saw a flash of red near her woods. She focused, leaning forward, and looked in that direction.

Esme.

It took a moment to realize what she was seeing. She stood there with the warlock, Marshall. He kept his distance from Migisi, but she knew he haunted her woods, keeping tabs on her. Of course, she was not the only witch under his influence. She wondered if Esme was as well. She hadn't considered it, especially since Esme had come from Canada. But he was Shadow incarnate. He could travel where he wanted to.

She watched as they talked. Marshall seemed to be listening, not a sign of his usual arrogance. She realized with more than a little anger that he seemed to be treating Esme as an equal, which he had never, ever done with Migisi.

They spoke for a few moments more, and Esme held her hand out. Marshall took it, and they shook. As far away as she was, Migisi could feel power wash over her. Whatever they'd just agreed on, they'd sworn on magic.

Migisi watched with concern, expecting... what, exactly? That Esme and Marshall would come through the door to hurt her or her child? That her doom would come as a result of that handshake?

Out in the woods, Esme gave Marshall a nod, and he answered with a bow, and then they turned and went their separate ways, neither of them sparing a glance for the house or Migisi.

"What are you up to, Esme?" Migisi murmured.

CHAPTER TWENTY-SEVEN

Sophie drove up the winding lane that led to the small stone chapel in the Copper Falls cemetery. She could already see a long line of vehicles pulled up along the side of the road near the chapel, mostly trucks and SUVs. She parked behind a rusty old Ford and got out, then maneuvered the gravel drive in her heels, focusing on not tripping and falling on her face.

It was better than focusing on her guilt. Or the fact that she'd see Calder. She'd already spotted his truck among the others.

She knew he'd moved out of his house. She'd watched from her living room window as he'd piled boxes into his truck, then hooked up the car he was working on and towed it away. Part of her was relieved; it would be too hard seeing him every day.

But mostly, she missed him. The fact that it seemed like her little ploy had worked was the only thing that made it even slightly okay. Since the morning after he'd "caught" her with Jack, she'd felt clearer, calmer. More in control. And from what she'd heard from Bryce, it was the same for Calder, even if he didn't seem to realize it. From what Bryce said, he was still mostly dealing with the end of what he'd had with her. It had worked.

But even that knowledge didn't exactly keep her warm at night.

She walked up the walkway to the chapel's stairs. Bryce, who was clearly there representing his wife-to-be, Cara, the twins' mom, Jean, and their grandma, Faye, all stood just outside of the chapel, talking softly to mourners as they entered. She'd only been to one shifter funeral before, but she knew from that experience that these events were not about mourning, really. The family would mourn in private, for a very long time. No, shifter funerals were about celebrating the life of the deceased, about remembering the joy. It was like a gift the community gave to the family, like a candle brightening the darkness.

It looked like any other funeral. The attendees were dressed in the customary black, befitting a solemn event. There would be tears shed. But the focus would be on joy.

When it was her turn to speak to the family, she reached Bryce first, who met her eyes, then gave her a quick hug. She hugged Cara tightly, for several long moments.

"Thanks for coming," Cara said softly.

"Of course," Sophie said. They'd been on the phone most nights, Cara pouring her heart out to Sophie as Sophie sat through another long, empty night. It felt like a paltry amount of help to give to her friend, considering that she was the cause of the mourning.

She hugged Jean, and the woman held her tightly, a warm embrace that Sophie knew well. Jean was a hugger.

She bent down to kiss Faye on the cheek and hug her, and Faye patted her cheek in that grandmotherly way she had.

When Sophie walked into the chapel, she noticed that it was full of shifters she knew from around town. Their pack, and at the front of the chapel, Jack sat with his brothers. She looked away from him quickly, her gaze immediately finding the one figure she both did and did not want to see.

Calder sat beside Jon a few rows from the front. He wore a dark suit, and it looked like he'd gotten a haircut. For a moment, all she could do was stand and stare at him, just the back of his head, his shoulders. It was as if she'd hungered for the sight of him, and now all she could do was take her fill.

Shaking herself a bit, she walked to one of the pews a few rows behind Calder and Jon and sat down. A few other women from the pack were there, and they greeted Sophie quietly. She nodded and sat down.

She tried not to stare at him, but she couldn't stop herself.

The organist began playing a song Sophie was not familiar with as the last of the mourners filed in. Mr. Daniels' casket sat at the front of the chapel, open, his hands folded serenely over his chest. Sophie looked away. That pose was one she'd had to see too often already, between her parents and David. More caskets, filled simply because the people knew her.

People started speaking. There were no prayers. It was a sharing of stories, memories of Russell Daniels. Sophie's mind wandered, and her gaze continued to come back to Calder.

At one point, when she was looking at him, he turned in his seat. His eyes met hers, and her heart stopped. He held her gaze for just a moment before giving his head a small shake and turning back around. He did not look at her again.

Once all of the friends and pack members who wanted to speak had done so, Russell's brother stood up and shared stories of growing up with Russell, making the assembled crowd laugh. He sat, and, to Sophie's shock, Cara stood up. His children weren't expected to speak, mourning as they were. And Cara, much more so than Layla, was a shy, quiet type.

Cara walked shakily to the lectern and looked at the crowd, meeting her mom's eyes for a brief moment, then Sophie's. Sophie tried to give her friend a reassuring smile.

"There is not much I can say right now. I want to thank all of you for coming and sharing your memories of my dad. I want to thank you for the love and support you've given my family over these past few days. This community is our family, and you've reminded us again and again why we love you all so much. We've seen a lot of darkness here lately," she said in a quiet voice, and Sophie froze. Cara's gaze met Sophie's again. "We've seen violence like we've never seen here before. Not in any of our lifetimes, anyway. We've seen loss. My family has been hit particularly hard by it, but we've lost others. Neighbors. Visitors. And it would be so easy to be angry right now. It would be *so* easy. It would be easy to look for simple answers, to lay blame where there is none." Cara met her eyes again. "None," she repeated in a determined tone, and Sophie realized then that Cara knew the guilt she'd been dealing with. "There is madness and evil in this world. But there is beauty as well. And believe me when I say that I know the difference, and I will continue to see the beauty, even when I want to rage." Tears slipped from Sophie's eyes, and she saw Cara blinking away tears as well. "And I want you all to remember that, too. Thank you," Cara finished, and then she stepped down.

Sophie swiped at her nose with a tissue she dug out of her purse, then blotted at her eyes. The assembly stood and watched them close the casket. Pallbearers, including Jack — as the alpha, it was an honor to have him serve as pallbearer, Sophie knew — and Bryce, flanked the coffin and carried it down the aisle as the mourners looked on. As they made their way down the aisle, the mourners filed in behind them. Cara's father was being cremated, as was typical for shifters of their local pack. Sophie watched as the pallbearers loaded the casket into the back of a hearse, and then they all stood, silently, and watched the hearse drive away, a final moment of farewell, shared together as snow fell yet again.

"Well. Isn't this cozy?" a voice she knew too well said behind them. Marshall stood on the steps of the chapel, in his customary black trench coat, a sly smile on his face. "All of Sophie's favorite people in one place."

Cara ran forward, ready to spring, and Bryce grabbed her, holding her back.

"You killed my father, you bastard," Cara screeched as she struggled against Bryce, trying to get to the warlock. Sophie started making her way to the front, and she heard the unmistakeable sound of the shift happening all around her.

"He's only the first. You can thank Sophie for your losses. All she had to do was uphold her end of a certain bargain," he said, malice glinting in hie eyes. People started trying to run, especially those with young children, and they were met, to everyone's shock, with an invisible wall. Marshall cackled. "Trapped. Plan on being here a while," he said. "Now. Who's going to die for Sophie's sins first?"

Sophie worked feverishly, drawing her power up and over the people around her, separating them from Marshall with an invisible shield.

Someone brushed past her, and she watched the twins' Grandma Faye stalk to the front, toward Marshall.

"Not today. Get behind me, Satan," Faye shouted, and in the next moment, she was leaping in a way that belied her many years, shifting to her wolf in midair, and when she landed, she had Marshall's throat in her mouth, having taken everyone, including him, by surprise. They fell back, and his screams and Faye's growls erupted around them. Sophie focused on forming her shield around everyone as she moved forward, watching waiting. And… there it was. Marshall panicked and tossed Faye off of him, trying to free himself, focusing on ending his pain rather than hurting Faye, in that instant. Sophie caught the old wolf with her magic and set her gently inside her shield.

Marshall stood, blood flowing from his throat, and he laughed.

"Is this the game we're going to play now, kitten?" He said in that vile voice, his tone twisting Calder's pet name, and she heard Calder's deep growl near her, closer than she'd realized he'd been. "You really think you can protect them from me?"

"Everyone stay near me. Don't try to charge him," Sophie instructed quietly.

"Gonna kill him," Russell's brother said.

"He'll kill you," Sophie said, still focusing on holding the shield. Faye's sudden attack had given her the opportunity to finish making it, surrounding everyone with her magic. It was the largest shield she'd ever even attempted, and she couldn't be sure it would hold.

"Oh, yes I will. Every single one of you." He looked into Sophie's eyes. "And I'll make it last a little longer, thanks to Sophie's little game here."

"You're not going to do that to me anymore, Marshall. You're the evil one here. Not me," Sophie said.

"We'll see."

And it began. He started throwing magic at her, at her shield, working to break it. The first blast had it trembling, and she focused harder, holding her hands out, her body rigid, her muscles tight. It was like wrestling with air, trying to keep the shield intact as Marshall hit it, again and again.

"Aw, the kitten's grown a backbone," Marshall taunted, striding around and attacking the shield from another angle. Sophie's teeth clenched as she held it against the onslaught. "I can do this all day, you worthless bitch. You are nothing."

He did it again, and again, and again, and Sophie felt sweat break out all over her body. Her breathing became labored, and she focused harder as the attacks came quicker. Those inside the shield could feel every impact, and each was met with screams and cries. Many of the adult shifters, those who didn't have children with them, had shifted and waited at the edges of Sophie's shield, ready to spring should the barrier fall.

Sophie knew they wouldn't be enough to save them. Marshall wouldn't be caught by surprise again.

She grunted and pushed her hands out harder, trying to build the shield stronger.

"So worthless. All of this pain. All of this death, because of one worthless whore," Marshall taunted as he blasted the shield again. "Remember that, as I kill you all. You would have lived, if it wasn't for Sophie." She heard Calder growl again, and then she felt a warm hand on her lower back.

"You've got this. I believe in you," he said quietly.

"Oh, gag me," Marshall sneered as he threw a harder blast at the shield. She didn't have any time to be grateful or touched by Calder's words, but that hand on her back, the reassurance and support it spoke of, gave her a little jolt of energy just when she'd started to feel her strength flagging.

"Every one of you will die. Slowly and painfully. And all because Sophie put her life above yours. She always has been a selfish bitch, though," he said as he casually blasted the shield again. Sophie felt it tremble.

It was going to break soon, and it was all she had.

She started panting.

"What's the saying? Sucks to be you," Marshall said with a feral grin as he blasted the barrier again.

Sophie felt it crack, and begin to crumble.

Sucks to be you.

Sucks.

You siphoned my power!

You know what you were doing! How do you think you managed to take Calder's curse?

Our powers are great. Limitless. Anything we desire, anything at all, becomes ours.

The shield started to fall, and Marshall laughed victoriously. The crowd around her started screaming.

Sophie focused on him, still holding what she could of the shield, and she pulled her power, rather than pushing it. She focused on him, and she could see the way his power coiled within him, in every cell, in every beat of his heart. She could see it.

She could see it clearly, the same way she'd seen Calder's curse. The same way she'd seen the magic that would make plants grow and animals heal.

She could see it.

And what she could see, she could control.

Sophie started pulling, absorbing.

Taking.

And she knew what she was losing, as well.

She grunted, and pulled harder, absorbing Marshall's Shadow magic a bit at a time.

"What the fuck are you doing?" Marshall screamed, and maybe it was the Shadow in her or maybe it was just a lifetime of living under his thumb, but she smiled at the sound of it. "Stop!"

With some of his power in her, it started to become that much easier to take the rest. It flowed into her, filling her, its oily slickness imbuing every part of her, obliterating anything that wasn't already Shadow.

Giving her everything he'd taken from so many others. It filled her, and he screamed.

He tried to run. She let out a low laugh, and used her power to throw an invisible wall around him, just as he had when he'd tried to trap the mourners.

The shifters seemed to sense that the tide was turning, and the males arrayed themselves around her, as if protecting her so she could finish what she'd started. Those with children fled, finally free of the trap Marshall had sprung on them.

Calder's hand still rested warmly on Sophie's back.

"Make the bastard pay, Sophie," Calder said.

And she did.

As the last bits of his power flowed into Sophie, Marshall screamed in a way that made her skin prickle. She wouldn't be able to take all of it, she knew. Taking all of it would kill him and, despite what she was, she refused to take a life.

Not even his.

But he could sure the hell go to jail.

"Be ready to grab him," she said, and she watched Calder and Jack both stride forward, each ready on one side of Marshall.

She stopped siphoning Marshall's magic, and he slumped to the ground, pale and trembling, still screaming, his nose bleeding. Calder and Jack each took one arm roughly and pulled him up. The town's three police officers were all in attendance, members of the pack, just like so many others. They shifted back and took Marshall from Calder and Jack.

Sophie slumped to the ground, trying to catch her breath.

Marshall's power felt like it was choking her, like she was gagging on it. Like she wanted to vomit.

The power of a Shadow lord.

She would never see the Light again, she realized as she watched the scene round her, the police, the shifters shifting back. Everyone looking at her while trying to look like they weren't.

Calder started to come to her, and she quickly scrambled up.

I want to be home, she thought.

And then, she was.

CHAPTER TWENTY-EIGHT

"I'll be out of here soon," Layla said with a smile. Sophie smiled back and settled herself into the chair beside Layla's hospital bed. "They said the swelling's gone down enough. There'll be physical therapy after, but at least I get to go home!"

Sophie nodded. She'd been slipping into Layla's room at the hospital when she was sure no one else was around. It was too awkward, after what had happened at the funeral.

"It'll be great to have you home. Bryce will be over the moon," she said, and Layla grinned. She sobered, then reached out, and Sophie took her hand.

"Why didn't you tell me about what happened at daddy's funeral?" Layla asked softly. By all accounts, Layla had woken from her coma at precisely the moment Sophie had taken Marshall's powers. Cara believed that Layla waking was thanks to Sophie, somehow, that Marshall had been keeping Layla from recovering. Sophie wasn't sure about that, but she did know she was thrilled to see her best friend awake and recovering. From what the doctors said, there was still some doubt about how well Layla would be able to get around; the injury had damaged her gross and fine motor skills. True to form, Layla was being philosophical about it. At least she had her life.

On waking, Cara had broken the news about their father's death to Layla. Sophie had hoped the rest of the story would wait for a while. Apparently, it hadn't.

"I didn't want to upset you more," Sophie finally said.

"Upset me? Sophie, you saved my grandma's life. Not to mention the lives of like, my entire pack. How in the hell could that ever upset me?"

"They were only in danger because of me," Sophie said quietly. "Your dad—"

"Not another word, Sophie, or I am gonna jump out of this bed and kick your ass," Layla said roughly, and when Sophie looked at her, her eyes were shining with unshed tears. "Marshall is the reason my dad is gone. Not you. Don't let his lies become your reality."

Sophie didn't answer, but she gave a small nod. Easy to say, not so easy to do.

"Bryce said he got out of jail. Escaped less than an hour after they locked him up," Layla continued.

Sophie nodded again, her stomach twisting. "I kind of figured he would. He still had some magic. I couldn't take it all," she said apologetically.

"So he'll be back," Layla said.

"To take revenge on me, or to get his powers back. Maybe both," Sophie said. "He's not likely to just give up. It's not his way. I won't let him hurt anyone," she promised Layla.

Layla gave her a gentle smile and squeezed her hand. "You aren't responsible for everyone, Sophie. You can't save the world."

Sophie was about to say something, when the door opened and Bryce walked in. He bent down and kissed Layla, and Sophie knew it was her cue to leave the two of them alone.

"Time for me to get back," Sophie said. She leaned down and hugged Layla, and then she nodded at Bryce and headed toward the door.

"Hey, Soph," Bryce said. Sophie stopped and looked at him questioningly. "You know he keeps calling you. Call the man back, okay?"

She shook her head. "He deserves something better. It's time for him to move on."

Bryce looked at her blankly. "Have you completely lost it? The man will never move on from you. You may as well ask him to stop breathing."

Her heart ached, and she didn't know what to say, in the end, she just walked out of the room, down the hall, and, in the next breath, appeared in her living room.

Solace and prison, all in one.

It had been two weeks. Two weeks, and her world was everything Esme had told her it would be: empty and dead.

She went out the back door and sat on the steps behind her cottage as snow fell on the world. None of it landed on her.

To the untrained eye, the world still looked the same. Snow covered the ground, and the forest rose in the distance. Only someone who loved the land as she did would see what she saw.

First, her land held no animal life. No squirrels or deer scurried in her woods, no owls hooted from her trees.

Not even the goats had remained. She'd arrived home the day of the funeral to find all three of them, even Merlin, gone.

Familiars were, after all, of the Light, and had no need for Shadow.

The trees in the distance had already begun to take the blackened, twisted form of those she'd seen around Esme's home. She scrunched up her face at the thought of Esme. If it hadn't been for her, Sophie never would have been able to break Calder's curse. She never would have been able to construct the shield that protected everyone at the funeral.

She never would have realized that she could defeat Marshall the way she had. She owed Esme an apology, and her thanks. And hopefully Esme wouldn't try to kill her on sight.

Sophie got up from the step and walked toward the woods. She followed the well-worn trail she always took. Once upon a time, she had habitually trailed her fingers along the trunks of trees as she walked past. Now, she tried not to touch anything for fear of making it worse. Of further speeding its death. No one had come to see her since the funeral, and, other than her stealth visits to see Layla, she had gone to see no one. She had stayed in her house and on her land. Cara still called every day, and they talked about normal things.

Mostly they talked about Layla.

Cara told her other things, too. That there hadn't been a single incident of violence in Copper Falls since that day, when before, the police had been over-run, the jail over-crowded, due to daily issues thanks to Marshall's influence. While Sophie was pleased, it confused her. She was just as Shadow as he'd been, now. She wrote the lull in violence off to winter's frigid temperatures keeping everyone inside.

They'd invited her for Christmas, and Sophie had gently declined.

So she talked to Cara, and she talked to Layla, and she watched her land die around her, and she sat, for hours on end, feeling Shadow writhe within her.

She ignored the other who kept calling her, despite how badly she wanted to hear his voice. He deserved to move on, and he couldn't do that if he was still holding onto her for whatever insane reason.

She walked the rest of the trail and came to the river, the falls. The boulder and its flanking oak trees.

She heaved herself up onto the boulder and remembered a humid summer day, the lips of the person she had known, even then, was the other half of herself.

At least she had the memories.

She watched as a nearby tree began to wither in her presence, the bark becoming gray and lifeless. She frowned.

Anything we want.

"Live," she murmured, and she waved her hand.

The tree's bark smoothed, thickened, and she tilted her head as she studied it. Wondering.

"Anything, huh?" she said quietly, looking down at her hands. "And what if I want life, Shadow? What about then?"

Of course, Shadow had no answers for her. She was coming to understand, bit by bit, that the only answers she was going to find were those buried deep in herself, in the centuries of magic she'd stolen from Marshall.

Well. It would give her something to do with her time, anyway.

She heard the snow crunching, and turned, ready to throw magic if she had to. She always expected Marshall to come back to her for his revenge. He would. She knew he would. He was not powerless, though he was a pale, weak version of what he'd been. And he was still Marshall.

But the shape that stepped out of the trees was one she dreamed over and over again, day and night.

Calder walked toward her, silently. In one easy movement, he leapt onto the boulder and sat beside her. Her body warmed, just having him close to her.

"Do you ever answer your phone?" he asked her, and she didn't answer, her voice unable to work around the emotions that rose in her at his closeness.

They sat in silence for a long time; the only sound around them was the rushing of the river. She could feel his warmth beside her in the cold. She wore a sweater. The frigid air no longer bothered her. Calder was dressed in a thick coat, gloves, and a hat. His blond hair peeked out from the bottom of his hat, and she curled her hands into fists, trying to fight the urge to run her fingers through that bit of wild, wavy hair.

"So. The curse is gone," he said finally, and she didn't answer. Sophie just looked straight ahead at the river. She wouldn't tell him anything about that. She didn't trust that it wouldn't come back if she told him the truth of it. He would have to live the rest of his life thinking she'd taken another.

"Don't suppose you want to tell me how that happened?" He asked, and she didn't answer. "Because I know you did it. You're just as sane as I am, which means it's really gone this time."

Still, she said nothing, but now she looked down at her hands and felt the trace of a smile curving her lips.

It was really and truly gone. She'd believed so, but hadn't dared to hope.

"You saved half of the damn town that day, Sophie. You're in control. So you did something to make that happen," he pressed, and still she said nothing. He took a breath. "We have some stuff to work through. Christ, do we have things to work through," he repeated in a low mutter. "But I think what we had... what we could still have together, is worth working for. Don't you?"

She heard him sigh, and then Calder pulled a glove off. To her shock, he took her hand in his, their clasped hands resting on her lap. He squeezed her hand gently, and the warmth of his flesh against hers was enough to break her. Tears flowed from her eyes. She squeezed his hand back.

They sat in silence, the tall oaks that flanked the boulder standing like enormous sentries, the river flowing ahead of them, the falls crashing in the distance.

"I'm Shadow. Completely," she aid after a while.

He squeezed her hand gently in his. He ran his thumb over her wrist in that calming, mesmerizing way he always had.

"I know exactly what you are, Sophie," he said, "I just wish you could see yourself the way I see you." The snow fell gently around them, blanketing the world, erasing the memory of autumn's decay, creating a blank slate for the promise of spring.

The End

Sophie will return in *Light's Shadow*,
the third book in the *Copper Falls* series.

Never Miss an Update!

Sign Up for Colleen's Newsletter.
http://bit.ly/colleensnewsletter

For backstory material, news, and upcoming events be sure to check out http://www.colleenvanderlinden.com

LETTER FROM THE AUTHOR

Thank you so much for reading *Shadow Sworn*! I hope you loved it. I've loved sharing the Copper Falls series with you.

I have a few people I want to thank, because no book happens in a vacuum.

I want to thank my amazing readers for your constant support. Your enthusiasm for these books and characters is what makes even the hardest writing days easier to take. Your emails, tweets, Facebook posts, and reviews never fail to brighten my day. Thank you from the bottom of my heart.

Thank you to my crazy-awesome beta reading team. You ladies never let me slack, and the input you give me makes each and every book stronger. Much love and many thanks to Susan Cambra, Shawna Cerda, Jo Dawson, Kristen Driscoll, Susan Emans, Jennifer G., Amber Hegarty, Brenda Hopkins, Krystin Hopkins, Sarah Leenart, Kathie Littlemore, Jayna Longstreet, Rachel Scott, and Sarah Wicks. You are amazing and I love you dearly.

Thank you to Ken and Amber of Ten Digit Creations for answering my questions about soap making during the writing of *Shadow Witch Rising*. Also, thanks for making the wax tarts that make my office smell so good when I'm writing!

Thank you to Elizabeth Hunter, Grace Draven, and the members of the Women of Urban Fantasy group for your friendship, support, and understanding. You get me, and it means a lot. Thank you!

Finally, I want to thank my wonderful husband, Roger, for being the one who believes in me most, and most importantly, when I can't seem to believe in myself. I love you. And thanks to my awesome kids for being their amazing, crazy selves. You're the best.

If you enjoyed *Shadow Sworn*, please consider leaving a review on Amazon or GoodReads. Those reviews make a huge difference, and I appreciate every single one of them. Thank you so much!

Colleen Vanderlinden
Detroit, Michigan
August 31, 2015

ABOUT THE AUTHOR

Colleen Vanderlinden is the author of the *Hidden* and *Soulhunter* urban fantasy series, as well as the *Copper Falls* paranormal romance series. The third *Hidden* novel, *Home*, was a finalist for *RT Book Reviews' Editors Choice Awards* for best self-published urban fantasy novel of 2014.

Her books have consistently received positive reviews, and *RT Book Reviews* has called her storytelling "electrifying."

She lives in the Detroit area with her husband, kids, demonic Basset hound, and two lazy cats. You can find out more about Colleen's books at her website, colleenvanderlinden.com, or follow her on Twitter, where she's @C_Vanderlinden.

The Hidden Series
Book One: Lost Girl
Book Two: Broken
Book Three: Home
Book Four: Strife
Book Five: Nether
Hidden Series Novellas
Forever Night
Earth Bound

The Hidden: Soulhunter Series
Guardian
Betrayer

The Copper Falls Series
Shadow Witch Rising
Shadow Sworn

Never Miss an Update!
Sign Up for Colleen's Newsletter
http://bit.ly/colleensnewsletter

www.ingramcontent.com/pod-product-compliance
Lightning Source LLC
Chambersburg PA
CBHW071121170626
46809CB00002B/448